ME & MY DOPE BOY

SHVONNE LATRICE

Other Works by Me:

Good Girls Love Thugs 1-5
Falling for a Hood King 1-4
Married to a Distinguished Thug 1-3
She's Gotta Have It 1-2
Me & My Dope Boy 1-3
Yazir & Nina 1-3
Forbidden Love with a Thug 1-3
You Needed Me 1-3
Shorty is in Love with a Real One 1-4
I Got Your Back 1-2
My Baby Is a West Coast King 1-4
Our Love Is the Realest 1-3
She Got It Bad for a Heartless Gangsta 1-4
She Got It Bad for a Heartless Gangsta: An AK Christmas
Hood Boyz Fall In Love Too 1-3
Nobody Can Love You Like Them Roughnecks Do 1-4
She Gave Her All to the Hood's Finest 1-5

Visit www.theshvonnelatrice.com for paperbacks!

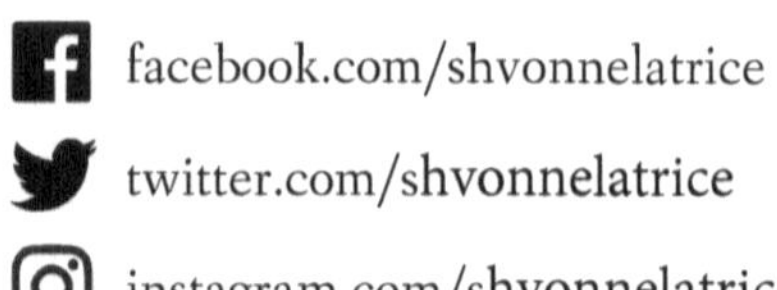
facebook.com/shvonnelatrice
twitter.com/shvonnelatrice
instagram.com/shvonnelatrice

$15.99

ISBN 978-1-966375-07-4

*S*UMMER HAD COME AND GONE, *and it was now time to start high school. I'd watched all the high school related movies during the summer, with my best friends Aysia, Willow, and Shannon. Luckily for Shannon and Willow, they were only going into eighth grade. They didn't have to deal with all the craziness that I knew came with high school in Baltimore.*

I had an older friend named Lauryn who was in eleventh grade at Patterson High School, and she'd gotten into three damn fights already. It's not like I was scared to fight, I just wasn't the type to go looking for them, and I especially didn't want to be constantly provoked.

I sat at the table playing around with my bowl of cereal, wishing there was some way I could be home schooled. My mother was a nurse, and my father was an engineer. They both worked five days a week so there was no way they could home school me. Even if they could though, I don't think they would.

"Non essere così giù Gianna, liceo è divertente. (Don't be so down Gianna, high school is fun)," my mother said to me in Italian. She was Italian and my father was full-blooded African American.

"Alta scuola non è divertente mamma. (High school is not fun mama)," I replied and scoffed. I got up from the table and threw my bowl into the sink.

My phone buzzed and I saw it was a text from Aysia telling me she and her mom were outside.

"Addio mamma e papà!" I called out as I rushed to the door.

"Speak English mi bella," my dad replied.

"Goodbye daddy," I chuckled at his attempt at Italian and kissed his cheek.

When we pulled up to school, there were so many people hanging around the outside. Aysia and I looked at each other, and then shook our heads with a smile. We said our goodbyes to her mother, and then treaded up the walkway.

"I see some fine niggas," Aysia smiled and nudged me.

"I bet you can't wait to pop that pussy on one of them," I smacked my lips at her and she laughed.

We went into the hallway, on our way to the counselor's office so we could get our schedules. As we were walking through taking in all the kids, I noticed all kinds of people. There were girls dressed in little to no clothes, and some people dressed like Dracula. All of a sudden, there were loud voices and ruckus, and I just knew it was a fight. To my surprise it wasn't a brawl, just a group of guys walking through. Everyone was acting like they were superstars or some shit. I rolled my eyes and leaned up against one of the lockers to watch the fuckery continue.

"Damn, he's fine as fuck," Aysia commented.

I looked at the one in the front, and Lord have mercy on my soul. He was about 6'2, with toffee colored skin, deep dimples, perfect teeth, and deep green eyes almost the same color as a leaf.

"You see something you like shorty?" he grinned at me, and I was so embarrassed as people started chuckling in the hallway. He bit his lip at me, and scanned me from head to toe.

I was wearing a regular white t-shirt, jeans, and Adidas. My brownish-red hair was hanging down my back, and I had bangles and a chain on. All the other girls including Aysia had on dresses and sandals, or shorts and sandals. I hated myself right now.

"I guess not," he smirked and then walked off with his friends, and a couple girls following like a pack of dogs.

"Got damn, who is he?" Aysia grinned as we watched them all walk away and out the building.

"That's Kendrick King, or KJ as we call him," some chick responded and popped her gum loudly.

"He's Kendrick King's son?" I frowned because I was surprised.

Kendrick King and his brothers were some big time drug dealers. People called them the fancy criminals because of the way they carried themselves. You would think their businesses were legit. Anyway, my mom said back in the day the King Brothers were every female's dream, including hers, but she was older than them. She had me at twenty-five years old. She said to never mention that to my father. I chuckled at the thought.

"Yes girl, out of your league though." She shot daggers at Aysia and me, and then switched off.

Once I got my schedule, I went to my homeroom, which unfortunately Aysia wasn't in. Thank God it was only for thirty minutes. I walked in and everyone was chatting it up and shit. People were sitting on the desks, throwing paper balls, just all kinds of shit. Lord please let these four years fly by, I thought.

The homeroom guide walked in, and right behind him was KJ and some girls. I looked to my left, and let out a sigh of relief when I saw the seat next to me was open. I hoped he sat there. Just my luck, some duck head nigga sat his ugly ass down next to me. I watched as KJ sat down next to one of his friends, and those thirsty hoes sat right around him. I sat back angrily, and stared straight ahead while the homeroom guide bullshitted at his desk.

"Aye homie, let me sit here." I looked over to see KJ asking duck face to sit down in his seat.

"Sure man," the guy hopped up and rushed over to KJ's old seat.

"Uhn un, KJ!" one of the hood rats called his name. He threw his hand up to tell her to be quiet.

"What's your name shorty?" he quizzed and then moved his desk right up against mine.

"Ooooohhh," the class said in unison.

"I'm Gianna, but my people call me Gigi," I smirked.

"Why I ain't never seen you 'round here before Gigi?" he frowned his gorgeous face up.

"I'm a freshman," I shrugged. He jerked his neck back and smiled.

"You're fourteen shorty?"

"Yeah, how old are you?" I wondered.

"I'm sixteen, in eleventh. I'm too old for you baby girl, but damn once you get a little older I want you," he nibbled on his lip and looked me up and down like earlier.

Age ain't nothing but a number! I yelled to myself.

"I'm mature for my age," I smiled. I wanted to convince him so badly. I'd never been horny in my life, but damn did I want him to fuck me. We stared at one another lustfully for a couple moments, and then he started laughing. He was beautiful.

"I'm sure you are, but the law enforcement don't see it that way," he shrugged and then scooted his desk back over.

For the rest of the thirty-minute homeroom, we sat there not saying a word to each other. KJ interacted with everyone else, as I wished to be two years older.

"Don't be giving in to these knucklehead niggas, not when you got a nigga like me checking for you," KJ said to me before walking out with his friend. The girls he was with stared me down and rolled their eyes at me. I gave them a nasty look back, and then walked out of the classroom after them.

I watched KJ walk off with his friends until I couldn't see him anymore, and then I rushed off to my first class.

A FEW WEEKS LATER...

High school was great now that I had something to look at when I arrived. Every morning I would walk through the halls with Aysia, excited to see KJ walking down the hall with his people. What made everything better is that now he would speak to me and hug me. I looked forward to smelling his cologne.

"Since when do you wear skirts to school Gigi, I thought you didn't care?" Aysia chuckled at me as we entered the hallway of school.

"I didn't but now I do, and I think you know why," I grinned at her and she nudged me lightly.

I heard KJ's best friend Lenny talking, and my heart started to beat fast because I knew KJ would soon appear. Aysia and I made eye contact, and a smile was spread across both of our faces.

"Hope you got an extra pair of panties Gigi, because I know them

bad boys are soaked," Aysia whispered, and I bucked my eyes at her playfully, making her giggle.

"Sup shorty," KJ made eye contact with me. I could tell he was high as hell, and it made him so much sexier. It was crazy because I thought I hated guys who smoked. "Walk with me to homeroom," he added after he gave Aysia a head nod.

He draped his arm around my shoulder, and I walked down the hall with him. So many people were looking at us, and I was nervous as hell. I had never been under so much pressure in my fourteen years. My hands were so sweaty I thought my books were gonna slide right out of them.

"Your hair smells good," KJ commented as we neared the classroom.

"Thank you. So does your chest," I chuckled and so did he. I liked that he didn't smell like a dime sack, nor did his breath. His lips didn't have any discoloration either.

Homeroom was bliss and too damn short. I went through my next four classes, wishing that KJ were in them. Luckily Aysia was in most of my classes so I had someone to sit with and talk to, instead of looking lonely and dumb. The only people who wanted to befriend me when Aysia wasn't around were crusty ass boys that KJ said were beneath me. The girls were way too jealous to wanna be cool.

BRNNGG!

It was lunchtime finally, so I rushed to the cafeteria to secure a table for Aysia and I. If you lollygagged too much, you would be standing for lunch. Once I got to a good table, I pulled out the chicken orecchiette my mother had cooked for dinner last night, along with a bottle of water.

"Excuse me, may I sit here with you?" some guy asked and sat across from me. He was a nice looking guy, with brown skin, a low cut fade, and he had on a windbreaker suit letting me know he played basketball.

"Umm, my friend is coming," I responded and half smiled.

"Damn, how big is your friend shorty?" he chuckled and so did I.

"So you must be new here, because I would've been seen your pretty ass," he licked his lips.

"Yeah, I'm a freshman. What grade are you?" I quizzed.

"I'm in twelfth, a senior," he smirked lustfully. "Man, you are too pretty for words, what's your name?" he asked and leaned in.

"Gianna," I smiled at him as he stared at me with sex filled eyes.

"Gianna, that's beautiful. Why don't you give me your number Gianna?" He pulled his phone out of his pocket.

Now, why did he think it was okay to date me, and KJ didn't? He was a year older than KJ!

"What's your name?" I questioned and then shoved some pasta into my mouth.

"How impolite of me, my name is Donny," he placed his large hand over his chest. He had to be about 6'5 and 150 pounds soaking wet.

I looked to my right to see if Aysia was near, and spotted KJ watching me from afar. He sipped his Gatorade and didn't break his stare. He finally stood up, and then waved me over to follow him.

"GIANNA," Donny said as I stood up and placed the top on my Tupperware to close it up. "Gianna!" he called again as I rushed off to follow KJ.

As soon as I hit the corner, KJ grabbed me and pulled me to the janitor's closet. He pulled the hanging string to cut on the very dim light, and then shut the door.

"What you doing out there Gianna?" he grinned with his sexy self as he neared me.

I backed away until I tripped over a gallon of some type of cleaner. KJ pulled me close to him, and then backed me into a wall.

"You like that nigga?" he asked me and I shook my head no immediately.

He stared down into my eyes, and I stared up into his green ones. He cupped my face, and then slipped his tongue into my mouth. My water and lunch slid out of my grasp and hit the floor, and I placed my *hands on his abs. We kissed heavily, and I wasn't sure if I was doing it right, but he didn't complain. I had only kissed one other boy in sixth grade. KJ pulled away, and I wanted to tell him to keep going.*

"Why'd you stop?" I wondered and he chuckled.

"Gianna, you're my girl. Well you will be, so can I ask you to stay to yourself?" he raised a brow and folded his arms.

"Stay to myself?" I repeated.

"Like don't be fucking with any other niggas. Not in this school, Baltimore, or the whole world," he explained and waited for my response.

"Wait, so you're not my man but you want me to not be with anyone else until you're ready to be my man?" I frowned.

"Something like that. I have my reasons Gigi, but I promise you I will make you my shorty," he neared me again and pecked me softly. "We can still talk on the phone, and text, and kiss, matter fact give me your number," he said and pulled his phone from his jean pocket.

I read it off to him and then asked, "Will you be staying to yourself too?"

"Don't worry about that. Just make sure you keep it tight for daddy," he said in a low tone, and my nipples got hard.

*H*E PECKED *me on the lips one more time, and then grabbed my hand so that we could walk back to the eating area. He sat me with him, and I waved Aysia over so she could sit with me and his friends. The whole lunch period he had his arm around me and acted as if we were boyfriend and girlfriend. After school, we went to get some food, and chilled until the streetlights came on, just getting to know one another and kissing. This happened everyday until the day he graduated. Little did I know, that was just the beginning of our "relationship".*

FIVE YEARS LATER...

"Oʜ ᴍʏ ɢᴏsʜ, KJ," London moaned as she fell to the side of me. I'd just gotten done dicking her sexy ass down like I had been for the longest. "Where are you going?" She frowned and sat up in the bed once she saw me sit up.

I ignored her clingy ass and walked to the bathroom to throw the condom away. I was a single man and didn't answer to any fucking body. I grabbed some towels from her linen closet, and then proceeded to take a quick ass shower. When I came back to the bedroom, London was sitting there with her pretty face twisted up. I just chuckled at her ass as I started to put my clothes back on.

"Nothing is funny, KJ!" She grilled me and squinted her eyes.

"It's actually very funny. You're mad for no fucking reason," I shrugged and frowned slightly.

"Because you be treating me like one of those little hoes on the block," she whined.

"I don't treat you like anything, but anyway, I'll hit you up later." I leaned down and kissed her cheek once I was dressed. I ain't have time for this bullshit.

"Am I gonna meet your mama soon?" She raised a brow at me.

I'd told her she could meet my mom one night when she was being stingy with the pussy. My mama hated her ass though, and I wished she'd never even found out about her.

"I told you she's tripping right now, but I got you," I smiled.

My mother had good reason to hate London... I guess. London was a sexy ass Mexican and Black chick, and was thick in all the right places. She was older than me though; fourteen years older to be exact. London was thirty-five, and my mother was thirty-nine, which explains why my mom didn't approve. I explained to her that London was nothing serious, but she didn't care, she didn't want me spending any of my time with her 'old ass', she would say.

I walked outside and squinted my eyes at how bright the sun was. It was summertime, and this afternoon was especially hot in Baltimore. I slid into my Panamera and sped off to my crib.

Currently, I was living with my mom and dad until my house was done being built. It was a big ass mansion with three dens, seven bedrooms, eight bathrooms, two kitchens, a pool, basketball court, gym, and spa room. The shit cost me major bread but it was nothing to a nigga like me. Anyway, I couldn't wait to be out of my parents' house because I needed the privacy to do as a nigga pleased. My mother was always hounding me about coming home at two and three in the morning or sometimes the afternoon.

I walked into the house and through the foyer, and I could still smell the pancakes my mom had just cooked. I walked out into the back area, and spotted my beautiful mother lying out on one of the lawn chairs in a two-piece bathing suit. Although a year away from forty, she didn't look a day over twenty-five. I shook my head and chuckled at she and my dad kissing like two horny ass teenagers. I used to think my dad was in their bedroom hurting my mom when I was little, and was devastated when I found out what they had really been doing all those years.

"Y'all need to get a room," I scoffed and they laughed.

"Look what the cat dragged in," my father stood up and slapped hands with me.

My dad was Kendrick King, one of the biggest- excuse me, not one of, but the biggest kingpin in the DMV area. He and my uncles Kendreeis and Kendon ran shit for the longest, but when it was time to hand over the reigns, it was given to none other than your boy. Now the King empire was run by my cousin Kaleeini, my little brother Kendrin, and myself. I'm sure you can guess who was in charge though.

"Where were you last night KJ?" my mom asked frowning. She pulled her long dark hair into a bun on top of her head, while waiting for my answer.

"I was handling business, Ma," I grinned and so did my dad.

"I hope you weren't handling business with that old hoe," she spat and folded her arms.

"If I am that's my business, Ma, I'm twenty-one," I chuckled at her ass.

She had some nerve coming at me like this when she herself got pregnant by my dad at seventeen, and then with Kendrin at nineteen. I'm way older than they were when all that shit went down.

"Watch your mouth KJ," she rolled her eyes.

"Chill out Nic, give him a break. He's already said that he and the girl aren't serious," my father chimed in to help me.

"I don't care! He doesn't need to be spending time with her! I should beat her ass for fucking on my baby," she responded.

"Ma, you know I got someone that I'm gon' be official with. Just wait on it," I said.

"Why not have a little fun? He's a twenty-one-year-old man," my dad shrugged.

"Oh, is that what you would have rather been doing at twenty-one, Kendrick?" My mom folded her arms and raised a brow at my dad.

"No baby, you know once I found you it was all about you," my dad bit his lip and then leaned in to peck her.

As always, she melted like a stick of butter and indulged in his kiss. My dad could tell my mom he made her a bowl of cereal, and she would think it was romantic as fuck.

"On that note," I said and then left them to damn near fuck by the pool.

"Is Daddy back there? I need some money," my little sister Kendria asked me.

She was fifteen going on thirty. She looked just like my mom but had green eyes, and I felt bad for any nigga that she, or our cousins Kennedy and Kaylie came in contact with. There were so many men in our family, and it was hard for a nigga to even get a hug from one of our sisters or cousins.

"Yeah, he's back there. What your grown ass need money for?" I stared into her jade green eyes.

"I wanna get my feet done," she giggled.

"For what?" I jerked my neck back.

"Because I'm a girl, KJ, that's why!" She rolled her eyes at me.

"It bet not be no nigga you getting them done for," I replied sternly. I didn't play about my little sister, and niggas knew that.

"Honestly, how could I even get around the nigga to show him my feet, the way y'all stay on my back!" She smacked her full lips and stormed to the back where my parents were.

I went upstairs and decided to take another shower, because the one at London's was just a quickie. I then brushed my teeth again, dressed, sprayed my cologne, and then dipped right back out.

As I walked by my brother Kendrin's room, I heard him going in on his phone. He must've been talking to his girlfriend, Willow. They fought like cats and dogs all fucking day, because she was crazy as fuck.

"You good, bro?" I roughed up my little brother Kendrae's hair as he played video games.

"Yeah, I'm straight. Where you headed?" He looked over his shoulder at me.

"To Kaleeini's. If Kendrin comes looking for me, tell him I left, aight?" I smiled down at him and he nodded.

Kendrae, or simply Drae wanted to be down so bad, but I felt he was too young. My dad did too, so it was really a no go. We always called him the break up baby, because my mom got pregnant with him while she and my dad were somewhat broken up. I'm not surprised because they fuck all the damn time. That was another reason I wanted to move out.

I pulled up to Kaleeini's condo, and then quickly got out and locked my car. As I was walking onto the curb, I spotted Gianna, or simply Gigi. Gigi was fine as fuck boy, got damn! She had a smooth light brown sugar complexion, long brownish red hair, and her body was to die for even though her titties were small. Her mom was Italian, and her father was black.

"Sup Gigi," I smirked and she half smiled while shaking her head.

"Hey KJ," she waved to me lazily.

"Where you going?" I wondered as I neared her and her friend Aysia.

"Why nigga?" She giggled and put her hand on her hip. She was wearing a yellow strapless dress and yellow sandals. I could tell she'd just gotten her hair straightened because I could smell the hairspray them places used. She may have gone to my mom's spot, because that's where all the bitches got their hair done.

"Because I wanna come with you," I half joked.

"Well you can't, carry on," she smirked up at me and I licked my lips.

Gianna was sexy as fuck, and I loved her personality. She was always doing her own thing and not like these other hood rats in Baltimore. She wasn't bourgeois as fuck either; she was right in the middle—just perfect.

"Aight, fine then," I shrugged and then walked off. I looked over my shoulder and just as I suspected, she was still watching.

You see, Gianna was my girl, but not my girl officially. Chicks that I fucked with over the years knew it too, and they couldn't say shit about it. When Gianna called or needed something, she was priority over any girl I was with at the time. We were like homies in love ever since the day I met her back in high school. I pretty much had her on the shelf waiting for me until I was ready to settle down. Niggas in Baltimore knew that she was off limits, and the niggas that did try and talk to her, she knew to turn them down. As soon as I was ready to be a one-woman man, I would cuff her officially.

My dad told me a while ago to never date a woman I was interested in before I was ready, because it would mess it up. I didn't know what he meant at first because he and my mom were damn near perfect, but as I got older I understood what he meant. I really loved Gianna and I didn't wanna be cheating on her and shit. When I got her I wanted to do right by her.

Me: *You coming through to Lenny's kickback tonight.* I shot Gianna a text.

Wifey: *Yep*

I WALKED into the kickback with my other homeboy Huey, and that shit was popping. I spotted my best friend Lenny and dapped him up, as he handed me a drink some shorty just made. As I sipped it, I spotted some nigga all in Gianna's face. I polished the drink off, and then walked up over there.

"So can I get that number or what?" he smiled down at her.

She was wearing a tight red dress that was nice and short. I hadn't fucked her yet for obvious reasons, but damn did I want to.

"Nah, she's good homie," I replied for her and wrapped my arm around her neck. I pulled her away while kissing on her neck.

"Move KJ," she nudged me off of her using her elbow. I pulled her into the dark hallway and pinned her up against the wall.

"Let's go in the room," I whispered before slipping my tongue into her mouth.

"You only wanna fuck me when you're high or drunk," she whined in between kisses.

She was right; I had just smoked a fat one while I was outside. When I was sober I wanted to save her, but when I was under the influence I wanted to fuck.

"Why you got niggas in your fucking face, Gigi?" I pulled away and asked.

"He literally just walked up to me KJ, and how do you think I feel when I see you fucking with all these girls while I'm at home lonely?" she pouted.

"But you know what's up though. They're just something to do until I'm ready for you," I grinned and kissed on her pretty face.

"Yeah, yeah, yeah, same story every time," she shook her head with a smile.

"And when I'm at the same party as you, I treat you like my girl anyway," I pinched her chin and she giggled.

I grabbed her hand and led her back out to the party. I found a seat on the couch, and pulled her into my lap.

"I love you, homie," she chuckled.

"Gimme some," I responded and she kissed my lips gently, while caressing my face with her soft hands.

I stood in front of my full-length mirror, giving myself the once over. Tonight, Aysia and I were going to KJ's summer party. Every summer he would throw this big ass party, and it was always turnt the fuck up. KJ was always throwing parties for random shit, but sometimes he threw them for occasions like Halloween or Christmas too. I was just going so that I could be around him; I didn't give a fuck what it was for.

I met KJ in high school, and I'd been in love ever since. He felt I was too young so he had no interest in being with me at the time. We were both under age, but he said once he turned eighteen, he couldn't have a sixteen-year-old on his arm anymore. We had an agreement I guess, so I really didn't fuck with anybody during high school, especially while he was still going there. We would hang out a lot, and we had spent many nights together sucking face until we couldn't anymore, but nothing else. He told me I was special and he didn't wanna go there with me yet.

I was fine with that shit, because I just knew once I turned eighteen he and I would become official, but boy was I wrong. When I became of age, another excuse came along as well. Now he didn't wanna 'mess us up'. He still wanted me to sit and wait for him, or in other words remain a virgin. I was so tired of sleeping alone, especially when I knew he was out smashing all kinds of hoes. I would hear through the grapevine that he had good dick, and shit, I wanted to know about it too! But I wanted it to be my dick only, and he knew that. He had a problem with committing right now, and he wanted me to wait until he didn't anymore. I rolled my eyes at the thought.

I then laughed when I thought about all the times he would drop what he was doing to come help me when I needed him. I remember I found out he was at some bitch's house, so I called him and told him I was hungry and sick. You should've seen that bitch's face when he brought me some food, and left her sitting outside for three damn hours while we cuddled and kissed. He had never told me he loved me yet, but I knew he did.

KJ and I used to text and talk on the phone everyday, as well as hang out a lot, but ever since he took over his father's drug empire we barely conversed. I usually only saw him if I was passing Kaleeini's, at certain functions, or when he would just drop by out of nowhere to make sure I wasn't getting dicked down. For some reason, even though our communication had dwindled, I still knew to keep 'it' on lock down for him. I was growing very tired though.

"Hurry up!" Aysia shouted to me as she stood in my doorway.

"Alright, dang, no need to rush," I chuckled at her anxious ass.

She had a major crush on KJ's cousin Kaleeini, and I knew she wanted to be there in hopes of pushing up on him. Aysia had a boyfriend named Brice though, so I wasn't sure how that was gonna work.

"I know you wanna look perfect for KJ, but damn," she taunted with a smile. I rolled my eyes at her because I didn't have a response.

Hell yeah I was obsessed with KJ, but every girl in Baltimore was. He was 6'2, had a toffee complexion, jade green eyes, deep dimples, perfect teeth, his hair stayed cut, and so did his body. I hated that bitches wanted him because I wanted him to my fucking self. I wasn't dumb though. KJ was a rich ass nigga and had plenty of bitches to bang out. I wasn't gonna be with anybody that would be smashing other hoes and cheating on me. So the fact that he wasn't mine officially was fine with me... at times.

"Gigi!" Aysia clapped her hands, snapping me out of my trans.

"Aight!" I yelled back to her and grabbed my purse. I was wearing a simple red dress, with red stilettos to match. I pulled my long brownish red hair into a regular ponytail, and wore gold jewelry to complement my look.

"Bye Mom, bye Dad," I smiled at my parents chilling on the couch watching TV.

"Addio Gianna, non stare troppo tardi. (Bye Gianna, don't stay out too late)," my mother pointed to me and I nodded before rolling my eyes.

"Sarò presto a casa madre. (I'll be home soon mother)," I responded. I was nineteen years old but she treated me like I was sixteen.

Aysia and I climbed into her black Toyota Camry, and took a couple pictures for the gram. She turned on Future's "Purple Reign" mixtape, and we turned up during the whole ride to KJ's party. When we got there, it was a line wrapped around the fucking corner. I prayed that we would be able to go right in, because I didn't bring a jacket or any extra shoes.

"Text KJ and tell him to let us up," Aysia nudged me and smiled.

She was wearing a black crop top with a black skirt and black heels. A simple glitter bronzer adorned her caramel complexion, accompanied by silver jewelry.

"What if he doesn't text back?" I laughed and pulled out my iPhone.

I knew he would respond, but he had his days when he would be on his bullshit. I also didn't feel too confident because we weren't in contact like we used to be.

"Gigi, KJ is in love with you, so he's gonna text back," she shook her head as she fixed her baby hairs in the visor mirror.

"He told you he loved me?" I quizzed.

"No bitch, I can just tell," she chuckled and I nudged her lightly.

"And when the fuck would I have sat down and had a conversation with him?" she added and laughed.

Me: *Hey KJ, do we have to wait in line?*

"Okay, I sent it," I took a deep breath.

"Stop acting like you're about to die," Aysia smiled at me.

I looked down at my phone and there was no response yet. I knew I shouldn't have text him. I hated to look stupid, and rejection was the main way you could look dumb. I blew out hot hair just as my phone buzzed in my freshly manicured hands.

KJ: *Nah shorty, tell Bolo at the front that you're with me.*

I read KJ's text and smiled. The thought of me being with him made me smile, even though I knew he didn't mean it like that... yet.

"Okay, let's go Aysia," I said before we both exited the car and then strutted to the front of the venue. People were frowning and making comments because we walked straight up to Bolo. "Hey, I'm Gigi and this is —"

"KJ already told me, have a good time, ladies," Bolo opened the door for us to walk in.

As soon as we got in, a lady with an earpiece grabbed my hand, and so I grabbed Aysia's. She led us through the party safely, and up to the balcony area where I spotted KJ, Kaleeini, Kendrin, and Kenzie. I slowly walked into the area as I watched KJ, his cousins, and his brother, turn up with a couple friends. There were some girls too, wearing damn near nothing. I knew my best friend Willow would have a fit if she saw Kendrin going in like he was right now. Kenzie was dating my other best friend Shannon, but he appeared to be on his best behavior from first impressions.

"Go say hi to your man," Aysia pushed me and I slapped her hand. Since KJ wanted to be surrounded by hoes, I would let him come to me!

"No bitch, I'm gonna sit right here and drink something if I can," I replied and she turned her lip up.

I didn't have my fake I.D. with me, so the waitress served me and Aysia these drinks called Shirley Temples. I swayed my body to

"Valet" by Eric Bellinger, and then all of a sudden some Gucci cologne hit my nose. I looked up to see KJ's fine faded ass.

"Why you come up in my shit and didn't speak?" He grinned with his sexy self.

"My bad, you looked busy," I shrugged one shoulder and drank from my straw seductively. He licked his lips and then sat down next to me.

"I ain't never too busy for you," he said in a low tone, and my body got chills like it always did when he spoke to me.

"Oh yeah? It doesn't seem that way," I raised a brow and cocked my head.

"How you figure?" He furrowed his brows.

"Because you haven't been hitting my phone or anything. We only talk when I text you, or your random calls you do to make sure I'm not fucking anybody. And the only time I see you is randomly or at your fucking parties," I pouted. I couldn't believe I was being so honest, but he looked so good right now. He wore a Burgundy crew neck, black jeans, a black snap back, and burgundy Nike Roshes.

"Alright, so if I asked your ass out on a date you would go?" He raised a brow making my pussy get wet.

I was the freakiest virgin you would ever meet. I was a virgin because I was waiting for his ass. On top of that, KJ had made it known that I was off limits to other niggas.

"So you wanna take me on a for real date? Not no bullshit nigga," I grinned and so did he, making his dimples appear.

"I'm offended Gianna, you know I wouldn't take you anywhere beneath Mickey D's," he laughed and I smacked his chest. It was so hard!

"I'm serious, Kendrick!" I said using his actual name. He had never asked to take me out before, so I was kinda happy that it seemed we were getting somewhere.

"I like when you call me that," he bit his lip and I blushed. I wanted to be with him now; I was tired of waiting for him.

"Answer my question," I whined.

"Yes baby girl, I'm gon' take you somewhere nice. You just be ready for a nigga like me, aight?" He stared into my eyes with his dark green ones. I just nodded my head. "That's Right" by E-40 and Ty Dolla $ign came on, and KJ took my drink out of my hand before sitting it on the table. "Lap dance," he demanded and I playfully rolled my eyes.

I stood up and he didn't miss one inch of my body as he eyed me. I slid into his lap, and his cologne invaded my nostrils even more. I held onto his kneecaps, and leaned forward before going to work. I looked over my shoulder at him, and he was smiling while looking at my ass; perfect. I continued fucking it up, and even got extra with it when I saw a couple hoes watching. Once the song switched, KJ wrapped his arm around my waist, and pulled me against his chest. He kissed the exposed parts of my back, making goose bumps appear on my forearms.

"Kendrick il mio amore (Kendrick my love)," I whispered.

"Stop saying my name like that girl, unless you wanna feel this dick," he whispered back to me in between planting kisses on my back and neck.

"Maybe I want to feel it," I looked down into his eyes.

I was still in his lap, so I could feel his rod hardening under me. I knew I shouldn't have come, because now my feelings for him had only intensified. I couldn't sit on his shelf of love any longer. He needed to be with me now or I was moving right along.

I LEANED over the balcony to stare down at the rowdy ass festivities going down in this venue. I shook my head and chuckled at all the people going in on the dance floor. My cousin KJ was a wild ass nigga. He loved to party, work, and fuck plenty of bitches. I admit it was fun most of the time, but I moved at a slower pace.

We were the sons of brothers Kendreeis and Kendrick King, and they ran the biggest drug empire here in Baltimore. Now that they had retired, it belonged to KJ, Kendrin, and me.

"There go shorty," KJ's best friend Lenny pointed over to one of the velvet couches.

Next to KJ and Gianna making out like some freaks, I saw Gianna's best friend Aysia pretending to be occupied with her phone. I knew she was feeling me, and I was definitely interested too, but I knew she had a dude.

We went to the same high school, and although she was a year under me, I always noticed her pretty ass. We officially met at a party KJ had thrown to celebrate him graduating from high school, and ever since then we'd been on some flirty shit. Every time I saw her at a party, we would always go somewhere secluded and just talk all night. I'd asked her for her number about one thousand times, and she always politely played me to the left because of her nigga.

She was dating this guy named Brice. He was a low-ball ass hustler; the type that got his money from robbing women coming out of shopping malls and shit. I wasn't sure how Aysia could like a nigga like myself, yet be with a trash ass nigga like Brice. Whatever the case was, I was done playing games. Either she was gone give me her number tonight, in preparation of moving on, or I was done.

"Be right back," I told Lenny and he nodded.

I walked over to where Aysia was, and pulled her up off the couch to take her to another one. I wasn't tryna be sitting next to KJ and Gianna sucking face.

"Damn Kaleeini!" Aysia giggled as we sat down on the couch.

"Put your fucking phone up, you ain't talking to nobody," I frowned and snatched her phone.

"Nigga, how you know I ain't talking to nobody?" She raised her perfect brow.

"Well, whomever you're talking to can wait because you're talking to me right now," I grinned and she blushed.

"Fine," she responded in a low tone, so I handed her back her phone. "But make it quick because you know my man may know some people up in this party," she said just as the deejay turned on some Baltimore club music.

"And then what?" I smirked. The thought of that nigga trying to do anything to me over Aysia was pure comedy.

"Then you might get beat up," she flashed her perfect white teeth.

"By whom?" I quizzed with a slight frown.

"Who you think!" She sucked her teeth.

"Aysia please, I could take you and there would be nothing your boyfriend could say to me about it," I stated seriously and honestly.

"Oh, you think you got it like that?" She asked with her head cocked. I could tell she was turned on by the look in her eyes.

"Yeah, pretty much. You ain't ready for me yet though, so I'll let him hold onto you for a little longer," I bit my lip and scanned her sexy ass body.

Her crop top had her toned stomach exposed. I was only twenty, and she nineteen, but she made me feel like proposing.

"Maybe you're not ready for me," she bantered.

"Why wouldn't I be? I know what you want and I know what you need," I responded and chuckled at my own words.

"Oh yeah?" She smirked.

"Yep," I nodded to assure her and we both laughed. "Damn you look good tonight," I ran my finger down her stomach.

"Kaleeini, stop," she touched my hand but didn't move it away.

"Stop what?" I questioned dumbly and moved closer to her pretty face.

"Pushing up on me, I have a man," she said in a low tone. Our faces were extremely close, so it was easy to hear her over the loud music.

"He ain't gon' be your man for much longer though, Aysia. You love him?" I inquired and she stared into my eyes.

"Kind of, I mean yeah, yeah, I do love him," she shrugged one of her shoulders.

"Are you in love with him?" I questioned further.

"You just asked me that," she replied smiling.

"No, I asked if you loved him. Loving someone and being in love with someone are two different things shorty," I corrected her.

"Sometimes I am and sometimes I feel like I'm not," she answered.

"So you gon' fix that?" I cheesed and so did she.

"I don't even know how you're gonna treat me. I don't wanna leave him for a player," she said and then ran her tongue over her perfect choppers.

"Player? You know I'm not a fucking player Aysia," I frowned.

"I know you're a young sexy dude, with a lot of money, and girls dying to be with you," she folded her arms over her perky breasts.

"So you think I'm sexy?" I laughed.

"That's all you got from what I just said!" She squealed.

"Answer the question shorty."

"You know I think you're sexy Kaleeini, especially with those eyes." She caressed the side of my face, and I kissed her palm.

"Let me get your number." I reached into my pocket and retrieved my iPhone.

"Kaleeini—"

"This is the last time I'm gonna ask you for your number, Aysia. You better take this chance to have a real nigga in your life," I told her sternly. She rolled her eyes playfully and then read her number off to me. "And you better answer every single time I call or text you, shorty. If you take too long to reply or anything, I'm dropping by your crib," I joked.

"You don't know where I live," she grinned.

"That's what you think," I winked and her jaw dropped.

I watched Kaleeini as he walked back over to join his cousins. He was so fucking sexy and aggressive, and I loved that shit. He seemed so right but I didn't wanna break up with my boyfriend, Brice just for Kaleeini to do me dirty.

I'd been with Brice for two years now, and at first everything was great. Over time, the relationship became more like a chore, because all we did was argue and shit. Sometimes I wouldn't even know what the fuck we would be arguing about.

Brice was diagnosed with paranoid schizophrenia about a year after we began dating, and at first he had a good handle on it so I didn't mind. He was taking his medicine regularly, but then he started doing cocaine. Because he was doing drugs, it pretty much made the medicine ineffective. He always thought I was cheating on him, or plotting on him to be killed by someone. That shit was saddening to me at first, but now I was just annoyed by it. I knew if I left him for Kaleeini, he and his family would think he was right all this time about me being a 'scheming ass hoe', as he would call me. Little did they know, their precious Brice was a cokehead, and stuck in an episode of delusion.

Anyway, Kaleeini was looking like the perfect upgrade, but I wasn't sure. I knew he had plenty of chicks he could pick from with his fine ass, so I was very weary. *Why did he want me?* I always asked myself. It seemed too good to be true.

I looked to my right and saw that Gianna and KJ had stopped kissing, and she was now out of his lap and sitting next to him. I got up and walked over so that we could leave. We'd been here for a couple hours now, and I had work in the morning.

"Gigi, you ready?" I plopped down next to her. She pulled her mirror from her purse and checked her smeared lipstick.

"Hell no, KJ said to come home with him," she sucked her lip with her freaky virginal ass. I could smell vodka on her breath, so clearly she'd had a couple sips of whatever KJ was drinking.

"Gigi! Are you ready to lose your virginity?" I asked.

"Nobody said anything about losing my virginity. We're just gonna go chill in a calmer setting," she replied.

"If you go home with a high or drunk KJ, you gon' be doing more than talking," I chuckled. She'd already put me up on game about how he only wanted some pussy from her when he was faded.

"Yeah, you're right," she sighed. She turned to him, and waited until he was done conversing with his cousin Kenzie. "Me and Aysia are gonna go KJ," she said to him in her sweet little voice.

"What? Why? Gianna, I thought you were leaving with me," he smiled showing his deep dimples.

"I—"

"Don't leave," he cut her off and pecked her passionately a couple times. This nigga was really putting his game down; I had to give it to him.

"Gianna, come on," I chuckled and lightly tugged her small waist.

"Man Aysia, leave your friend alone and go dance or some shit!" KJ cackled and I shook my head at him.

"Nope, come on Gigi," I pulled on her arm.

We stood up together and KJ was mouthing something to her, I guess trying to convince her otherwise.

"I will see you on our date, KJ," Gianna half smiled and he smacked his lips.

"Don't bring her ass!" he called after us and I flicked him off.

"Good thing you came girl, because I definitely would've went home with him," Gianna huffed as we walked outside of the venue.

"And let him fuck?" I smiled and she twisted her mouth up like she was thinking.

"You know KJ has a way with words, so shit, probably!" she laughed and so did I.

"Girl, that whole family has a way with words," I exhaled as we neared my whip.

"What you mean? You must've had a deep conversation with Kaleeini again!" she yelped and then started twerking.

"Get your crazy ass in the car!" I shook my head and slid into the driver seat. "Anyway, yes, Kaleeini pulled my ass to the side and damn near deebo'd me out of my fucking number," I said once we were both inside the car.

"Isn't this like the tenth time he's asked you for it?" Gianna quizzed as she put on some ChapStick.

"Yes, and he told me this would be the last time, so you know my ass quickly read that shit off," I chuckled and so did she.

"So what about Brice though? You know you can't have both guys, Aysia," she said.

"And I don't want both. I want Kaleeini, but I'm not trying to leave what I got for something that may not be for sure," I sighed and made a left.

Gianna didn't know about Brice's illness whatsoever. Keep in mind though, his illness alone was not why I wanted to end our relationship, it was the way he was handling it.

"I get it. But don't miss out on something better just because you're comfortable. How would you feel seeing Kaleeini boo'd up with another bitch?" She questioned and I thought about it for a couple moments.

"How would I feel before or after I beat her ass?" I half joked and we burst into laughter.

"Exactly, so quit playing games boo," she replied.

"I know you ain't talking! Your ass been in love with KJ ever since you were fourteen years old, and here we are five years later and he still ain't your man," I smacked my lips.

"I know, I'm working on it," she grinned.

"Well work faster, y'all are super cute together," I stated.

"I'm not gonna chase him though. He knows I fuck with him, but he needs to prove to me that he wants me too, and not just for a kiss buddy like he's been doing," she sighed.

"I agree. If he wants you wants you, he will make it known. Ain't he fucking some older chick?" I wondered.

"Yes, on top of like seven other girls. I think she is like forty or some shit," she chuckled.

"Damn! Ain't his mama younger than that?" I frowned and bucked my eyes.

"Yeah, she's thirty-nine," she nodded.

"You know all the history on KJ I see," I nudged her with my elbow.

"Shut up, we've just been associates for a long ass while," she poked her lips out and stared out the window.

"Well, hopefully you guys become more than that. I have a feeling this summer is about to be wild as hell!" I lightly tapped the steering wheel and Gianna nodded in agreement. I pulled up to her parents' condo, and she kissed my cheek before getting out. "Bye boo," I said out the window before pulling off.

As I was driving, I heard my phone ringing. I quickly glanced down and turned my lip up when I saw it was Brice. A part of me was hoping that it was Kaleeini.

"Hey," I answered my phone dryly.

"What's up? I been blowing your line up all fucking night, Aysia! You better not be out fucking a nigga!" Brice shouted in my ear. "I saw a car drive by my crib twice in a row, you bet not have set me up either!"

"I'm not fucking nobody, and I didn't set you up, aight? I told you I was hanging out with Gigi tonight, Brice," I rolled my eyes as I came to a red light.

"Come over then," he said in a calmer tone.

"I'm tired, I will come over tomorrow after work," I exhaled heavily and disconnected before he could respond.

My phone buzzed and I looked down to see his name on it. It buzzed the whole way home and when I got there I saw I had four-teen missed calls, and twenty-seven text messages.

Brice: *Who was that in the background when I called?*

Brice: *I seen a nigga in the background of your picture on Insta-gram Aysia... I ain't no dumb nigga!*

Brice: *Stop hanging with Gigi's hoe ass!*

I read the text messages as I sat in my driveway. I wasn't sure how much longer I could deal with his ass.

THAT PARTY GOT wild as fuck, especially after Gianna left. I didn't want her little sexy ass to go, but then again, maybe it was for the best since I was gone off weed and alcohol. I would've been hot if I had taken her home and fucked. Gianna was my baby, and I wanted her when I deserved her.

Anyway, once she was gone, all kinds of fine shorties showed up, and me, my cousins, and brother were definitely enjoying their company. What can I say though? I'm a single man. As for Kendrin and Kenzie, they deal with their relationships how they want to. I ain't the type of nigga to be spending time keeping niggas on the good foot. It wasn't nothing but harmless flirting anyway.

I slipped my hoodie over my head, and slid my feet into my all black Nike Huaraches before coming out of my room. Two more weeks and a nigga would be in his own fucking home. I walked down the stairs right when my mom's best friend Christy walked in. She was actually a cousin through marriage, but she seemed more like an aunt. She, my mother, Kaleeini's, and Kenzie's mother were all best friends, so maybe that's why.

"Hey Aunt Christy," I flashed her a smile and gave her a hug. I kissed my mom on the cheek before hugging her as well.

"Where is Pop?" I quizzed.

"In the office," my mom replied and then led Christy to the kitchen to talk some more. I went to the back to see my father because he said he wanted to talk to me.

"Good morning," I said as I walked into his office and closed the door behind me.

"Oh finally, sit down," he said and started clicking shit on his computer. I did as he asked, and then waited for him to finish whatever he was clicking on.

"Aight, so how is everything going?" He squinted his eyes and stared at me.

"It's going great, as usual," I replied and shrugged.

"And you're making sure to pay attention to everybody and everything, all the time?" He asked.

"Yes Pop, damn," I chuckled.

"I'm serious, KJ, I wanna make sure that you're not too focused on shorties and partying to the point where you're neglecting your priorities," he stated.

"Look, before anything I'm a King man and you know we always handle business. I don't party or fuck with any shorties until I know my business shit is in order. Speaking of business, I got that Colombian connect I told you about," I said to ease his mind.

"Oh, word? I guess I don't have to worry about you as much as I thought," he grinned and I shook my head.

"Yeah, you're retired and now I run things, so you should let it be that way. Relax your nerves, man," I responded and he nodded.

"Excuse me," he laughed. "Well that was all I wanted to speak to you about. I just wanted to see where your head was at," he added and popped some gum into his mouth.

"I appreciate that and I promise Dad, if I need help, which I won't, I will let you or my uncles know," I reassured him as I stood up.

"Cool, where you headed?" He wondered.

"To check on the status of my shipments, and then to my house to just look at it," I answered.

"Yeah, it's time you go, you're giving your mama high blood pressure every time you come home at one and two in the morning," he chuckled and so did I.

"I know. And speaking of Mom, give her a break one of these nights, I'm tired of hearing y'all asses every time I walk by you guys' room. That's another reason I'm moving!" I half joked and we both laughed.

"Your mama is used to me by now, she's good," he nodded and grinned. We dapped each other up and I walked out.

Nobody liked to hear their mama getting fucked, even if it was by their father. Some nights I wanted to walk in there and make sure he wasn't fucking her all kinds of crazy ways. Ha. The thought of him doing anything outside of missionary to my mother had me a little bothered. It was bad enough that I knew she was giving him head when I only heard him moaning.

I walked outside to our huge roundabout driveway, and hopped into my car. After checking on my shipments and house, I decided to go visit this shorty named Zaria. She was fine as fuck and could suck a mean dick. She was kind of clingy, but it seemed like all the girls I fucked with became that way after awhile. That's why I would go weeks without talking to them sometimes, trying to break that attachment. It didn't work as well as I thought though.

I pulled up to her crib, and jogged up her walkway. I always popped up unannounced because I didn't give a fuck. I wanted my dick sucked when I wanted it, and the fact that she may have been busy didn't matter to me. I banged on her door lightly, and a few moments later she opened the door wearing little ass jean shorts and a spaghetti strapped top.

"Look who finally decided to show up," she rolled her eyes and then walked into her house.

I watched her ass as I followed behind her. We both sat down on the couch, and she was mugging me like a muthafucka. I burst into laughter because that shit was funny for some reason. I guess because she thought her being mad was gonna make me become nigga of the year.

"Why you mad, shorty?" I squeezed her thigh and she smacked my hand away.

"Because you haven't answered any of my texts or calls, and then you just show up out of nowhere!" She yelled.

"Damn, you that mad because I ain't hit your line or respond to you?" I frowned. She acted like she couldn't fuck with other niggas.

"Why wouldn't I be?" she raised her brow. Her smooth golden skin looked extra supple, so she must've just gotten out of the shower.

"Well for one, I'm not even your man," I shrugged and looked around her place using my eyes only.

"You sure in the fuck act like it though!" she shouted.

"What? How?" I jerked my neck back. I did a lot of shit, but acting like someone's man wasn't one of them. Even Gianna couldn't say that, and I showed her the most love and affection.

"You come here and fuck me all night, then I cook for you and shit. I don't do that for just anybody," she rolled her eyes.

"Sounds like you act like *my* woman, but I don't act like *your* man," I pursed my lips and stared at her.

"I hate you, nigga," she sucked her teeth.

"So what, now you ain't gon' give me any?" I asked in a calmer tone. Fighting with her was not the way to get in her panties.

"Apologize and I will," she smirked with her arms still folded.

"What you take me for shorty? I ain't gon' apologize for nothing," I squinted my eyes. She just looked away from me, still frowning.

I scooted closer to her, and then gently pulled the straps of her top down to expose her plump breasts. I took one of her nipples into my mouth, and then sucked them hungrily.

"Aaaahhhh," she cooed softly as I devoured her nipples.

I unbuttoned her jean shorts while getting my fix, and then pulled them down along with her panties.

"Come show him some love," I told her and she got her sexy naked ass on her knees.

She pulled my dick from my jeans, and then took it into her mouth. She deep throated it like the professional she was, and I threw my head back to enjoy it.

"Mmmm," she purred as she glided her warm wet mouth up and down my shaft.

I gripped a handful of her twists, and bounced her head up and down on my dick at the pace I wanted. After releasing into her mouth, she swallowed it up and then stood to her feet. I pulled a condom from my wallet, and then slid it down onto my rod. I grabbed her small wrists, and then pulled her into my lap. She grabbed my dick, and then positioned it at her opening. We stared each other in the eyes, and I bit my lip as she slid her self down onto me.

"Oh my goossshhh," she whimpered and frowned.

She was super tight, letting me know she had definitely been saving the pussy for ya boy. If that's what she wanted to do, I wasn't gon' stop her.

She placed her palms on my shoulders, and I placed mine on her waistline. I guided her up and down on my dick, until she finally took control.

"I hate that you got such good dick, KJ," she cried out as she rocked her hips on me. She had some good ass pussy, but it wasn't good enough to lock a nigga down. I squeezed her ass so hard that I felt her pussy lips spread. "Aaahhhh!" she called out as she rained down on me.

I turned her around so that her back was to me. I placed her legs on the outside of mine, to give me more access to her opening, and then I went ham. I had one hand on her shoulder, and the other on her waist, as I drilled into her from behind. She was crying out like a wounded animal as I fucked the shit out of her. I saw her small hands grip the couch cushion, as her caramel face turned bloodshot red.

"Mm," I mumbled as I felt my nut rising. Soon after, I released into the condom. She drenched me again with her juices, and slowly wound her hips on me as she let it all out. I gripped her breasts from behind, and played with her nipples as I caught my breath.

"I fucking love you," she panted. I ignored her because I didn't give a fuck.

She finally got off of me, and I got up to go clean myself in the bathroom. Once I was finished, I came out to the smell of tacos. She knew that was my favorite food, and I knew she made it so that I would stay.

"Smells good," I commented as I sat at the table in her kitchen.

"I went shopping yesterday just in case you came by," she smiled at me and then went back to cooking the meat.

"Thanks shorty, I don't need you going out of your way for me though. You be getting the wrong impression when I let you do that shit," I sighed and pulled out my phone.

"No, I was tripping earlier. I just missed you, that's all. I know you don't want anything serious right now, but when you do, I want you to know where you should go," she walked over to me and tried to kiss my lips but I moved.

"You know I don't do that kissing shit," I rubbed her ass and then squeezed it.

I didn't kiss and I didn't eat pussy when it came to these hoes. I'd met a cute little shorty back when I was fourteen, and we were both virgins. She was sixteen, but you know that didn't stop me from getting her. I pretty much got with her so I could learn to fuck and eat pussy. That was the last girl whose pussy I ate. I fucked her for about a good six months constantly, and then I broke up with her. I realized I didn't need her anymore, after a time I ate her pussy to the point where she was trembling. She missed school the next day because of how hard I dicked her down too. She was devastated when I dumped her, and probably still hates me, but at least she knew how to suck dick after me. Ha.

I WAS SITTING in the conference room of our building because KJ had called a meeting with everybody. He said he had some good news and I couldn't wait to hear. Anytime he had good news that meant we would be making more and more money.

"So we got that Colombian connect y'all, which means we will be getting more shipments than usual. That also means we're gonna be pushing way more product per week, and we all know what that results in," KJ grinned and so did I.

"Results to more fucking bread, bro," his little brother Kendrin smiled and nodded.

"Exactly. Now everybody is gonna have their same position, but now we need Drew and Lenny to be on shipment duty as well," KJ said.

Drew, short for Kendrew Jr., was part of the team as well. We had so many family members that there wasn't really a need to recruit anyone outside of the family like my dad and uncles had to. We had a few outsiders, but besides Lenny and Tesean, they were in lower positions.

"Sounds like a plan," Drew nodded.

"Kaleeini and I will continue to double check the money count, and Kendrin and Tesean will keep an eye on the traps. Everybody needs to make sure that they're being very thorough, even though I'm gonna go through everything with a fine toothed comb," KJ said and everyone nodded. "Alright, well that was all I had to say for now, so remember Tuesday at 3am is the first shipment aight?" He said.

We all stood up to leave the conference room, and I felt my phone chime in my pocket.

Aysia*: Hey.*

I smiled at my phone, and just decided to call her pretty ass.

"What you call me for nigga? Who said I wanted to talk on the phone?" She giggled.

"I don't wanna talk on the phone either, I wanna see you. Where you at?" I quizzed as I hit the alarm to unlock my car.

"I'm at home painting my nails," she responded sweetly.

"Get dressed and I'm gone come scoop you," I said and then disconnected before she could protest.

I drove to Aysia's mom's condo, and then texted her to tell her I was outside. A couple minutes later, she emerged wearing jeans, a t-shirt, and sandals. Her dark hair was hanging down, and as always, she had her baby hairs slicked down.

"I hate that you just decided we were gonna see each other," she smiled and pushed her hair behind her ear.

"Yep," was all I said as I pulled away from the curb. I drove to my condo, and then quickly parked in my space. I got out the car, and she was still sitting inside cheesing. "Get your ass out the car!" I said and knocked on my car window. She sucked her teeth and then climbed out.

"You brought me here why? I'm on my period," she chuckled.

"Ain't nobody tryna fuck, so calm down with the lies shorty," I laughed and opened my door for her. We walked into the living room, and she plopped down while taking in her surroundings.

"This your hoe crib?" she wondered and I laughed as I sat down next to her.

"Nah, this is where I'm living until I find a nicer house. I don't feel like I really need a house though until I get a family and shit, but my dad feels like I do," I replied.

"So you don't have a hoe crib?" She cocked her head.

"If you're asking if I have other places around town, the answer is yes, but not for the hoes, aight?" I nudged her lightly.

"You know I'm supposed to see my nigga in like an hour, and you fucking kidnapped me," she smiled. Her smile was so fucking pretty. Everything about her was pretty.

"Well, when he calls looking for you just let me answer," I said and she giggled.

"So what do you want from me, Kaleeini?" she asked seriously.

"I want you to be my girl, but I need you to drop old boy first before I spend any serious time with you," I said.

"So you want me to break up with him, just so you can date me? What if you realize you don't like me? I'm gon' be assed out!" She poked her full lips out.

"I highly doubt that we won't end up being a couple, but you just have to take that chance. Who would you rather be with? Me or that corny ass nigga?" I raised a brow.

"To be honest Kaleeini, I really like you and I would love to pursue something with you but I'm used to Brice," she shook her head.

"So you're scared is what you're saying?"

"Yeah," she responded in a low tone, almost like there was another reason as well.

"Why though? You think I'm that bad of a guy?" I quizzed.

"No, but I know you're a hot commodity around Baltimore, Kaleeini, and there are plenty of girls waiting for you," she shrugged and played with my dreads.

"But look who I'm chilling with," I stated and a smile crept across her face.

"It seems too good to be true though. Like I'm just Aysia and you're Kaleeini King," she scooted closer to me and sat Indian style.

"In my eyes, I'm just Kaleeini and you're Aysia Terrence," I smirked and so did she. "Nah, but I get what you're saying shorty. How about you spend some actual time with me, and we will go from there? But as long as you got a boyfriend, just know we can't be as serious," I told her.

"I know, but I wanna hang out with you still and feel you out," she said.

"I wanna feel you out too," I bit my lip. Damn did I wanna feel her out. My dick got hard just from looking at her.

"Kaleeini!" she squealed and tapped my chest.

I leaned my face closer to hers, and she pecked me gently. She pulled away and we stared each other in the eyes for a couple seconds. I grabbed her face, and then slipped my tongue into her mouth. We began kissing passionately, and I pulled her into my lap to straddle me. I put my hands under her shirt, and she stopped me.

"I'm just resting them here," I grinned. She threw her hands over my shoulders and we resumed kissing.

This was *my* girl, and little did she know, I was gonna be taking up all of her fucking time. I just hoped Brice wasn't a sore looser type of nigga.

ONE WEEK LATER...

I WAS WALKING through the mall with my friend Willow, but I wasn't even in the mood to shop. Willow was KJ's younger brother Kendrin's girlfriend, and we'd been friends since middle school like Aysia and I. I kind of wanted to pick her brain and see if she had seen KJ with anybody recently, because his dog ass hadn't hit me up or asked me out on a date like he'd promised. I was trying not to care because he wasn't even my nigga, but damn, I wanted his stupid ass. However, it was obvious he didn't want me right now, and if he did, it wasn't for the right reasons.

"So he hasn't brought a girl to the house?" I asked Willow as I sifted through some shirts.

"KJ? Hell no, the day he brings a girl to his mama and daddy, pigs will be flying," she chuckled.

Hearing that was bittersweet; it was bitter because it just proved how much of a pit bull KJ was and would always be. It was sweet because that meant no other girl was occupying his time seriously. I knew he was fucking on hoes, but that's the thing, they were just hoes.

"That's good, I guess," I shrugged.

"Why don't you just call him, Gigi?" Willow placed her hand on her hip.

She had a light cinnamon complexion like me, and always wore her hair in two long ass French braids. She had a mole like Marilyn Monroe, long eyelashes, and big full lips that she kept covered in gloss. She had Kendrin's name tattooed on her hipbone, and she always found ways to show it. She was beyond possessive of her nigga. She would always introduce Kendrin as simply her boyfriend, and then wait for someone to try and differ.

"I'm tired of vying for him, Lo. I'm just gonna wait it out. If we end up together then so be it, but I'm not in the business of chasing niggas." I turned my lip up at the thought.

"Even ones that look like KJ?" She grinned and popped her gum.

"Yes, even sexy ass ones with dark green eyes and dimples," I said and my nipples got hard just at the thought of how bomb he was. Fuck, why couldn't I have him?

Willow and I shopped a little more, and then we got some food before heading home.

"Call me tomorrow so you, me, Aysia, and Shannon can go to breakfast!" she yelled out of her window and I nodded.

As I was walking up the steps of my parent's condo, someone gripped my body from behind. I tensed up, dropping my shopping bag, but then the familiar cologne hit my nose.

"Get off me, KJ!" I pried his hands off of my body, and then picked up my shopping bag.

"What you get?" he smiled and snatched my bag. I rolled my eyes as he sifted through my new things.

"Just these two cheap ass dresses?" he taunted and smirked with his cute ass. "Why didn't you get some cash from me before you went shopping?" he questioned.

"Give me my shit, asshole!" I grabbed my bag back, and then turned to go to my door.

"Damn Gigi, come here," he tugged on my arm and turned me to face him. "Why are you so mean today? You got your period?" he asked seriously.

"No," I replied being short.

"Then what's up, shorty? I missed you," he cheesed and I couldn't help but smile back.

"How do you miss me when I haven't heard from you since the party?" I raised my brow.

He looked so good wearing a navy blue short-sleeved button up, jeans, and Jordan's. His hair was freshly lined up under his hat, and his neck and wrists were both iced out.

"I been handling business, but look, let daddy take you out tonight," he offered.

"I'm busy," I lied.

"You ain't fucking busy! Put on one of your little ten dollar dresses you just bought, and come on before I change my mind," he joked.

"I don't care if you change your mind, nigga! Who said I wanted to go?" I furrowed my brows.

"I'm kidding beautiful, go change," he said in a low tone, and squinted his alluring eyes. I inhaled sharply, taking in his cologne, and then turned on my heels just as my mother emerged.

"Kendrick, la bello! Oh honey, come give me a hug!" my mom waved KJ over, and I rolled my eyes as I walked past her into the house. She and my dad loved KJ, because they thought he was so sweet.

"Mrs. Daniels, how are you? You're looking younger every time I see you!" KJ complimented my mom and she giggled like a schoolgirl.

I left my parents to drool over him in the living room so that I could get ready. I peeled off my jeans and sweatshirt, and then grabbed one of the new dresses I'd just bought. For his information, this shit cost me $50! I put the black strapless dress on after taking off my bra, and then went to the bathroom to clean my vagina. I didn't know why I was doing that, but I just felt the need to. After refreshing myself, I slipped on a black lace thong that I'd gotten from

Victoria's Secret. I put on my same gold jewelry, and then ran my flat iron over my brownish red hair that lightly swept my tailbone. I wanted to cut this shit, but I knew my mom and KJ would have heart attacks. KJ always threatened me when I said I was gonna cut my hair. I put on my nude gloss, some black strappy stilettos, and then sprayed my Juicy Couture perfume before going into the living room.

"Oh, you guys are leaving?" my father asked, still smiling at a joke he and KJ were laughing at.

"Yes Daddy," I said in a somber tone.

"I'm taking Gigi to dinner, if that's okay with you guys." KJ looked back and forth between my parents.

"Absolutely son!" my dad beamed and my mother grinned in agreement.

"I'll be back by ten," I waved them off.

"Oh, nessun coprifuoco- excuse me, no curfew tonight, we know KJ is gonna look after you," my mom chimed in, surprising the fuck out of me.

We walked down to KJ's car, and he opened the door for me. As soon as I got in, the smell of sweet cinnamon hit my nose. It always smelled like cinnamon buns in his car.

"You smell good," he said once he got in on the driver said. He leaned over and planted the softest kiss on the side of my neck. I immediately felt my river gates open down between my legs.

"Move KJ," I nudged him playfully.

"You ain't even kissed me yet," he said as he buckled his seat belt.

"Since when do I kiss you?" I turned my lip up jokingly.

"Since I met your cute ass, come here," he said and I pushed him off. He just laughed at me, and then started the car.

On the way there we listened to Miguel, and he kept looking over at me. I stared out the window the whole ride, because I was still mad at him. I hated that he thought everything was supposed to be on his time. I wanted to put my foot down, but as soon as I saw him my spine would turn to cooked spaghetti.

We pulled up to Sotto Sopra, an Italian restaurant on Charles

Street. The last time I came here was my prom night. KJ had brought me here to ensure my prom date didn't take me to some hotel and smash. He refused to admit that was the reason he took me to eat, but I knew him.

KJ parked right in front of the restaurant, and then he came around to open my door. He helped me out of the car, and then closed the door behind me. I started to walk off, but he pinned me against the car and started tonguing me down. I tried to resist at first but it was no use. I lightly hugged his torso, as he gripped my face in his strong hands. By now, my thong was soaked. He finally pulled away and stared down into my eyes. He pecked me once more, and then grabbed my hand so that we could go inside.

"Somebody ain't wearing panties tonight," he commented and squeezed my round ass.

"Stop KJ!" I slapped his hand and he laughed. "I *am* wearing panties! It's called a thong nasty!" I scowled as we walked up to the door.

"Prove it," he grinned and I pushed him gently.

Once inside, we were seated and then we promptly gave our drink and food orders to the waiter. We were both pretty hungry so we didn't want to take too long.

"So why'd it take forever for you to ask me out?" I quizzed and sipped my water.

"I told you I was busy, shorty," he smirked.

"Busy smashing hoes, that's for sure," I scoffed.

"Handling business more so; plus, you ain't my woman yet," he responded.

I hated when he told me I wasn't his girl. Especially because he would go the fuck off if I ever said that to him. Trust me, I'd done it before and he blew up. In his eyes, he was kind of my nigga but I wasn't his girl.

"Yet? Who said I would ever be your woman?" I turned my lip up.

"You are gonna be my girl, and my wife, and my babies' mother," he said and shoved some bread into his mouth.

"Well, you're gonna have to do better than what you're doing if you want me," I told him.

"Like chase you?" He frowned.

"Something! I feel like I'm always sitting here waiting for you to want me! And then right after I get any attention from you, you just put me back on the shelf again," I pouted.

"It ain't even like that, Gigi. I want you, babe, I just don't wanna hurt you," he stated honestly.

"By cheating on me?" I asked.

"That, and the fact that I'm a busy guy. I want you when I'm ready, because otherwise I may mess it up." He took my hand into his.

"I can't sit here and wait for you, KJ! I'm gonna meet someone else, watch," I took my hand from him and sat back. This date was pointless in my eyes, because clearly he and I weren't gonna get anywhere. I was so over being his little wife on hold.

"You don't need to date anybody else, Gianna! You've been single this whole fucking time! Just stay that way for a little bit longer, and I promise I'm gon' wife you, shorty, I swear," he said it as if it was a good idea.

"I'm tired of being single, KJ, so the next guy that hits on me, I'm giving up my number if I like him," I raised my brow.

"And I'm gon' murk his ass," he chuckled. "Soon as I get word, I'm having him bumped off. Take an innocent person's life if you want to," he stared into my eyes.

"This isn't fair, KJ! You can't keep me on hold like this," I whined.

"You think I'm gon' sit back while some other nigga bangs you out? Fuck out of here!" he waved me off. I stayed silent until the waiter finished setting our food down.

"Well like I said, you're not gonna have a choice," I reiterated and twirled some pasta onto my fork.

"Where is all this bullshit coming from? You were fine, and now you're tripping for what? You gon' always be in love with me Gianna, ain't no point in wasting another nigga's time," he gritted.

"I'll get over you," I shrugged one shoulder.

"Gianna, what do you want from me shorty?" He set his fork down.

"I want you to grow up, KJ," I folded my arms. "Real men don't put girls on hold until they think they can be faithful! They just become faithful!"

"I am growing up, but I can't become Prince Charming overnight, baby," he pleaded. "I refuse to be with you and fuck around with other girls. Ain't that enough for now?" he frowned.

"I don't wanna talk about it anymore," I sighed and then went back to eating my food. We sat there in silence for a while, as we both devoured our dishes.

"Would you guys like dessert?" the waiter asked.

"No, we will take the check please," I spoke up and KJ stared at me before shaking his head and sighing.

He paid the bill, and then we walked out to the car. He opened the passenger side for me, and then he got in on the driver's side. I couldn't take it anymore, so tears spilled down my cheeks. He'd just shattered all my hopes and dreams tonight, and I was sad as fuck. Something I had planned on happening had just died.

"Gianna, baby, please don't cry," he leaned over closer to me.

"I can't help but fucking cry! This whole time I thought you would be for real about us, but you're not! You wanna play the field until you've had enough, and then you want me to wait around! Well I'm not, KJ! I'm moving on, and I'm done with you!" I sniffled and wiped my face. "Niggas been waiting for me to stop being dumb for you!"

"You ain't done with me," he said. "And you shouldn't be worried about other niggas! You ain't being dumb, you're my shorty and you know that. You act like when people ask me about you I deny how I feel about you," he added.

"Watch how done I am with you, KJ. I can show you better than I can tell your ass." I wiped the new tears that had come down, as my leg bounced repeatedly.

He exhaled heavily, and gently pulled me over the center console and into his lap.

"You wanna be my girl that bad?" he asked and moved my hair out of my face. I ignored him and looked down at my hands. He kissed on my shoulders, and then my collarbone. "Tell me, Gigi," he said in a low tone.

"Tell you what?" I looked into his face with my wet one.

"Tell daddy you wanna be with him," he nibbled on his bottom lip, and then put my hair behind my ear while rubbing my thigh.

"I wanna be with you, Kendrick," I finally said, letting the tears fall where they may. How many ways did I have to tell him and show him that?

He moved my arm from being in between us, and then pulled me close to kiss him hungrily. I cupped his smooth face, as he positioned me so that I was straddling him. He felt between my legs, and moaned once he felt how soaked I was.

"You still new?" he quizzed in between kisses, and I simply nodded. He knew the answer, but I think he just liked hearing it. He gripped my ass cheeks and crushed me closer into his body. "I want you, shorty, but you gotta work with me, aight?" He stared up into my eyes and I nodded. "So I'm your man now?" he cheesed.

"Yeah," I replied and my voice cracked slightly.

"I wanna fuck you so bad right now, but your first time should be in a bed with roses and shit," he said and then cleared his throat.

"I don't care where it is, as long as it's with you," I responded.

"You better stop talking like that," he laughed. "But nah, I want it to be special for you, shorty," he sucked my bottom lip. "But damn," he commented as he felt my pussy again. My little lace thong was wet as hell. "Get back in your seat before I change my mind," he said, and I climbed off of him and giggled.

He took me to the movies and then home. We'd made it official, but you never knew what anything meant when it came to KJ. I guess I would have to wait until the morning to see the difference.

I was sitting outside of my mom's condo, inside Kaleeini's car. He and I were kissing like two long lost lovers, and although I knew Brice would be coming to see me in a little bit, I didn't stop him.

"I love kissing you," I whispered in between kisses.

"Same," he replied. I finally pulled away once I got a glimpse of the clock, which read 8pm.

"Let's go to the movies," he offered. We'd just spent all day at the park, and then we'd went out to lunch.

"I can't Kaleeini, I have to get ready for bed. I have a job interview in the morning," I lied.

I hated to lie because I knew it would only bring harm in the end, but I had to. I wanted Kaleeini to take me seriously, and I knew he wouldn't if I still had Brice.

The first few weeks Kaleeini and I hung out, I realized I didn't want him talking to anyone else, so I told him I let Brice go. Now, here I was dating two different niggas, and I knew it would end badly. I wasn't sure how to let Brice go, and I wasn't sure if I should yet.

"Aight, well hit me up when it's over with," he smirked and I nodded.

I planted a kiss on him and then got out of the car. I was blushing and feeling hot all over from spending all that time with him.

I went inside my home, and checked my mom's room to make sure she was gone. I freshened up, and about fifteen minutes later, Brice was banging on my door like the police. I rushed towards it and he banged on it again.

"Okay, damn!" I shouted and flung the door open. Brice mugged me and then barged into the house.

"Fuck you been doing all day?" he questioned and plopped down on the couch.

"I've been out with Willow, Gigi, and Shannon," I lied and sat down next to him.

"You smell like men's cologne," he growled and twisted his mouth up. I guess my 'freshen up' session was in vain.

"You're fucking paranoid, Brice," I waved him off and then picked up the remote control.

I pressed the channel-up button, and then suddenly Brice pounced on me. He wrapped his hands around my neck, and squeezed as tightly as he could.

"You cheating on me, bitch? I know some niggas were following me today, and I'm sure you sent them! You're tryna get rid of me for another nigga!" he screamed in my face and shook me by my neck. I clawed at his hands as I gasped for air, but nothing helped. I kicked wildly as he continued to squeeze with all of his might. "Answer me, you hoe!" he barked in my face, letting spit fly everywhere. He then burst into laughter at the sight of me losing oxygen, before he finally let go.

"Get the fuck out!" I hollered when I caught my breath. This nigga had never put his hands on me before, but I knew it was just a matter of time.

"I ain't going no fucking where!" he hollered. "I know you gon' have some nigga slide through here as soon as I leave, Aysia! You selling my pussy?" he squinted his eyes.

"Leave Brice, or I will call the fucking police, nigga," I stated calmly while still panting.

His facial expression went from angry to sad in a matter of seconds. "I'm sorry baby, I ain't mean to choke you. But what do you expect when you come in here smelling like men's cologne?" he shrugged.

"Maybe because I was at the mall shopping for a gift for my daddy!" I lied.

"Damn, my bad shorty," he said and reached over to try and touch my face. I slapped his hand down.

"Get out, Brice! I'm done," I said and stood to my feet. I couldn't deal with this shit anymore. He wasn't my boyfriend; he was a walking, talking, stress.

"Aysia, baby, come on. It was an accident," he neared me and pulled me close. "I love you and I'm sorry, aight?" He kissed my forehead.

I dropped my face into my hands, and he rested his chin on the top of my head. "I can't do this anymore, Brice," I sobbed. I was so tired of the shit we went through. His antics were running me low.

"Do what? I told your dramatic ass I was sorry Aysia, damn!" He let me go and shoved me back.

"Dramatic? Nigga, you almost killed me!" I yelled.

"Get the fuck over it! You should've let me know you were out shopping for your father when I first asked your ass about the cologne smell! Maybe then I wouldn't have had to discipline your ass!" he shouted down into my face.

I stared up into his light face and shook my head. The boy that I once loved was long gone. I knew it was because of the cocaine he snorted every now and then, but I knew if I said something he would go crazy. I walked away from him and opened my front door, just as my mom walked through wearing her nurse scrubs and carrying groceries.

"Oh, hey Brice. Aysia, are you okay baby?" She squinted her eyes in confusion at my disheveled mane.

"Yeah Ma, I'm good. Brice was just leaving," I said not taking my eyes off of him.

"Alright, well I'm gonna start on dinner," she said and walked past me towards the kitchen. Brice glared at me, and then walked out the door.

He turned around to face me, and as soon as he got outside he said, "I'm gon' give you some time to cool off, Aysia. You know you don't want me fucking with another bitch," he smirked. "That's why you be having muthafuckas follow me, hunh?" he laughed.

I slammed the door in his face and then went to get my phone.

Me: *This nigga choked me!* I sent to a group text with Gianna, Shannon, and Willow.

Willow: *Brice?*

Shannon: *Brice?*

Gigi: *Brice?*

They all replied at different times, but very close to one another.

Me: *Yes!!!*

After filling them in on the details, Gianna and Willow decided to come over. "So what happened?" Gianna asked.

"Girl, he smelled Kaleeini's cologne on me," I sighed.

"Still, he shouldn't be putting his hands on you," Willow frowned.

"I told his ass I was done." I looked at them to see their reactions. I didn't know if I was, but I wanted them to think so for now.

"About time, bitch!" Gianna laughed and put her hand up for a hi-five.

"So what's up with you and KJ?" I smiled. I didn't want to talk about me anymore.

"For real, last time I checked you said he was your man," Willow smacked her lips.

"And he still is my man. I feel like I'm in a dream because we talk all day, and he sees me damn near everyday," Gianna blushed.

I was so happy to hear that, because Gianna had been in love with KJ for the longest, but I just hoped he wasn't trying to play her.

She said he wanted to wait until he was ready, and he didn't seem too ready the last time I checked.

"Have y'all fucked?" I quizzed.

"Not yet, but I feel it coming," she half smiled.

"KJ hasn't hit yet? He may be smashing someone else," Willow raised both of her brows.

"Lo, stop it," I glared at her.

"Look, Gigi is my girl, and I'm tryna keep her from looking dumb. You know KJ loves to get that dick wet, so if he ain't fucking you then who is he fucking?" Willow continued. I hated to admit it, but she was right.

"Rain on my fucking parade, why don't you," Gianna sighed and laid back on my bed.

"I'm not trying to boo, I just want you to be up on game," Willow shoved some gum into her mouth.

"Like you are with Kendrin?" I asked and we all laughed.

"Exactly, baby girl. Kendrin don't get shit past mc, because he knows I will straight gut his sexy ass." Willow popped her gum and cocked her head to the left with her ghetto ass.

"Don't we know it," I chuckled.

We continued talking until my mom called us for dinner. I knew this summer was gonna be a crazy one, and it was just getting started.

Tonight, my family was having a big ass party for my cousin Kenzie. He'd gotten a basketball scholarship to Morgan State University, so we wanted to celebrate for him. He'd gotten it awhile back, but his parents, my Uncle Kendon and Aunt Jessica, really wanted to do it big for him so it took months to plan.

"Are you ready, baby?" my mother walked into my room.

She was wearing a red dress with matching red stilettos. I swear if you didn't know she was my mom you would think she was in her twenties.

"Yes, let me just get my shoes," I replied and leaned down to kiss her cheek.

"Okay," she turned around and walked out.

After putting on my shoes, I prayed silently that my girlfriend Willow didn't act a fucking fool tonight. My whole fucking family would be there, and I did not want to be embarrassed.

See, Willow had been my girl for about a year and a half, and I loved how obsessed she was with me, but sometimes she took that shit too far. She was always looking to beat a bitch down over me, and it was a fucking turn off sometimes. But like my pops told me, crazy girls had the best pussy and Willow was no exception.

I shook my head and then grabbed my phone to slip into my pocket. I walked downstairs to see my mother, father, little brother Kendrae, and my baby sister Kendria waiting for me.

"I'm gon' drive myself because I need to pick up Lo," I told them as I descended the stairs.

"Why didn't you say something before having us wait!" Kendria spat and then stormed outside. My dad and I laughed at her, and then we all exited the house together.

Once in my car, I sped to Willow's house after letting her know I would be there soon. I pulled up to her crib, and then took a deep breath before sending her another text. She came down minutes later, wearing a tight black number and looking sexy as hell. She had taken her usual French braids down, so her hair was loose and wavy.

"Hey daddy," she said as she got into the car and poked her lips out. I pecked her gently, and then groped her smooth thigh.

"Be on your best behavior tonight, Lo," I pointed my finger in her face, and she pretended to bite it before laughing.

"We're not going any fucking where until you promise not to act a damn fool tonight." I threw my car into park.

"Okay Ken, damn," she turned her lip up and then looked out the window.

"Give daddy another kiss," I said before leaning over to suck on her neck. She chuckled and then turned to peck me. She smelled like candy, and I couldn't wait to fuck later on.

I pulled off from the curb, and swerved through the streets of Baltimore until we finally reached my grandpa, Kairio's house. We always held functions here, because they had the biggest and safest house. I pulled into the parking structure area, and then got out to open Willow's door. We walked hand in hand to the elevator, where I put the code in before getting on. The elevator took us to the bottom floor, and when the doors opened, it was like a fucking club but with the lights on. Everyone in my damn family was here.

I looked at Willow and gave her a knowing look so that she would know I meant what the fuck I'd said earlier. I spoke to my brother who was chilling with his arm wrapped around Gianna. He was halfway drunk all damn ready. I then said what's up to Kaleeini, Aysia, and my other three thousand cousins as well. My famous cousin, Kayden King was here too, so you know Willow was anxious to meet him. Once we finished chopping it up, I headed over to congratulate Kenzie. He was standing next to Willow's best friend and his girlfriend, Shannon.

"Congratulations bro!" I shouted, and we embraced each other after slapping hands.

"Thank you, man," he nodded as Shannon and Willow embraced. I spoke to his parents, and then grabbed a couple snacks that were being served.

A couple hours into the party, KJ had led all the young people to this big ass room in my grandparents' house. He turned on some music, and everyone started turning up. My brother lived for fucking parties. When "Gettin It" by Iamsu came on, shit really got fun.

Outside of family, there were some girls and dudes I didn't recognize, so I'm guessing they were Kenzie's friends. After dancing our asses off, Willow, Aysia, Gianna, and Shannon went to the bathroom for some reason.

"I'm Lisa," some chick walked up and introduced herself to my big brother.

"Sup Lisa," KJ grinned and then sipped some more champagne. She went on to introduce herself to Kaleeini, Kendrae, Kendall, Drew, Lenny, and then myself. Just my luck, when I was shaking her hand, Willow was coming back.

"I'm Willow, Kendrin's girlfriend," she raised a brow and moved the girl's hand out of mine.

"Oh hey, my bad," the girl said and laughed.

"What the fuck is so funny?" Willow folded her arms.

"Lo, chill out," I said and tried to sit her little ass down, but she was too strong when she was angry.

"It's just funny how pressed you are when all I did was introduce myself," Lisa replied, clearly not understanding how crazy my girl was.

"Bitch, you better watch your fucking mouth!" Willow shouted and cracked her knuckles.

"Or what? Girl, don't make me fuck your nigga and send him home to you to stick his dick in your mouth," the girl taunted.

"Okay, now *I'm* getting mad," Gianna chimed in.

"Aye, come here and be quiet," KJ yanked Gianna down into his lap, and locked her in place. Shannon and Aysia were also being restrained, thank God.

Willow all of a sudden tied her hair up, so the other girl shook her head. She clearly didn't know how serious Willow was. I stood up and grabbed Willow from behind before she could strike the girl.

"Put me down, Kendrin!" she shouted and kicked as I carried her away.

I sat her down outside the room, and then she Allen Iverson'd my ass, and charged old girl back in the room. She straddled the girl and started going in, causing all kinds of commotion. I rushed over, picked her ass up, and quickly carried her out of the room, just as my parents, aunts, and uncles came to see what the fuck was going on. My dad was looking at me disgusted, as I carried my unruly ass girlfriend out of the room. She was screaming obscenities and kicking wildly. I took her to a half bathroom, and sat her ass down on the closed toilet.

"Fuck is wrong with you, Lo?" I shouted in her face after locking the door behind me.

"Excuse me? That bitch was all in your face!" she grimaced.

"I told your ass to behave! You're embarrassing me in front of my family, for what? Because the girl introduced her fucking self?" I frowned down at her. I was so mad I could punch her ass right now. She was lucky I was brought up right, or her head would've been in that toilet.

"Kendrin she—"

"Shut the fuck up! Get yo' ass up and let's go right fucking now!" I screamed in her face.

She stared up at me for a couple seconds, and I could tell she was scared of what I was gonna do to her. She finally got up off the bathroom floor, and followed after me like an ashamed puppy. I didn't even have the courage to face my family as I rushed her crazy ass onto the elevator to leave. I opened my car door for her, and slammed it closed once she got in. Just as I was about to get into my car, my mother called my name. I exhaled heavily and then walked over to her.

"Don't bring her to anything else until you can control her. Your father told me to tell you this," she caressed my face.

"I know he's thinking I'm some little punk," I replied.

"Probably," she chuckled. "But mommy doesn't," she kissed my face.

"Way to make me feel better, Ma," I tittered. I hugged her and then kissed her face, before jogging back to my car.

"She hates me, hunh?" Willow asked as I backed my car out.

"Nah, my dad is just mad as hell right now. He had to send a message through my mom," I shook my head.

"Kendrin—"

"Willow, just shut up right now. I'm taking you home," I cut her off.

We drove in silence until I reached her crib, and I ignored the tears running down her face. I hit the unlock button, and waited for her to get out.

"I'm sorry baby, can I have a kiss?" she asked after taking her seatbelt off.

I clenched my jaw and ignored her as I stared straight ahead. Grinding my teeth was the only thing keeping me from backhanding her right now.

She released my seatbelt, and then started to unbutton my pants. She took my dick out, and then deep throated me.

"Lo, baby, stop," I moaned although I wanted her to keep going.

She drenched my dick with her spit, and worked her jaws up and down my shaft. She came up and sucked the life out of my tip, before taking my ten inches back into her mouth. I felt her tonsils on my head, and it made my pelvis tighten. She licked and massaged my balls with her small hands as she groped my dick.

Willow had a fucking Master's Degree in Dickology. Although a virgin when I met her, she could suck and fuck like nobody's business now. Some chicks just had it in their blood, and didn't need much practice; Willow was one of them. Her eagerness to please me made her a mind blower in the bedroom.

I massaged her scalp once she took my dick back into her mouth and sped up her sucks. "Aww fuck!" I cried out and shot my seeds into her mouth.

She swallowed it up like a shot of Patrón, and then picked her head up to wipe her mouth. I was tired of this same routine, but it was too damn hard to leave. I loved her ass and the sex was amazing.

A WEEK AND A HALF LATER...

I WAS SITTING at my vanity trying to fix my hair into my usual two French braids, but for some reason I couldn't do it. I kept thinking about Kendrin and how I embarrassed him in front of his family. I planned to be on my best behavior, but that stupid hoe got the best of me. As usual though, I felt super dumb in hindsight. After that night, Kendrin and I barely talked, even though he acted as if everything was okay after we fucked.

I blew out hot air, as I finally was able to complete my hairstyle. I grabbed my purse and then got into my car so that I could go pick up my friends. We were gonna go eat at Salt on Pratt and Collington for lunch, so that they could help me keep my mind off of Kendrin.

As I sat outside of Shannon's house, I decided to shoot him a text.

Me: *Good afternoon daddy.*

I placed my iPhone into the cup holder, and stared out the window until I felt Shannon and Gianna tugging on my door handles. I hit the unlock button so that they could get in, and then checked my phone. There was no text from Kendrin, so I rolled my eyes and cranked up my car.

"He's still tripping?" Shannon asked me and I nodded.

"Has Kenzie said anything?" I asked her and she shook her head no.

"I thought you said he was giving you short answers? He's not answering now?" Gianna asked as I drove to Aysia's house.

"Yeah, he was giving me short fucking answers, but now I get late ass responses or no response at all," I sighed and my stomach started to feel knotted.

I loved that nigga and I didn't know what I would do without him. He didn't understand, like I was really trying to be calm and cool, but I know how bitches are. Kendrin was 6'1, had a toffee complexion, with jade green eyes, perfect teeth, and dimples. On top of looking good enough to eat, he was rich as fuck.

We'd been dating for a little over a year, and when we first started he cheated on me. I remember he was supposed to pick me up from school one day, and he didn't show up. While I was waiting, a girl named Cecilia told me she saw him riding around the hood with some hoe named Janet that was in college, and I was devastated. She offered me a ride to the girl's home, and just like she said, Kendrin's car was parked out front. I went nine thousand on him and the girl, breaking the windows to her condo and her car. As soon as she walked out, I whooped her ass as Cecilia watched, and Kendrin tried to pry me off of her. Later on, I found out that Cecilia had a crush on Kendrin, but when she found out her cousin Janet had bagged him first, she decided to sabotage their little rendezvous by using me.

By saying that, I was insecure as fuck, but I still tried to suppress it for him. Girls were always in his ear, blowing up his phone, posting dumb shit on the gram, and all kinds of shit, so hell yeah I was jealous as fuck. I shook my head at my thoughts as I pulled in front of Aysia's condo.

On the way to go eat, the three of them indulged in conversation, but all I could think about was my man. I was so worried that he didn't wanna be with me anymore. The thought alone made my stomach hurt.

We finally got to the restaurant about fifteen minutes later, and we all quickly got out.

"So what you gonna do, Lo?" Aysia asked me as soon as the waiter walked away.

"I don't fucking know," I shrugged and checked my phone for what seemed like the fiftieth time.

"He'll get over it, he loves you," Gianna half smiled at me and I shot her one back. She was always so positive and I loved that about her.

"Yeah, just give him some time," Shannon added as she shoved some food into her mouth.

We conversed for a couple hours and then I dropped them all off. As I sat outside of Gianna's house, I dialed Kendrin. I couldn't go to sleep without talking to him at least a little bit.

"Hello," he answered with his deep sexy voice.

"What are you doing?" I asked.

"I'm relaxing. I just finished setting up a part of my condo," he exhaled.

"Oh, I forgot you moved this week," I said somberly. I was kind of mad he didn't ask me to come over to his new place.

"So what's up?" he quizzed as if he was ready to get off the phone.

"Kendrin, what's up? You've been ignoring me and shit, so what, you're done with me now?" I started to cry at the thought.

"I don't know Lo, you be going too far, baby," he responded.

"I know and I'm sorry, but I'm trying Kendrin," I cried.

"You say that shit every time, Willow. I can't keep doing this shit with you every fucking week," he barked.

"Let me come over," I sniffled.

He exhaled heavily and then finally said, "Hurry up. I'll text you the address." He disconnected shortly after.

I smiled to myself and then waited for the text to come through. Once I got it, I clicked it so my phone could lead the way. I pulled up to his new condo, and texted him to let him know I had arrived. He walked out wearing basketball shorts, socks, Jordan slide-ins, and a t-shirt. His hair was freshly cut, and he looked so fucking good. Once I neared him, I could smell his cologne. He raised his arm to hug me and I could also smell his intoxicating deodorant. After our hug, he led me inside and closed the door behind me.

"This is nice," I said in a low tone.

"Thank you. I still need to get it together. I'll be happy when I get my house though," he said and sat down on the couch. I sat next to him, and then rubbed his hand.

"Baby, I'm sorry, and if you give me another chance I promise I won't act up again," I said sweetly.

He stared at the TV, ignoring me. Tears started to come out of my eyes again, so I stood up to leave. He got up almost simultaneously, and pinned me against the wall. I stared up into his dark green eyes, and sniffled.

"I'm gon' break your fucking neck if you ever act like that again, shorty," he said sternly.

"I won't—"

I couldn't even finish because he had jammed his tongue into my mouth. I caressed his face as I relished in the moment. Just an hour ago I thought I'd lost him forever, and I was happy that, that wasn't the case.

He picked me up, and I wrapped my legs around his waist. He carried me to his new bedroom, and laid me back on the bed. He pulled down my shorts and thong, and then took my clit into his warm mouth. I spread my legs some more, and pushed my pussy into his face. He feasted on me like it was the best meal he'd ever tasted, and then slipped his fingers into me.

"Kendriinnn, ahhhh," I whimpered as he fucked me with his mouth and fingers. I released and he licked up all my juices. I sat up and let him remove my top and unhook my bra.

"I love you, girl," he said before roughly kissing me.

"I love you too, daddy," I smiled and sniffled again.

He massaged his dick, and then rubbed it on my lips before I took it into my mouth. He humped my face in a circular motion until he came, and I drank it up. He bent down to flick his tongue over my nipples, and then turned me over on all fours. He slipped inside me, and then began pounding away. I was soaking wet, so he was calling out to the high heavens. I gripped the sheets with my teeth, as he slammed into me from behind.

"Aaahhh, aaahh, babyyyy," I purred.

"Tell me you gon' behave," he demanded as he slipped in fast and pulled out slow.

"I'm gonna behave," I cooed. He spanked me hard, and then leaned down to bite my ass cheek. I loved when he bit me like that.

"Whose pussy is this, Willow?" He gripped my waist tighter, and then ran his tongue along my asshole.

"Yours, Kendrin," I moaned loudly as I exploded.

"Aarrggghhh," we called out together as he filled my body up with his cum. He slowly slid out of me, flipped me on my back, and then yanked me by my ankle. He climbed in between my legs and kissed me hungrily.

"I love you, baby," I whispered in between kisses.

"Sʜɪᴛ," I grunted as I slid the condom off of my dick. London was lying next to me panting heavily.

I felt bad as hell for fucking her now that Gianna was my girl, but what was I supposed to do? There was no way I could let Gianna be with another nigga, but then again, it was hard for me to just be with one girl, especially since I hadn't fucked her yet.

I'd been holding out because I didn't wanna damage her, but I knew I couldn't wait much longer. I was also tired of feeling like shit on rye bread every time I busted a nut with another bitch.

"Look London, I need to talk to you," I said when I came back from her bathroom.

"What's up babe?" she grinned.

"We can't do this anymore, aight?" I frowned. I didn't care whether she agreed to this or not. The least I could do was try to be faithful to Gianna.

"What? What the fuck are you talking about KJ? I haven't seen you in weeks, and you come and tell me you're not fucking with me *after* I give you some?" she glared at me.

"If that's how you see it. I see it more as a goodbye fuck," I half joked. She knows she would've still given me some pussy even if I had told her beforehand.

"But London, I'm in a relationship now, so I can't fuck around with you anymore," I said as I started to get dressed.

"I thought we were in a relationship!" she hollered with eyes of fire. I gave her a look as if she had two heads sprouting from her neck.

"Stop being stupid shorty, you knew you weren't my bitch. We go weeks without talking sometimes, you said it yourself," I laughed at her delusional ass.

"Whatever KJ, just leave," she sniffled and wiped her face. I didn't argue because I was leaving anyway. I hoped she didn't expect me to coddle her, because I would need to give a fuck in order to do that. I finished getting dressed without saying a word, and then left.

I had to go to Hawaii for a meeting, and I thought it would be a great little getaway for Gianna and I. I felt bad for fucking around on her, even though she had no idea. Not only that, I'd been neglecting her a little for the past three days, so I wanted to make up for that as well. Next to cheating, the worst thing I could do was make her feel like being with me was not what she wanted.

Once I pulled up in front of my newly finished mansion, I dialed her number.

"Hey baby," she sang into the phone.

"Sup shorty?" I chuckled. I loved how happy she became whenever I called her on the phone.

"What are you doing?" I quizzed.

"Nothing, I just came back from the nail shop," she replied.

"Pack a quick bag, I want you to come somewhere with me," I said.

"Where to?" she asked.

"To Hawaii," I responded and got out of my car so that I could go inside my house to get ready myself.

"Ooh, I—"

"You scared to travel with your man?" I questioned.

"No," she said in a low tone. "Give me like an hour though," she added.

"Alright, one exact hour and I will be outside your crib," I told her. I didn't know what she needed an hour for, but since I had to shower and pack, I agreed.

"Okay, bye," she disconnected.

I looked at my phone and saw London and Zaria, along with a couple other bitches had texted me. I went in and blocked all their numbers for the time being, because I didn't want them to hit me while with Gianna.

I cleaned myself up, and then packed a few things for the trip before going to get my girl. As soon as I pulled up, I dialed her ass.

"Coming," she answered and then quickly hung up.

I waited for a while and then I saw her come down wearing a crew neck, jeans, and the Jordans I'd just bought her. Her long hair was hanging down messily, and she was carrying a black bag. As soon as she got into the car, I dipped my tongue into her sweet mouth.

"You missed me?" I asked and she nodded with a half smile. "I missed you too," I said before pecking her again. I stared at her pretty ass for a little bit, and then put the car in drive.

I drove to the port, and then we boarded the plane to Hawaii. My private jet was decked the fuck out, and I could see the amazement in Gianna's eyes. All the seats were black, and the carpet was red and plush.

After we ascended into the air, I unbuckled both of our seatbelts and then led her to the bed. I laid down, and she smiled down at me nervously. I then cut on my playlist that I'd made for the trip.

"Come here," I patted the bed, and she slipped out of her shoes and laid down with me. "Ain't you hot?" I questioned and then began pulling her crew neck over her head before she could even answer. She wore a thin t-shirt underneath, so I slipped my hands under it.

I then pulled her closer to me, and as soon as our noses touched, our tongues became entangled. I ran my hands up and down her backside, before stopping at her ass and squeezing.

Damn, I wanted to do all kinds of shit to her. She caressed my face as "Feelings" by Adrian Marcel played softly over us. Our tongues were so far down each other's throats, that I was waiting to feel her tonsils. I forgot where I was as I became so enthralled in our kiss. This almost thirteen-hour flight seemed way shorter with her here with me.

Once we arrived, we were greeted and taken to my vacation home by limo.

"Wow KJ, this is beautiful," Gianna smiled as she looked around the home.

"So are you," I said and hugged her from behind. I started kissing on her neck, and groping her little body. Damn, I wanted to fuck her all over this place. "You hungry?" I asked her.

"Yes, you gonna cook for me?" she grinned.

"Fuck no, shorty, we gon' go out," I said before pressing my lips against hers. I couldn't keep my hands off of her, nor could I keep a soft dick around her. "Go get dressed so we can go to dinner," I told her.

We got dressed and chose to eat at this place called Hali'imaile's. Everyone said it was good as hell, so we thought we'd try it out.

Gianna was wearing a canary yellow dress that hugged her perfect physique. She wore her long ass hair in a ponytail, and a little flower in her head for the occasion. From looking at her body, I knew after tonight she would be a virgin no more.

"Why are we here?" she questioned after the waiter dropped off the crab pizza we ordered for an appetizer.

"I have some business to take care of," I responded.

"Oh," she said somberly.

"Why you say it like that?" I wondered.

"I thought you were bringing me here like as a couple thing," she smacked her lips and then flashed her pretty smile.

"I did, shorty. I only needed to be here for two days, but I brought you earlier so we could spend some time together," I said.

"Oh good," she squinted her eyes playfully.

"I know I haven't been spending much time with you lately, but it's because of work. That's why I wanted to do this for you," I said.

"Thank you, baby," she blushed. "See, I told you that you could be a good boyfriend," she chuckled.

I cleared my throat because my cheating was bothering me for some reason. This is exactly why I didn't want to make her my girl, because now shit was messed up already. I wanted to be honest with her like my dad had advised, but I couldn't just yet.

After we ate, we went right back to the house since it was late and we were pretty tired. I dimmed the lights in the whole house, and then lit a couple candles so that we could still see.

I pulled Gianna close and started to kiss her gently. I was beyond ready to pop that cherry. She stopped me, and then grabbed her bag before darting to the bathroom. I smacked my lips and shook my head as I undressed down to my boxers. I hoped she wasn't on no *I don't wanna fuck* shit, because my dick was so hard you could snap it like a potato chip.

As I laid in bed deleting the nudes from random hoes in my Instagram DM, I heard the bathroom door open. Gianna stood in the doorway wearing a red lace bra and matching red lace panties. Her cinnamon vanilla complexion glistened from the candlelight, and her brownish red hair brushed against her perfect body.

"Come here, Gigi," I whispered as I sat up.

She walked to me slowly, looking like she had come straight from heaven. As soon as she reached me, a hint of sugar hit me, which I guessed was her perfume. I grabbed her waist and admired her body from head to toe. She had small but perfectly round breasts, a nice flat stomach, and a plump little ass. I knew her body was perfect, but I had never seen it this way, only in tight clothes. She dropped her red robe, which was hanging off her shoulders anyways.

"Gigi, you look so beautiful, baby girl," I said in a low tone and she cheesed. "Is this why you needed an hour earlier?" I asked.

"Yeah, I had to go to The Gallery and buy something nice for you," she responded and flipped her long hair to the other side.

I pulled her into my lap, and she straddled me. I caressed her smooth thighs and gripped her ass in my hands. I loved this girl. I planted kisses on her collarbone, which smelled so sweet.

"I love you, Kendrick," she whispered my name so perfectly.

I turned around and laid her on her back. I unhooked her bra, and then slid it down her arms. I scooped her breasts into my hands, and sucked on her nipples hungrily. I tugged on her thong as I continued to lick and suck her nipples. I sat up so that I could pull her panties down and off, and once I did, I admired her pretty pussy. I got down on my knees, kissed her stomach softly, and then trailed the kisses down to her pussy to kiss her lower lips. I did that a couple more times, and then started to suck on her clit. Her back arched, and I spread her legs wider so I could feast on her better.

"KJ, aaahh," she whimpered and rubbed my short hair.

I lapped up her juices, and sucked on her clit like a piece of candy. I didn't wanna use my fingers because I wanted my dick to be the first thing inside of her. I pushed her legs back towards her, and hooked my mouth onto her vagina. I sucked the life out of her and she screamed loudly. I kept eating her pussy until my chin hairs were soaked. I finally let her clit go, and then ran my tongue down the length of her center. I then just softly French kissed her pussy like I loved it, as she cried out. The smell, the taste, the feeling, everything was just perfect. Her legs were trembling, and her body was drenched in sweat already. I stepped out of my boxers, and then climbed in between her legs after putting her in the middle of the bed.

"You ready?" I asked her as I tongued her down.

"Yes," she purred.

"It may hurt but I promise I will start to make you feel good," I said and she nodded.

I sat up to get a condom, but changed my mind as I stared at her sexy ass lying there naked. If I was gonna be her first, I wanted to be her first everything. I positioned my eleven inches at her opening, and I saw her grab the sheets next to her.

"Relax, Gianna," I said. I was about to try and push myself inside her, but I laid down closer to her first. I wrapped my left arm around her body, making us become so close it seemed like we were one. I took my right hand, and used it to rub my dick between her slit. "Tell me you love me again," I said. I wanted to distract her a little bit.

"I love you," she smiled and her body relaxed under mine.

I smiled back at her, and then pushed my head into her opening. It wouldn't let me in, so I put her legs in the nooks of my arms. I didn't really need to hold my dick because it was on brick status right now. I pushed with all my might, and finally I broke into her.

"Uuuuh, uuuh," she called out as I continued to push the rest of my dick inside of her. Whatever was in my way was getting knocked the fuck down as I forced entry.

I had never felt pussy this tight, wet, and snug in my life. Not even the girl from when I was fourteen, and she was a virgin too.

"Shit," I commented once I was all the way in. I hoped I had enough time to pull out. At this rate, I would be exploding in seconds.

I slowly began to stroke her, and her pussy was gripping the hell out of my dick. I had to say a silent prayer to the sex gods so that I would have some stamina.

I saw a tear roll out the side of her eyes, so I licked it up and then sucked on her lips as she whimpered. The feeling of her hard nipples against my body made my dick even harder.

"Damn, Gigi," I moaned as I humped her slowly in a circular motion.

She draped her arms over my shoulders, just as I slipped my tongue into her mouth. She moaned into my mouth, but it was muffled since I was tonguing her down.

"Aaahh, ahhh, ahhh," she cooed softly into my mouth. I felt her burst, and it just intensified what I was already feeling.

"Yes, do that again, Gigi," I whispered to her. "Can I go faster?" I asked her and she shook her head no. "Baby, do you know how good you feel?" I closed my eyes and groaned.

I had to bite down on my lip to keep from crying out like a bitch.

Got damn! I'd had some good pussy in my days, but this right here was crack. I had to look down between her legs as I stroked, to make sure that this was just regular pussy I was in. That was a bad idea, because the sight almost made me nut.

"Ken-Kendrick," she stammered over my name as she stared up into my eyes. She was so beautiful.

"I told you I was gonna make you my wifey," I said before crushing my lips against hers.

Despite what she said, I sped up just a little. She dug her freshly done nails into my back. Usually I didn't like bitches doing that, but Gianna was my baby girl so she got more privileges. She locked her legs around my waist, and that's when I couldn't help myself. I started beating it up and she came hard as hell. She was soaking down there, and I knew I was about to explode. She hugged my neck tightly as we kissed passionately. I slammed into her every now and then, and after a few hard pumps I was nutting all in her by accident. There was no way I could pull out. I had never cum so long and hard in my life. I felt like everything had been pulled out of me. I never understood when niggas would say the pussy was too good to pull out until now. I felt like she fucked me, and not the other way around.

We laid there kissing for a cool minute, and then I finally got up off of her. "I'm sorry I didn't pull out baby," I said as I scooped her up. She was too sore to walk.

"I'm on birth control," she whispered.

"Since when?" I frowned.

"Since you made me your girl," she chuckled lazily.

I kissed her soft cheek, and carried her to the bathroom. I ran a bubble bath, and then placed her in it. I climbed in as well, and then pulled her to me so she could straddle me.

"How you feeling?" I questioned.

"Sore," she smiled and pushed her hair behind her ears.

"Did you like it?" I quizzed and squeezed her ass.

"Yes, because it was you, and I love you," she looked into my eyes intensely.

"Say it again," I bit my lip.

"I love you, Kendrick," she reiterated.

"Again," I pecked her.

"I love you, Kendrick," she giggled.

"Gimme some," I told her and she slipped her tongue into my mouth. After our bath, I had to sample that shit again before we passed out.

———

THE NEXT MORNING, I woke up early as hell so I could shower, brush my teeth, and go get some breakfast for my shorty. The pussy was so good she had a nigga running to get her food to wake up to.

After getting the food, I went back to the house. When I got there, she was coming out of the shower looking good as hell.

"I was looking for you," she smiled and adjusted the towel around her body.

"I went to get you some food, babe." I held up the bag for her to see, and then walked to the kitchen to put it on some plates.

She walked into the kitchen, and sat at the table wearing an orange dress. She had combed her hair down into a long braid.

"You sweated out my press," she chuckled and smoothed down her edges as I sat down at the table with her.

"Sorry, shorty," I grinned and she shook her head at me.

"It's okay, it was worth it," she ran her tongue over her teeth.

"Look at you already acting like a nympho." I kissed from her hand to her forearm slowly, and I felt goose bumps rise against my lips.

"Only for you," she replied in a low tone, and I felt my dick start to harden.

I just started eating my food, because in a minute she would have me living in Hawaii, cooped up in this house fucking her all day.

When we were done, I went out onto the balcony to make a couple business calls. I was meeting a business partner from Mexico in two days, and I had to set a few things up with the team I called out here.

As I finished my last call a couple hours later, I looked to my right to see Gianna standing in the doorway. I smiled at her sexy ass, and she walked over to me slowly. She got down on her knees, and immediately went for my zipper.

"You know what to do with that?" I raised a brow.

"No, but I wanna find out," she responded and released it from my pants.

I smoothed her hair back as she stared at my size. She took the tip into her mouth, and started sucking on it like a piece of candy. I leaned back to enjoy the show, and to let her get more comfortable. She began to take more of me into her mouth after swallowing her spit.

"Don't swallow your spit shorty, just let it flow freely," I told her.

She went back to sucking me off, and as I had explained, she let her spit do it's own thing. My dick was covered in her saliva, and she was slurping me like a little professional. I had to sit up because it was getting good as fuck.

"Baby, just like that," I moaned. She gagged very lightly, and that shit turned me on even more. "Pull your dress down," I panted.

She did as I asked, and the feeling of her sucking my dick in combination with seeing her in a white thong only, had my pelvis tightening. I slipped my dick out, and rubbed it on her lips before pushing it back into her mouth. She went ham on it like she was tryna suck the gold out of it. I stood up, and then began humping her face in a circular motion, before releasing. She tipped her head back a little to take it down. I snatched her up by her arm, and then picked her up while kissing her. She wrapped her legs around my waist, as I carried her inside to bang her out.

I HAD CALLED KJ six times already, and that nigga had yet to answer my fucking call. He'd blocked my cell number so I was using my house phone. I was so angry I didn't know what to do. I had given this damn boy everything, and he had the nerve to come up into my crib and tell me had a girlfriend? Nigga, please.

I met KJ at my friend Tanya, son's birthday party about a year ago. Tanya's son was the same age as KJ, so I initially was not interested in him, even though he was gorgeous. When he first approached me, I could see all in his eyes that he just wanted to fuck me, and I was too smart for that so I brushed him off. He took the rejection well, and never looked back. After having my ear to the streets a bit, I realized I'd made a huge mistake; KJ was a boss ass nigga with a lot of bread. I just knew once I put this pussy on him, he would've been putty in my hands.

Over time we got closer, but he would never spend the night or anything. He would hit me up, fuck me, and then leave right after, pretending he had an emergency to tend to. Next thing you know, I'm the one sprung off of his young ass. He had me wrapped around his finger, and no matter how many times I told myself that I was done, he always changed my mind. KJ was fine as hell, and had dick that would make you direct deposit your check into his account.

All my friends shook their heads at me when I told them about KJ. They always complained that I was only a few years younger than his mother, and that he had been fucking with plenty of women. I tried approaching him about the many bitches he stuck his dick in, and he straight laughed in my face. One girl in particular was named Gianna.

Gianna was KJ's little pride and joy. Anytime her whack ass called, he would hop right up and go do whatever she had asked. I remember one occasion, he was deep in my guts and spotted her name flash across his phone on the dresser. Why did this nigga stop fucking me, get dressed, and leave? Nothing beats the time I dissed her ass and he almost broke my jaw by squeezing it, and then gritted in my face to never speak her name again.

I was really trying to hang in there, and just knew that he would eventually realize what he had in me. I was a real woman, not some little teenager like Gianna. She couldn't do for him like I could, and he would soon see that. I wanted him, I craved this little nigga, and I was gonna have him.

I plopped down onto the couch, and pulled my phone out quickly when it buzzed. I sighed when I realized it was just an email, and remembered he'd blocked my cell phone. I stared at the TV, not even paying attention to the movie playing, before I finally grabbed the cordless to call him again.

I inhaled sharply when I heard the phone pick up, followed by a lot of rustling, and then the close of a door.

"Hello, baby?" I questioned into the phone.

"Yo, what the fuck you blowing my phone up for?" KJ barked into the phone. I was so happy to hear his voice that I wasn't too bothered by his tone. How did he even know this number was mine?

"I-I missed you, and the way you left yesterday morning left me feeling uneasy," I responded in a whiny tone.

"What can I do to get you to leave me alone? Because in a minute I'm gon' have somebody take care of you," he exhaled heavily.

"Are you serious? We've been together for months—"

"Stop saying we were together, London! We were occasional fuck buddies shorty! You living in a fucking fantasy world right now, and you need to wake the fuck up!" he growled.

"So that's it, Kendrick?" I sniffled. I didn't even realize I was crying until a tear landed on my thigh.

"Oh my gosh, yo. I swear you're getting on my fucking nerves with all the drama- what's up babe?" I could tell he pulled the phone from his mouth. "Go back to bed, I'm coming," he added and then I heard the faint sound of a door closing.

"Are you with another bitch?" I screamed so loud my own ears rang. I was already crying so hard that my vision was blurry as hell.

"Whoa, bring yo motherfucking voice down, girl. Secondly, are you honestly checking me? I've never even taken you out or spent the night over. You couldn't possibly feel or think that I was your nigga, and if you did, I feel sorry for you because you got some mental problems," he stabbed me with each word he spat.

"But I thou—"

"You running me low London. Move on ma, damn," he hung up on me, and I began to pant heavily.

How could this be happening right now? Although KJ would go weeks without speaking to me, I was scared to go on without him. Knowing that he would never be popping up or hitting me up randomly, cut deeply.

I hugged one of my decorative couch pillows, and then laid down horizontally. I stared at the wall as tears raced down my cheeks at an alarming rate. I closed my eyes and prayed that right now was simply a nightmare, and that I would soon wake up.

I FOUND it hilarious that Aysia thought I believed her about Brice. I'm not sure what type of nigga she took me for, but it must've been a dumb one. I used her little lie to my advantage though. Since she was 'broken up' with old boy, I would be extra touchy-feely and she couldn't say shit. There were no more 'stop I got a man' excuses, unless she wanted to put herself on blast and be honest. It was bittersweet though, because although I was able to basically treat her as my girl, the reality of the situation was that she was still *his* girl.

Tonight I was about to teach her ass a lesson though. I was gonna force her to make up her mind right in front of me and Brice. After tonight, either she would be mine and mine only, or I would be washing my hands of our *flirtationship*.

"Hey boo," this chick named Erica got into my car.

Before Aysia and I got closer recently, Erica and I were fuck buddies and nothing more. She was cool to chill with, and definitely cool to smash, but I just didn't see her as the wifey type. I was picky as hell when it came to women, and unfortunately, Erica didn't make the cut.

"Sup shorty," I smirked at her before putting my car in drive.

We headed to Landmark Theatres to see a movie because I knew

Aysia and Brice would be there on a little date of some sort. This would be the last one though, so he'd better enjoy it.

Honestly, I'm surprised he didn't think she was cheating, because she spent six days out of the week damn near, laid up under me. I hadn't hit yet, but I knew that was soon to come and I couldn't wait. I had fantasized about all kinds of shit that I wanted to do to her pretty ass, and I could wait until it came to fruition.

Once I parked, Erica and I got out and purchased tickets to some movie. I wasn't listening when she ordered them because I was keeping an eye out for Aysia. Right after we got the tickets, I saw Aysia and Brice standing in line to get snacks. Aysia was wearing jeans and some revealing ass top, showing her sexy stomach. *Show-time*, I told myself.

I made sure to get in line right next to the one Aysia was in, and also made sure to contain my smile. I couldn't wait to see her jaw hit these theatre floors.

"Can I get whatever I want?" Erica quizzed with a grin.

"Of course shorty, anything for you," I winked down at her.

As soon as the words left my mouth, Aysia snapped her neck to look over at us. I made eye contact with her, and she was glaring hard as fuck at me. I knew she was angry as fuck, and that's just what I wanted. She was so mad that she hadn't even realized I caught her in a lie about Brice. Neither one of us said a word as we waited in line and purchased snacks. She kept looking at me when Brice wasn't paying attention though, really letting me know that she would rather be in Erica's spot.

Right when I got situated in the movie, my phone was jumping.

Aysia: *For real nigga? I'm glad I didn't leave Brice for you.*

Me: *Me too, enjoy the movie.*

I locked my phone and chuckled lightly.

Not even five minutes later, Aysia was calling. I stood up to go out of the theatre, and right when I put my phone to my ear, I saw her standing there. I ended the call and so did she.

"What the fuck, Kaleeini? You are such a liar," she shook her head with glazed eyes.

"I'm a liar? I thought you broke up with Brice?" I frowned and folded my arms.

"I did but, we-he-"

"Shut the fuck up with them lies Aysia," I scoffed and turned around to walk away.

"Wait Kaleeini," she grabbed my arm with her small hands.

"What Aysia? I don't have time for your fucking games. Go be with that bitch ass nigga of yours, I'm off you," I hissed and she stared up into my eyes.

"So you don't want me anymore?" she asked and sniffled.

"Nope, not unless you tell that nigga it's a wrap with me standing here," I shot her an evil grin.

"Kaleeini."

"Aysia, do it or I'm done with you," I stated sternly. As if God was on my side, that fuck nigga came out looking for Aysia.

"Baby, what's going on?" he questioned and touched the small of her back.

"Uh, umm, Brice-"

"Who is this?" he frowned and looked me up and down. He looked a little off to me, but I couldn't put my finger on why.

"Tell him who the fuck I am, Aysia," I snickered.

"Brice, this is Kaleeini-"

"Kaleeini!" Erica came from the theater looking for me. I put my hand up to signal for her to stop talking. She just stood there next to me, and we both stared at Brice and Aysia.

"Continue Aysia," I said and yanked her over to me. I hugged her tightly from behind, and started kissing on her neck. I was tired of seeing him touch the small of her back.

"Aye nigga, what the fuck wrong with you!" Brice shouted and charged me.

I quickly pushed Aysia behind me, and waited for him to make a move. He stopped once he got close to me, and panted heavily with his fists balled up.

"Tell him who I am Aysia," I repeated without taking my eyes off of him.

"Brice, this is Kaleeini, and he's my man now," she said still standing behind me.

"Nigga, what the fuck!" he shouted and shoved me backward.

Erica and Aysia screamed once they saw me deliver a right hook to his face. Blood flew from his mouth, and he stumbled and knocked over a trashcan.

"Security! You guys have to go!" one of the theatre workers yelled before calling security over his walkie talkie again.

I snatched Aysia up, and then threw Erica some money for a cab or some shit. We booked it out of the theatre, and then quickly got into my car before speeding out. I wasn't trying to have any run-ins with security or the police.

"You are crazy!" Aysia screamed to me and pouted. She knew she was happy that she could be with me freely now.

"You like that shit," I smirked.

"No, I hate it," she grinned and caressed the nape of my neck. I drove her to my place, and then we got comfortable in the living room after we made some margaritas.

"So, am I really your girl?" she asked as we interlocked fingers.

"I don't know, you got a bad reputation with me. You need to make that shit up to me first," I replied.

"Okay, I will. And then when I blow your mind, what will be next?" she asked and straddled me.

"We'll just have to see," I responded and bit my lip. Mission accomplished.

It was around 10pm at night, and I was lying in bed with KJ at his new house. It was huge as hell and I knew he'd paid a lot of money for this shit. The foyer was huge with white marble floors, and his high ceilings had chandeliers hanging from them. The one thing I loved was all the paintings he had on the walls. You could tell he put a lot of thought into choosing them.

We'd just gotten done fucking, and he was in the bathroom relieving himself. I loved being his girl and being with him all the time, but a part of me wondered what he'd been doing before he took my virginity. Willow was speaking the truth when she said KJ loved pussy, so I wasn't sure how he was getting by without any during our first weeks together.

"Look at you," he grinned once he came out of his bathroom, and then hopped into the bed with me. He got between my legs and slid his tongue into my mouth. He threw the sheet out of the way to expose my naked body, and then let his dick rest between my legs.

"KJ," I said and moved my face away. I couldn't hold it in any longer, so I had to ask.

"What?" he responded and stared into my eyes. His green ones were such a pretty shade of dark green. Although the room was dark, the moonlight from the windows made it easy to see one another.

"Before we had sex, were you doing it to anybody else?" I asked and caressed his smooth toffee colored skin.

"You're asking if I cheated on you?" he frowned and I nodded my head. "Why are you asking me this?" he quizzed still frowning.

"Because you weren't trying to with me, so I'm sure you were getting it elsewhere," I said.

"What would you do if I said I was doing dirt?" he whispered and stared at me. I swallowed the lump in my throat, and my stomach started to feel queasy. I knew getting our relationship off the ground would be hard but damn. "What would you say?" he asked again and kissed the area right below my small breasts.

"I don't know KJ, I would feel all types of ways. I would be mad, sad, disappointed—"

"And what would you want to happen after that?" he questioned further. I was crying by now and he wiped my tears away.

"I would want you to apologize to me, and promise to never do it again, and mean it," I sobbed and sniffled. He wiped my falling tears again, and kissed my lips gently.

"You wouldn't leave me?" he asked and searched my eyes with his own.

"No," I said somberly. "But if it happens again I will," I added and looked into his eyes. He inhaled sharply, and then nodded. "You know I love you, Kendrick, but I can't let you treat me this way. Don't you love me too? If you do then don't keep breaking my heart," I cried. A part of me knew that finally being his girl was to good to be true. To think KJ could be faithful was pure bullshit.

He sighed and looked off to the left. He was still lying on top of me, between my legs. He caressed my hair, and then made eye contact with me again.

"Gigi, before we went to Hawaii, I was messing around with other girls. I didn't wanna have sex with you because I wasn't sure if I could be with you at this time in my life. I made you my girl because I didn't want you talking to anyone else, but at the time I wasn't sure if I wanted that. Not that I don't want you because I do, but I didn't wanna be cheating on you and shit. I care about you, baby, and I *am* in love with you, that's why I wanted to wait until I could do right by you," he said and the tears really started to pour from my eyes.

We hadn't been together that long and we were already breaking up. "But, the more I hang out with you as my girl, the more I'm seeing that I can be faithful to you. So Gianna, I'm sorry for cheating on you, shorty, and I promise it won't happen again. Stop crying, because I love you, aight? It's only gonna be me and you from now on, I swear baby girl," he finished, surprising me. He had never told me that he loved me. I always told him, and I just assumed he felt the same. It felt good to hear it though. "And sooner or later, I'm gonna marry you and all that shit, aight?" He smiled and reached under me to squeeze my ass, making me giggle. "Tell me you love me and that you gon' always be down for me," he said and nibbled on his bottom lip with his perfect teeth.

"I love you, Kendrick, and I'm gonna always be down for you," I replied and tapped his nose lightly with my pointing finger. I felt his dick harden, and then start to push into me. "Aaah, aaah," I whimpered.

"Mm," he moaned softly. "This pussy is mine, Gianna. You better not even let another nigga smell it," he groaned as he worked himself in and out of me.

"I won't," I half whined before he pressed his lips against mine, and then bear hugged my body without losing his stroke pace.

THE NEXT MORNING, we got dressed around 10am because we were gonna go have brunch with his parents. I'd met them before, but not to the point where we'd sat down like we would today. I was a little scared to meet them formally, because KJ said he'd never brought a girl to meet them like this before. I hoped his mom wasn't one of those weirdly overprotective ones, because I didn't feel like dealing with that. As for his dad, people feared him, so naturally I was scared to meet him too. On top of that he was very attractive, and KJ and his brother Kendrin looked just like him.

A lot of people thought KJ and Kendrin were twins, and they hated that shit. KJ just had a little more facial hair, but if you didn't know them you probably couldn't tell them apart. Another detail was that KJ had his mother's name on his arm.

"Chill out," KJ chuckled as he stuck his key into his parents' front door. I smoothed down my orange dress, and then did the same to my edges. KJ shook his head at my nervousness and then kissed my lips. "Ma!" he called out over the big ass mansion.

A couple moments later, a beautiful woman with caramel skin and long dark hair appeared. She was wearing a white dress with thin straps; his mother was beautiful and very youthful.

"Where is Dad?" KJ asked her just as his father hit the corner.

"Hi, Mrs. King, I'm Gigi- Gianna," I stammered slightly. I remembered my mother told me to never introduce myself with my nickname.

"You can call me Nic honey, and I remember you," she smiled and flashed her pretty teeth.

"Mr. King," I stuck my hand out to shake his, and I was pretty sure he could feel it trembling.

"Hi again, Gianna," he smiled and his green eyes sparkled.

"I'm sorry Gianna, my husband naturally charms everyone," Nic cheesed and then playfully patted Mr. King's chest.

We all chuckled and then followed her to the huge back patio where there was a table covered in food. It was shaded with a huge white umbrella so that the sun wouldn't burn us up. KJ pulled my chair out, and Mr. King did the same for Nic.

"Gianna, we've heard a lot about you. It's good to finally sit down with you instead of just the hi and byes like usual," KJ's father smiled. Damn, I hoped KJ aged as well as him.

"You've heard a lot about me?" I repeated and raised a brow. It felt good to know that KJ had mentioned me to his parents prior.

"Yeah, ever since KJ was in eleventh grade he has been saying, 'Ma, don't trip, I have Gianna and I'm gonna marry her'," she quoted him and chuckled.

"Ma, come on, man," KJ smiled, making his dimples appear.

"Yeah, we were worried that he didn't inherit my good taste in women," Mr. King added and we all chuckled.

"So Gianna, are you in school? Or what do you do?" Nic asked me.

"I'm not in school, no. I want to be a stylist, so right now I do freelance jobs for photo shoots," I replied nervously. KJ told me she had a Master's Degree, so I was hoping she didn't judge me.

"Really? So you're really into fashion?" she cheesed.

"Yes, I love it. I have subscriptions to just about all the high fashion magazines," I replied and sipped my lemonade. We were having lemon chicken angel hair pasta, and it was so good.

"That's nice honey, and it sounds like fun," she nodded and winked.

"KJ tells me that you're half Italian," Mr. King chimed in and squinted his eyes at me.

"Yes, my mother is Italian and my father is black. KJ told me that Mrs. King, excuse me, Nic was a quarter Italian," I responded.

"Yes, my father was half like you," she nodded with a smile.

"Oh, he passed away?" I wondered.

"Mm hmm," Mr. King replied, and then he and his wife chuckled lightly before he planted a small kiss on Nic's neck.

We ate and talked for the rest of the lunch, and soon enough I was relaxed. His parents were way nicer than I assumed. Being around them just made me want to be with KJ even more, because I admired their relationship. Hopefully, one day we would get married like he'd promised. It wasn't possible for me to be any more in love with him.

"Well, it was nice meeting you, Gianna," Mr. King said as we all walked towards the door. I hugged and kissed him and his wife.

"Oh sorry, I think I got some lipstick on your cheek," I told Mr. King. "I don't want to upset Nic," I taunted and the four of us cackled. Nic began to clean it off for him.

"Maybe back in the day, but she knows what's up now," he replied making us all chortle heavily.

"See, I told you it was gonna be all good," KJ smirked at me once we got into his car and onto the road.

"And you were right as always, KJ," I rolled my eyes playfully. He grabbed my hand in his, and then kissed the back of it gently. "I love you, Kendrick," I said in a low tone.

"I love you too, shorty."

Tonight, I wanted to lay out all of the works for Kaleeini. I knew I was on thin ice with him after lying about Brice, but I was happy that he was still interested in me. Especially because he could've easily given me my walking papers, and had someone new on his arm within the same hour.

It was crazy because he could have any bitch in the DMV area, yet he wanted to be with me. I wasn't gonna question it too much, because I enjoyed being with him too. Also, I didn't want him to start wondering why he liked me and change his mind. I chuckled at the thought.

I'd booked a one-bedroom suite at Staybridge in Linthicum, and cooked a meal for us to eat about twenty minutes ago. This room had taken a nice chunk out of my already small paycheck, so that nigga had better appreciate it. My baby was worth it though, so I didn't mind spending the coins.

I texted Kaleeini the hotel and room number, and then I hopped in the shower to get fresher for my baby. I then changed into the lingerie one piece I'd bought from Victoria's Secret, which was barely there. I put a few loose curls into my hair, and then put lotion on my body from my neck to my feet before spraying my perfume. I lit some candles from Bath and Body Works, and then laid on the bed to wait for Kaleeini to arrive. *I should've left him a key at the front*, I thought.

Fifteen minutes had passed, and I was starting to get anxious. *What if he was standing me up?* I thought to myself. Maybe he had finally realized he could possibly do better. No fuck that, I was a catch no matter how fly the nigga was.

I picked my phone up off of the dresser, and checked to see if he had texted me. There was nothing there.

Me: *He's not here.* I sent to the group text.

Shannon: *How long have you been waiting?*

Gigi: *Give him some time.*

Willow: *Call that nigga!*

I chuckled at Willow, and then locked my phone. I kicked off my heels, and right when I did there was a knock at the door. I quickly slipped the heels back onto my feet, and then double-checked my appearance in the mirror. I could use a few curls, but I still looked perfect nonetheless.

KNOCK!

KNOCK!

He banged on the door again. I looked out the peephole, and I smiled when I saw his sexy ass. His dreads were down, but he had his hood on, making them protrude through the front. I opened the door, and put my hand on my hip. His seaweed colored eyes lit up while smiling, and then he walked into the room.

As soon as I closed the door, he picked me up and lifted me in the air. "Wait, we need to eat," I giggled as he kissed on my collarbone.

"I'm about to eat right now," he said in a low tone, before laying me on the bed.

"No Kaleeini, I spent a lot of time on the food," I nudged him off of me.

"Alright, and you better know how to cook. I'm gon' be mad if I'm missing out on pussy for some burnt chicken and wilted salad," he taunted and we both burst into laughter.

He sat down at the little table in the room, and I lifted the silver top on his plate. There was a lemon Rosemary chicken breast, with cheesy mashed potatoes, and steamed carrots with glazed walnuts.

"Damn Aysia," he commented and lifted his fork. I sat down in my seat, and then started to eat as well. "Thank you for this shorty. Is this just a one-time thing?" he asked.

"Me cooking for you?" I quizzed and dabbed my mouth with the cloth napkin.

"Nah, pulling out all these stops and shit," he answered before eating the carrots.

"I always do nice things for my man," I responded and ate some of the chicken.

"Oh, so I'm not special? I don't want shit that you've done for that nigga." He dropped his fork.

"Chill Kaleeini, I have never done *this* like *this* for him," I cheesed. "I'm going that extra mile so I can get on your good side, remember?"

"Good, and you better not be doing this for anyone else," he said and resumed eating.

"And what about you? All the stuff you did for other girls," I said.

"Does it seem like I've done anything for any other girls?" he raised a brow. "Shit that whole movie fiasco was way out of character for me. I never chase a woman like that shorty," he scoffed.

"Not even Erica?" I stared him down.

"Only thing I've done for her is dick her down," he replied.

"Well, I don't want you dicking her down anymore," I smirked.

"Who do you want me to dick down then?" he smiled.

I got up out of my seat and then straddled him. "Take a wild guess," I whispered.

He polished off his glass of champagne, and then got up with my legs still wrapped around him. He put me down, and then I stepped out of my heels. I turned around and lifted my hair so that he could help me out of my lingerie. Once he unsnapped it, I pushed it down to my ankles before stepping out of it. He kissed my back and neck, and then turned me to face him.

"Damn," he said in a low tone as he took in my physique. "Aysia, you are so bad," he spoke softly.

He grabbed my face, and then started tonguing me down. In the midst of our kiss, I unbuckled his jeans as he stepped out of his sneakers. I pulled back to help him out of his hoodie and shirt, and finally this fine ass nigga stood naked in front of me. His toasted vanilla complexion was covered in tattoos, and cut the fuck up. His dick was swinging, and damn was I pleasantly surprised. I just knew he had a small dick because everything else was bomb, but boy was I glad to be wrong.

I tied my hair up, and then got down on my knees. "You about to put in work, hunh?" he chuckled at me, referring to me putting my hair up.

I gently grabbed his dick, and then began to suck on the tip like a Popsicle. Once I had it nice and lubricated, I took his full dick into my mouth, and played with his balls.

"Shit, shorty," he called out in a low tone as I worked my jaws. I closed my eyes to enjoy the moment, and my baby started moaning loudly as hell. I felt his strong hands grab my bun, and I smiled on the inside because I knew I was doing a good job. "Damn, do that shit Aysia," he grunted and then spilled his seeds down my throat. He picked me up, and then brought me to the bed. He laid down on his back, and then pulled me to his face. "Sit on my face," he told me.

I had never done that before, but I wasn't gonna protest. I mounted his face, and then slowly lowered my pussy to his mouth. He gripped my waist, and then began to suck on my clit softly.

"Mmmm," I purred and then clutched the headboard.

"Ride it," he demanded and I did so. I wound my hips onto his mouth slowly, and he ate my pussy like I hadn't just cooked a big meal for him.

"Oh my gosh, Kaleeini," I whimpered. This shit was feeling too fucking good. I think it had become my new favorite foreplay action. "Uuuh, uuuh," I cried out as I released.

He put me on my back, and then got between my legs. He got off to get a condom from his jeans, and then rolled it down. I was dripping at the thought of him entering me.

"This is the last dick you gonna know," he smirked at me as he gently smacked his dick against my wet center. I spread my legs some more, and pushed my pussy towards his rod. His head almost went in, and we both let out a soft moan. "I like how you take control," he bit his lip.

He pushed himself inside me, and I felt it in my stomach. I couldn't even move at first. We interlocked our fingers, and then he pinned my hands above my head. He worked in between my hips, hitting my spot back to back.

"I'm cumming already," I whined and he smirked. After I gushed on his pole, he let out a soft groan.

"You're so damn wet right now," he said before sucking on my lips. He pulled out, and then put me on all fours. He kissed down my back, while pushing his dick into me from behind.

"Aaah, uuuh," I cooed once he made his way inside me. I bit the pillow as he pounded me from the back. You could hear the sound of him going in and out of my drenching center from here to Timbuktu.

"Fuck!" he called out and squeezed my ass roughly.

"Uuuggghhh!" we both screamed out as we exploded. After catching his breath, he pulled out of me and went to flush the condom. He brought me a warm towel to wipe with, and then he took it back to the bathroom for me.

"I knew that pussy was fire," he chuckled as he climbed back into bed with me. "That nigga hasn't touched you in a long ass time. That pussy was way too tight," he added.

"I think the last time was probably ten months ago," I giggled nervously because ten months ago, I was not a willing participant in our sex session. I stayed because I knew it was Brice's illness and not him.

"Good, just making room for your real future," he kissed my forehead and I nodded in agreement.

"So do you forgive me now?" I questioned as I laid on his chest.

"Nah."

"What? Why Kaleeini?" I frowned and sat up.

"I'm just kidding, come here," he yanked me down, and then kissed me passionately. "Yes, I forgive you. Tell me whose girl you are," he said in between kisses.

"I'm yours, Kaleeini," I panted because the kiss felt so good in combination with our warm naked bodies touching. He started to kiss down my body, until his mouth reached my clit. I couldn't be any happier.

TODAY, my brother KJ and I were gonna go do an unexpected drop by on one of the traps. For the last couple of pickups, the money had been short. So either these niggas were pocketing the money or pocketing the drugs, and either way we weren't having that shit.

I literally felt bad for niggas when they would try to cross us, because I wondered if they were actually dumb enough to think they were gonna get away with it. No nigga or bitch has ever been able to get one over on the Kings, so I don't know why muthafuckas continued to try. They needed to learn to respect what they could never be, and fall in line if we allowed them to be down; simple.

We pulled up and parked across the street, but a little ways down. Just in case something popped off unexpectedly, we didn't want to be right across the street from the scene.

"Damn, you ready?" I chuckled at KJ after he secured his piece in his waistline.

"I stay ready nigga," he smirked at me. "You'll never catch your boy slipping."

We walked up to the house nonchalantly, in order to make these niggas think that everything was okay. We ain't wanna rush up in there because it was still sunny out, and the few people around would become alarmed.

"Oh KJ, Kendrin, what's up?" this dude named Casey smiled, and so did the other two workers we had in this specific trap.

"That's what the fuck I'm trying to figure out," KJ smiled and the three of them looked at one another while stuttering. "Come walk, with me, Ronald," KJ grinned and waved him over to us.

"Aye man, I don't even—"

"Let's go," KJ cut him off.

I wasn't one to talk much. I felt in times like these there was nothing to say. I had always been like that. Growing up, I was never that nigga who was barking and arguing with other dudes. If I was approaching you, I was swinging because there were no words at that point. I was still the same way whether it was shooting or fighting. I wasn't an arguing ass nigga, and I even tried to be that way with my girlfriend Willow. She was the only one who could get some words out of me, but that was only because I couldn't hit my shorty.

We left Casey and Aaron back inside the house as we walked across the street and climbed into the car. We drove in silence until we reached our warehouse, and I swear I heard every lump that Ronald swallowed on the way. KJ parked, hopped out, and then ordered for Ronald to get out as well.

"Man please—"

"Quit fucking crying!" KJ barked and I just chuckled.

My brother could always spot a snake in the room before anyone else. I had no idea who it was, but clearly KJ knew it was Ronald.

"Sit down." KJ slammed a dirty chair in the middle of the warehouse room for Ronald to sit in. Ronald did as he was told, and I saw he was already tearing up. "Be honest, are you smoking my product?" KJ folded his arms and waited for him to respond.

"I-I just been having a hard time at home. You know my baby mama cheated and—"

"Save all that shit for Maury, homie," KJ sucked his teeth and then let out a deep sigh.

Seeing niggas try to cross us was annoying as hell. You just wanted to smack the shit out of them for being so stupid, and ending their life over a couple thousand dollars or a temporary high.

KJ pulled a bag out of his jacket pocket, and then lit the blunt it contained. Ronald stared up at him, still sniffling like a little bitch.

"I promise it won't happen again K—"

"Shut the fuck up, I'm thinking!" KJ shouted over him and he jumped. After taking a couple pulls on the blunt, he passed it to me and immediately pulled his gun from his waist.

POP!

POP!

Ronald's head split open, and KJ chuckled. "Bitch ass nigga," he mumbled to himself and then looked at me. We both burst into laughter, and then I took my phone out to dial Syrus and Dave for clean up.

After they took care of Ronald, we left so that we could go chill with Kaleeini and Kenzie. Kenzie was going off to training camp soon, so we wanted to kind of enjoy his last days here for a while.

"So what's up with you and Gigi, bro?" I asked KJ as I ashed the blunt in the car's ashtray.

"What you mean what's up with Gigi? Same thing that's always been up, that's me," he smiled as he made a left turn.

"That's yours officially, or what? Because Mom and Pop said y'all ate lunch and shit," I raised a brow. KJ had always claimed Gianna, but not on anything official, so this was surprising to hear.

"Yeah, it's official," he replied.

"I thought you said you were saving her until you could settle down?" I frowned in confusion. I knew this nigga was not ready to be anybody's husband at all.

"I know, but she got to talking about she gon' start fucking with other niggas, so I had to change my plans," he chuckled.

"So you've been good or what?" I quizzed.

"Not at first, no, but now I am. I been told you she was the one, so

I'm gon' turn in my player card early," he winked at me as he parked in front of Kaleeini's condo.

The King men loved women, but my father was right when he said we knew early on if a girl was the one. I had only been on one date with Willow and I knew she was wifey for sure. And I have been with plenty of women in my nineteen years. Same with KJ, he knew Gianna was it back when they met in high school.

"Damn, you must've finally taken that V card," I laughed and so did he.

"Yeah, remember when I took her to Hawaii with me?" He looked over at me and I nodded. "That's when it happened, and man, that shit was so good I almost proposed to her," he half joked and we cackled.

"Well that's good to hear, now Ma can rest. She was so worried you were gonna get one of these hood rats pregnant," I shook my head.

"Never! You know Dad instilled in us early to strap up unless she was our shorty," he huffed and I nodded in agreement.

"Did you with Gigi?" I wondered with a grin.

"Hell nah!" He burst into laughter and we slapped hands. "I was going to but I was like fuck that, this is my girl," he responded.

We got out of the car, and as we walked up Kaleeini's steps, we saw his parents, our Uncle Kendreeis and Aunt Morgan walking out of his crib.

"Hey," we all said and greeted them.

"I cooked food and bought groceries because you know Kaleeini ain't never got shit," Aunt Morgan taunted and we chuckled.

"Thank you, did you make cinnamon buns too?" KJ inquired. She would always make one pan for him, and then another pan for everyone else to share.

"Just for you," she smiled and kissed his cheek, and then she and our uncle continued to walk out. Kaleeini's younger brothers Kendall and Kendlan followed behind, and we greeted them as well. When we walked in, Kaleeini and Kenzie were already stuffing their faces with food.

"Damn, it better be something left," I turned my lip up and followed KJ to the kitchen.

"So are you excited?" I asked my cousin Kenzie once KJ and I returned to the living room with our plates.

"I am, but then I'm not happy about waking up at 4am to train and shit," he shook his head.

"Is Shannon gonna visit you?" Kaleeini asked.

"Yeah she is, and y'all know I'm gon' be looking forward to that shit," he bit his lip and we cackled.

"I'm gonna miss you, baby," Shannon caressed my face as we laid in my bed.

"I'm gon' miss you too, shorty," I replied and pecked her soft lips.

Shannon and I had been together for a cool minute, and I loved her sexy ass. She was slim thick, had smooth brown skin, and long ass dark hair. I planned to make her my wife one day, even though there were some things in the way.

"How long will you be gone again?" she quizzed and twisted up her pretty face.

"Just one month, and I'm only gonna be in Virginia so you can visit me," I responded and sat up in the bed.

"I'm gonna visit you a lot baby," she smirked.

"Make sure you call me first though, aight?" I raised my brow at her and she nodded. I kissed her lips once more, and then got up to get ready for the shower. "Let's get cleaned up before my mom, dad, and sisters come home," I told her and walked to the bathroom within my room.

I turned on the shower, and then climbed in to let the water hit me. She got into the shower with me, and I squeezed her petite round ass.

"You're so pretty," I pursed my lips before darting my tongue into her mouth.

"I thought we were getting cleaned up, Kenzie," she whined and giggled as I lifted her up and brought her down onto my dick.

"We are... after this," I replied. "Damn," I commented at the feeling of being inside her.

I cupped her ass cheeks and moved her up and down my shaft. She draped her arms over my shoulders and started to suck on my lips.

"Aaahh, aaahh, Kenzie," she whimpered as I tugged on her bottom lip.

I gripped her tighter, and then began to slam her down onto my dick, and soon after we both exploded. I kissed her hungrily for a couple moments and then let her down. We cleaned each other up, and then got out to get dressed, just as my parents and sisters arrived.

"I hope all your stuff is packed," my mother said to me, and I nodded before kissing her cheek.

She was a firecracker, and my dad said she had been that way since they were younger. He said Cuban women were crazy and to never date one. I thought that was hilarious.

"Look Shannon, I'm gonna run some errands baby, and when I'm done I'm gonna call you, okay?" I smiled and so did she.

"And don't you forget to do so." She put her arms around my neck, and leaned up for a kiss.

"I could never forget about you," I spoke honestly. Shannon was my world, and there was no way I could be without her. She turned around to leave and I smacked her ass.

Once she was gone, I ran upstairs to change my clothes, and then hopped into my car. I sped the whole way to my destination, and then quickly exited my vehicle. I went up the walkway and rang the doorbell.

"Hey daddy," my other girlfriend Rosalind answered the door, wearing some short ass dress.

"Sup shorty," I cheesed down at her and pulled her close. I backed her into the house and closed the door behind me.

Alright, so yeah I had two girlfriends. Rosalind was my girlfriend first, but when I saw Shannon I couldn't pass her up. I got invited to Gianna's birthday party, and that was the first time I laid eyes on Shannon. I tried the whole night to not approach her, but I couldn't help it. The longer I stared from across the room, the prettier she got. I finally said fuck it, and told myself I would just smash and pass, but after spending time with her I was on it. I so badly wanted to trade Rosalind in, but I couldn't do that.

My family knew nothing about Rosalind, and for some reason she never asked about them. She was okay with not meeting my parents and shit, I guess. Shannon on the other hand, kind of had a shoe-in because she was friends with my cousin's girlfriend Willow and KJ's little boo, Gianna.

"I don't want you to leave," Rosalind pouted and then started kissing on my neck.

"I don't wanna leave you either baby, but it's only for a month," I grinned and so did she.

I loved Rosalind a lot, but Shannon had ultimately stolen my heart. I knew the day that I had to choose it would be Shannon, but for now, I wanted and had them both. Shannon's and my connection was so natural, and I could spend hours just talking to her. Rosalind on the other hand, I didn't talk to as much, but I could dick her down for hours for sure. Anytime I had something where I was to bring a date, Shannon was the one to attend. If you asked around Baltimore who my girlfriend was, everyone would say Shannon Breaux. I was surprised no one had mentioned it on TV during one of my games or in interviews, but I was thankful nonetheless in case Rosalind tuned in. She didn't watch much TV.

"I cooked some food for you," Rosalind smirked.

"Make me a plate then, shorty." I plopped down on her couch.

She switched off into the kitchen to make me a plate, and I checked the time on my phone. I had a strict ass schedule when it came to managing two fucking girlfriends. I replied to a text that Shannon had sent me, and then put my phone away just as Rosalind returned with my plate of food, looking good enough to eat her damn self.

She was light skinned, and had long curly hair. I didn't listen to my dad when he said to stay away from Cuban women, especially ones that looked like Rosalind.

"So what's your plans for us, Kenzie?" she asked as she watched me eat.

"Umm, what you mean? You're my shorty," I leaned over and kissed her cheek.

I hated when she tried to have these *where are we in the relationship* talks, especially because she definitely wasn't in the running for a ring on that finger.

"I know, but when will shorty get a ring or something, papi?" She played with my chin hairs.

"Once I get drafted into the NBA, you know I'm gonna marry you, girl," I lied. Shannon was to be my wife, but damn I wished I could have them both so that I wouldn't hurt Rosalind. On the contrary, keeping Rosalind would hurt Shannon, and her feelings were more important than Rosalind's. Ain't this fucked up? Maybe because Rosalind was my girl first.

"You better," she giggled and then sat back. I set my plate to the side, and then reached up her dress to pull her panties down. She was so sexy, and it was hard not to want some pussy when I saw her.

"What are you doing?" she smiled.

"I'm about to make love to my girl," I said before tugging them down her thighs.

Gianna, Shannon, Aysia, and I had just come from the nail shop and were about to go have lunch. We decided to meet up because we needed Gianna and Aysia to spill the newest tea in their love lives. I was nosey as fuck and always wanted to know what was up. I had no qualms about coming right out and asking either.

"Gigi, you start first since you never told us what happened in Hawaii," I stared her ass down.

Ever since KJ made her his girl, well officially, she'd been MIA because she was always up under him. I was happy though, because everyone was waiting for them to get together officially. I would've been pissed if he had had her waiting like that just to make another girl his bitch.

"Stuff happened," she replied and blushed.

"Stuff like what?" Shannon smiled.

"Well, we flew there on his private jet, and that part in itself was just bliss. We made out, ate snacks, listened to music, and talked the whole way. Well most of the way, it was thirteen-hour flight damn near, so we did nap a bit. The first thing we did when we got there was have a nice little dinner, with pleasant conversation of course." She sucked her teeth and chuckled. "Then we went back to the vacation home, and KJ lit some candles in the room and stuff. We started kissing and shit, but I stopped him so that I could go change into my lingerie that I'd just bought."

"Aww shit!" Aysia clapped her hands together.

I was on the edge of my seat with this shit right here. Gianna had been a virgin forever, so I was hoping she finally knew how great of a creation dick was, especially a King man's dick.

"Yeah, so, I changed and then when I came out... we had sex," she smirked and shrugged one shoulder like it was nothing.

"And how was it?" I grinned.

"It was bomb when he was eating my pussy, but then it hurt bad as fuck when he first fucked me. But by the third time that night, it wasn't as much pain and was feeling good. My pussy got sore though. Anyway, I liked it every time because it was with him," she responded giddily.

"How cute," I said and she squinted her eyes at me playfully.

"Did he strap up?" Shannon asked.

"Damn, do you really need all those damn details?" Gianna frowned.

"Fine then," Shannon giggled.

"He smashed out raw," Aysia blurted and we laughed hard as fuck.

"You sucked his dick yet?" I questioned and we all stared her down, awaiting her answer.

"Yes I did, and it's not as hard to do as I thought. He came in my mouth though," she whispered the last half and snickered. "It didn't taste like anything though," she added.

"Damn bitch, you a little freak bitch already," Shannon commented, making us laugh loud as fuck. We paused and looked around the restaurant, and people were staring at us like we were some ghetto hood rats.

"Now you," I said to Aysia.

After she put us up on game about she and Kaleeini, we finished eating our lunch. I thought it was dope that we were all dating men in the same family.

We went and got ice cream from Uncle Wiggly's, but then went our separate ways after KJ called looking for his precious Gianna. I didn't mind because Gianna was finally getting what she wanted out of that nigga.

On my way home, I decided that I would stop by and see Kendrin. I missed his sexy ass even though I'd just seen him last night. I called his phone, and he picked up immediately.

"Sup shorty," he said.

"Hey daddy, I wanna come spend the night," I smiled as if he could see me.

"I told you that you don't have to ask me that Willow, come through baby," he replied in his sexy tone. I loved that he lived alone now.

"Okay, be there soon," I giggled happily and hung up.

I got to his condo about five minutes later, and when I parked I saw him coming outside.

As I was crossing the street, some hoe ass bitch said, "Hey Kendrin," and waved all seductively. I sped up my walking until I made it to the curb.

"Sup China," Kendrin nodded towards her.

"What you doing out—"

"Don't worry about what the fuck he's doing out here," I raised my brow at her once I'd made it over by them.

"Oh damn Lo, chill out," she chuckled and looked back at her friends. How the fuck did she know my damn name?

"Willow, come on, don't start this shit," Kendrin tugged on my arm.

"Yeah, get your little Chihuahua, Kendrin," China waved towards me and I just couldn't contain myself.

WHAM!

I punched her ass in the nose, and then we started going at it. She grabbed a handful of my hair as I wailed on her face. She was screaming at the top of her lungs, yet she had a good grip on my French braids. She kicked me in the stomach, so I kicked her ass too, and she flew into a tree. She screamed loudly as fuck, and clutched her sore back as blood dripped from her nose. I charged her but before I made it, Kendrin grabbed me by my waist and carried me inside. I wanted more of that bitch!

"What the fuck is wrong with you!" he screamed down into my face.

"Are you serious? Did you hear what she said to me?" I hollered back at him.

"So fucking what! She's just jealous of you and you fed right into that shit! You cannot keep stooping to the same level as these bitches, Willow!" he yelled. I just looked away and folded my arms. "Now look at your fucking face, that shit is all scratched up and shit," he said holding onto my chin. "And your hair is all messed up."

"I'm still cute as fuck," I responded, still frowning.

"Willow, I think we need some time apart," he said catching me off guard.

"What? Why Kendrin?" I started to tear up.

"I told you I couldn't deal with this shit any more man. You out here fighting every got damn day, and for what? I'm *your* nigga and you know that, yet you out here acting like you need to prove something! These bitches know what's up, Willow!" he frowned. "That's why they come at you like that, and you fall for it every fucking time!"

"Okay, I get it!" I wiped my tears. I couldn't let him break up with me.

"No, you really don't. You say that shit every time, but you really don't get it. I'm a nigga of a certain caliber Willow, and the girl on my arm can't be fighting like she's on Jerry Springer every time some random hoe says something she doesn't like," he said.

"So it's over now?" I panted heavily as more tears ran down my cheeks.

"Yes, for now. I need some time to think on if this is really what I want babe, it's just too much. Our relationship is supposed to be a joyful addition to my life, not a hassle," he replied.

"You don't love me anymore?" I questioned as my tears drenched my face.

"Nah, I do love you, that's why I'm telling you we need to go on a break instead of just breaking up with you. I need a mental break, and you need a physical break," he laughed wryly.

"For how long?" I sniffled.

"I don't know. It may be for good," he stared down into my eyes.

"No Kendrin, I'm sorry, I promise. I won't say nothing or fight nobody," I sobbed like a little child about to get their ass beat.

"Go home, Willow." He shook his head and then walked to his door to open it.

I stared up at him for a little bit, and then walked towards the door. I stopped once I reached it and looked up into his handsome face. I caressed it and then leaned up to kiss his lips. He let me but didn't kiss me back. I turned around slowly and walked back to my car. He closed the door behind me, and as I was crossing the street, China yelled "Sent you home already?"

I just ignored her stupid ass and got in my car to go home. Once I got home, I locked myself in my room and cried myself to sleep. I hoped Kendrin changed his mind soon, because there was no one else out there for me.

Tonight was the last night that Kenzie would be in Maryland, so he and I were gonna have a nice romantic dinner. I don't know why I was so sad when he was only gonna be gone for a month, but I was. Kenzie and I had been Siamese twins since the day we met damn near, so I hated that he would be away from me. He was for real my lover and one of my best friends, and I just loved the fuck out of him.

I buttoned my halter dress around my neck, and then put on my earrings. I sat down on the bed and grabbed my phone, so that I would know when Kenzie had arrived. I blew out hot air as I thought about this month that we wouldn't be able to see one another every-day. I was so attached to him. Also, a part of me hoped no bitches would be able to push up on him while he was away. Hoes saw dollar signs when Kenzie was around, because they all knew he was NBA bound. I would slice a bitch up in a minute about my nigga though.

"You okay?" my dad peeked his head into my room.

My mother had run off after she decided motherhood was too much. I was thankful that she got pregnant by a great guy though. My father was the best dad a girl could have.

"Yes Daddy, thank you," I smiled at him and closed my clutch.

"Just checking, how late will you be out tonight?" He quizzed.

"I'm not sure, do I have a curfew all of a sudden?" I asked him with the raise of an eyebrow.

"No, I just like to know these things, but have fun tonight baby girl. A month is gonna fly by like that," he snapped his fingers.

"I know, I'm good," I half lied. He walked in, kissed my cheek and then walked back out. My phone buzzed and I looked to see that it was Kenzie telling me he was outside. When I stood up, I heard a knock at the door.

"Kenzie, hey," my dad answered it just as I entered the living room. "I'm happy you're not one of those guys that honk for the girl from outside," my father said and folded his arms across his chest.

"Not at all," Kenzie smirked with his sexy ass. He turned his attention to me, and his green eyes beamed once he took in my appearance. "You look beautiful short- Shannon," he grinned. I chuckled at him almost calling me shorty in front of my father.

"Have a nice night, and good luck at camp Kenzie," my dad said. I took Kenzie's hand, and we walked down to his car where he opened the door for me.

We drove to The Capital Grille, and on the way there we vibed to some Chris Brown. When his song "2012" came on, I gripped Kenzie's hand in mine. We both loved that song, and would always listen to it.

Once we were seated at our table, we immediately started kissing passionately. "I'm gonna miss you," I said in a low tone.

"I'm gonna miss you too, but remember we're gonna be facetiming and shit, and you're gonna visit me, right?" He bit his sexy bottom lip.

"You know I am, baby," I smiled and stared into his eyes. For some reason, all of that shit didn't sound like enough. I was used to being all in his grill all day, except when he had practice.

"You know I love you no matter what right?" He said.

"You better, and what do you mean no matter what? There aren't any bitches at camp right?" I half joked.

"Hell nah there ain't. Shit, I wish," he taunted and I lightly tapped the back of his head.

The waiter walked over to take our order, and then once he left we resumed our conversation.

"Well good, but yes, I love you no matter what happens too," I said.

"No matter what?" he raised a brow.

"Yes, and forever and ever," I grinned.

"That's why you're gonna be my wife, shorty. You'll ride with me 'til the wheels fall off, won't you?" he smirked and then scanned my body.

"I sure will. We'll be like the modern day Bonnie and Clyde," I draped my arms over his shoulders.

"Ooh, I like it when you talk like that. We may have to start doing some role play or some shit," he kissed on my chin.

"That sounds fun. I may surprise you when I come visit you next weekend," I replied.

"Next weekend?" he jerked his neck back.

"Yes, that's what I planned," I responded.

"Baby, I planned for you to come the weekend after. You know the first weekend we're getting settled in and everything," he pecked me.

"So next weekend?" I asked to clarify in a somber tone.

"Yes, next weekend, and I promise it'll be worth the wait," he cheesed.

"Oh yeah?" I raised a brow.

"Most definitely, you may need to roll that sexy ass body around Baltimore in a wheelchair when I'm done with you, shorty," he hugged my waist tightly.

"Ooh, I may order it early," I said before slipping my tongue into his mouth.

We ate dinner, and then talked a little while after. We went out to the car, and then I waited as Kenzie booked a hotel room on his phone.

"I can't wait to come back and get my own place," he said as he cranked up the car.

I couldn't wait either. Even though his parents, Jessica and Kendon were cool, we couldn't be fucking like we wanted to in his room. The most we would do were quickies, or wait until the whole family went out. The only thing I liked about the quickies was that the thought of getting caught made me cum faster and harder.

We arrived at Lord Baltimore Hotel, and he jogged around the car to my side to open the door. He was such a gentlemen and I loved that about him. We checked in and then went up to the beautiful suite.

"Kenzie, how much was this?" I squealed. He was always doing nice things for me, and spending a lot of cash on me too.

"Only the best for my shorty, so don't worry about all that," he said and pulled me close.

He dipped his tongue into my mouth, and pushed my dress up to my waist. He lightly pushed me onto the bed, and then yanked my panties down to my ankles. Once they were off, he latched onto my clit and began taking me to new heights. I was head over heels for this nigga, and nothing or no one could change that.

I WAS so ready to turn the fuck up tonight. My cousin, Kaleeini was throwing a costume party, and that shit was about to be fun as hell. I wasn't the type of nigga to dress up, so I just decided on black jeans, a black crew neck, black Nikes, and this little black half Batman mask that Gianna found for me. She wanted us to match, and I didn't mind such a small item.

"What do you think?" Gianna walked into my bedroom wearing a black latex cat suit, with black thigh-high boots on.

She had an eye mask on, and a white wig that hung down her back. The bodysuit hugged every curve on her little slim thick body, and for a minute I wanted to strip her out of it.

"Damn, keep that on when we get back," I said and then grabbed a handful of her ass.

She definitely had on a little ass thong under it. She giggled when I groped her, and then headed out of the room so that we could leave. "Aye come here," I tugged her back to me and then maneuvered my tongue into her mouth. After getting my fix, I pulled back from her. "You know better than to not give me no love," I nibbled on my lip and she smiled. She pecked me again and then we left the house.

When we got to the venue, you could hear the music blasting

from the fucking outside. There was a crowd of people outside, some waiting to get in, and some people just hanging around bullshitting. Thank God Kaleeini had valet set up, because trying to find a park over here would've been too fucking crazy.

"Hi KJ," some thick Spanish chick waved to me.

I think I smashed her before, but I wasn't too sure. I ignored her and I felt Gianna staring a hole through the side of my face. I was trying to pretend I didn't notice her, but a smile crept across my face so she knew I did.

"Chill out," I said and grabbed her close to me. I kissed her temple, and she rolled her eyes up in her head.

Bolo was working the door like he did for all of our functions, so he just nodded and moved out the way so me and my shorty could get in. "Jumpman" by Drake & Future was blasting as we walked through the packed ass venue. There were strobe lights and shit going everywhere. There were so many girls in just lingerie, trying to pass it off as a costume by adding devil horns or bunny ears.

People were grinding and freaking each other on the dance floor, as I protected Gianna from the crowd. It was hot as hell already, but I was glad that we would be going to VIP. When I got up there, I saw Aysia sitting on Kaleeini's lap, Kendrin chilling with Drew and Lenny, and then Willow and Shannon sitting by one another.

"Hey guys! Gigi, you look sexy!" Shannon beamed when she neared Gianna and I. She was dressed as one of them slutty nurses.

After greeting she and Willow, I walked over to sit in between Kaleeini and Kendrin, and said what's up to my boy Lenny and cousin Drew who were in the midst. I pulled Gianna down into my lap, and let my hands roam all over her body. For some reason I couldn't get enough of her. I've never met a girl that I wanted to fuck every breathing moment. I guess because I had never been in love before, and also had never come in contact with such good pussy.

"Kiss me," she whispered and I did so. Her perfume smelled so sweet, and it was something I wanted to smell forever.

"Let's dance, Gigi!" Willow shouted, I guess trying to get

Kendrin's attention. He didn't pay her ass any mind, and I could tell it bothered her.

Gianna, Aysia, Willow, and Shannon got up and started dancing to "Work" by Rihanna, and damn I couldn't keep my eyes off of Gianna. We made eye contact, and although she was a little ways from me, I could tell she was dancing for me. My dick started to get hard as I watched her move her little body in that tight ass contraption. One of the VIP waitresses poured me a drink, and I sipped it as I kept my eyes locked on my shorty. I mouthed come here, and she slowly walked over to me. She sat down into my lap and I moved some of the wig hair out of her face.

"You're so beautiful shorty, you know that," I said and she blushed.

"I love that you tell me that all the time," she replied.

"Because it's true. You know I been doing right by you like I promised," I said before kissing her soft neck.

"You better be nigga. You would be miserable without me," she grinned and showed off her perfect white teeth.

"I really would," I chuckled lightly.

"I would be miserable without you too, that's why I waited for you," she caressed my face.

"I'm glad you waited for me, that pussy is too good to be giving to other niggas," I licked my lips and squeezed her ass.

"I didn't wanna give it to anyone else," she said in a low tone.

"Tell me what I wanna hear." I planted a kiss on her lips as Miguel's "How Many Drinks" poured through the speakers.

"I love you, Kendrick, and I'm gonna always be down for you," she responded and smirked.

She pulled my bottom lip into her mouth, and I slipped my tongue into hers. I could taste the passion fruit juice she had been sipping on. She cupped my face as we kissed so hard I thought our lips would burst.

Suddenly, Gianna was yanked backward and I saw London standing there. "So this is the bitch you left me for?" she screamed.

She was wearing a short red dress with devil horns. Gianna hopped up quickly, and shoved London backward.

"Don't approach my fuckin' man, bitch," Gianna spat. I quickly got up and sat Gianna down next to my little brother Kendrin.

"Aye, where the fuck is the security?" I barked as I looked around the little VIP area.

Kaleeini went to the entrance of VIP and went in on them, causing them to come over towards us. In the meantime, London was yelling all kinds of shit while being restrained by Lenny. Kendrin was restraining Gianna, who was trying her hardest to fuck London's ass up. I rushed over to Lenny, snatched London up, and rushed her into the nearest bathroom in the VIP area. I didn't even check to see what gender it was for, and honestly I didn't give a fuck.

"Fuck is wrong with you, hunh?" I hissed. My blood was boiling like a muthafucka right now. I wanted to knock her ass out for coming in here and touching Gianna like she actually meant something to me. The nerve of this bitch to be acting like we were in a damn relationship.

"How dare you leave me to be with that young hoe!" she shouted back to me. "I gave you everything, KJ!" she added as her tears began to ruin her makeup.

"Kendrick," Gianna walked into the bathroom.

"Gigi, go sit back down outside," I put my hand up to stop her from talking.

"What—"

"Gigi, go!" I yelled sternly. She paused for a couple moments to glare at me and London, then she left. I turned back to London and backed her into the wall. "You don' lost your fucking mind running up on me like that shorty. I'm not that nigga; trust me. I don't know what type of muthafucka you're used to but you should know by now that I'm a different fucking breed. That girl out there is my baby and there ain't shit you can do to change that. You were a fuck buddy and you knew it from jump. Don't approach her and damn sure don't put your hoe ass fingers on her again, or I will have you burned down to ashes and thrown into the nearest sewer, you got it," I gritted. I was dead serious too. I wouldn't even throw her fucking ashes in a river. I would flush that shit down my toilet after dropping a deuce. She stared at me with tears running down her cheeks, and shook her head at me.

"I still love you, and I will be here when you come to your senses KJ," she sniffled and then tried to walk around me. I grabbed her by the neck and slammed her into the wall.

"That ain't what the fuck I wanted to hear," I said. "I asked you if you understood what the fuck I just told you," I sneered.

"I understand," she sobbed hysterically. I flashed her a smile, and then let her neck go.

"Now walk up out of this party. I bet not see you no more tonight," I backed away and then opened the bathroom door. She was crying so hard her body was shaking, but she walked that ass up out of there like I'd ordered her to.

I treaded back out looking for Gianna and I didn't see her. I didn't see Willow either, only Shannon and Aysia.

"Where is Gigi?" I asked her friends.

"She asked Willow to take her home," Shannon replied and then looked at Aysia.

"The fuck, why?" I frowned in confusion.

"She just said that she was done with you and your cheating ass," Aysia responded and shook her head with a sympathetic expression.

I snatched the mask that I had on off, because I had forgotten it was on. I know London thought I was crazy as fuck keeping this shit on.

"Where did they go?" I asked.

"They went to Valentino's to eat," Shannon said. Aysia nudged her for telling me, and Shannon just shrugged.

I turned around and then dapped up my brother, as well as Kaleeini, Drew, and Lenny, before leaving. I forced valet to get my car before a couple of other people who'd already requested theirs, and then I sped out of there.

I pulled up to Valentino's, and damn near got out before the car was all the way in park. I walked in and ignored the lady asking me how many to be seated. I spotted Gianna sitting at a table with Willow across from her, and her wig was sitting next to her. I stormed over there, ready to snatch her ass up by her arm.

"Let's go Gigi," I said and she jumped when she saw me.

"Fuck you, go be with that bitch," she spat and then put some pasta into her mouth.

"Gianna Isabella Daniels, I'm not gon' ask you again, let's go," I said again as Willow watched with her eyes bucked.

"Kendrick Dreaux King Jr., I said fuck you and I'm not going," she rolled her neck at me, and I wanted to knock fire from her. I chuckled out of anger, and then scooped her ass up. "Put me down!" she shouted as I carried her crazy ass through the restaurant.

"Sir! Put the young lady down!" some guy yelled. I ignored his ass and continued outside.

I threw Gianna into the car, and then got in and sped off. We didn't talk the whole way to my home, but I really didn't care. Once I parked in my roundabout driveway, I went to her side and she hit the lock button before folding her arms. I just hit my alarm to unlock it back, and then quickly yanked the handle and pulled her out.

"Take me to my parents' condo!" she screamed at the top of her little lungs, as I carried her to my door and inside my house. I took her upstairs, set her down, and then locked the bedroom door. "I'm leaving," she said and tried to walk to the door.

"Man, sit down," I lightly pushed her onto the bed. "I'm sorry about what happened earlier shorty. That girl is just a hoe still trying to hold onto something she ain't had in a while," I knelt down in front of her. "When I told you to leave the bathroom, it was because I was handling it, baby," I said and rubbed her thighs.

"Why were you in there so long?" she asked, still scowling.

"Because I was making sure she understood not to approach us again, or it would be her ass," I responded. She looked away and then back at me. "I told you I'm doing right by you, baby, you have to believe me. You know I love you and I wouldn't do anything to lose you, Gigi," I said before kissing on her collarbone, while unzipping her suit down the front.

"You swear?"

"I swear," I nodded and pulled the suit down her smooth cinnamon thighs. She had on a white lace thong and the matching bra, looking so fucking sexy. I planted kisses on her flat stomach, and then her thighs while spreading them open.

"KJ, I have something to tell you," she moaned.

"Tell me," I replied and started to pull her panties down.

"No, stop and listen." She tried to move my hands but I had a good grip on her underwear.

"I can multitask," I smirked up at her, and then kissed her pussy through her panties.

I put one of her legs up so that her foot was flat on the bed, and then continued kissing and inhaling the scent of her center through her panties.

"KJ," she panted.

"What baby? I'm listening," I whispered as I moved her panties to the side to kiss her bare lower lips.

"We-we've been ha-having a lot of sex," she stammered as I begin to French kiss her pussy, while holding her panties to the side. I pushed the leg that was propped up, outward for more access.

"I know... I can't get enough of you," I said in between licks and sucks.

"Aaah, aaahh," she purred. I wanted more, so I pulled back and yanked her panties off roughly. I placed her thighs on my shoulders, and then went back to eating my favorite meal. "KJ!" she cried out.

"Mm hmm," I replied to let her know I was still listening while my mouth was occupied.

"I'm pregnant," she finally said. I stopped working my magic, and pulled away to look up at her. "I know it's soon, and I promise I was taking my birth control everyday. I don't know what happened KJ. I swear I didn't do this on purpose. I even set an alarm—" I cut off her motor mouth with a deep kiss.

"You're gonna have my baby?" I asked to clarify and she nodded. I started laughing, and a smile spread across her face. I dropped down and kissed on her flat stomach a couple times. "I love you, Gigi," I said as I kissed her soft lips constantly.

"I love you too," she said in between kisses.

"I told you that you were gonna have my kids. And look at you tryna break up knowing you're carrying my baby," I smiled at the thought of her crazy ass, and she chuckled.

I stepped out of my shoes, and then took off the rest of my clothes while she watched closely. I reached behind her and unhooked her bra. She moved to the center of the bed, and I got on with her to get in between her thighs. I kissed her inner thighs, and then went back to her lips. I wiggled my way into her snug hole, and we both let out a soft moan. Her beauty and my love for her seemed to intensify now that I knew she was pregnant.

"I love you, Kendrick," she cooed as we continued to make love.

My younger brother Kendall and I were at Uncle Wiggly's getting ice cream so we could catch up. I was a busy guy, especially now that I had made Aysia my shorty, so I always liked to make time for my little brothers.

"So how is senior year so far?" I asked him after paying the cashier.

"It's straight, I like that we got more freedom and shit," he replied and I chuckled.

"Yeah, I loved my senior year because I didn't do shit really, and was ditching like a muthafucka," I said.

"But when I graduate, you and KJ should put me on," he nudged me.

"Have you talked to Pop about that?" I raised my brow at him.

My father Kendreeis had done this drug shit with my uncles Kendrick and Kendon for the majority of his life, and he hated for me to get into it, but he couldn't stop me. I knew if Kendall came to him trying to live the same life, he would have a fucking fit. It's not like he looked down on the art of pushing weight because his whole blood-line did that shit, including my grandfather Kairio. He just didn't like all the dangerous shit that came with it. He told us my uncle Kendrick was brushed with death at least three times, but it just let me know to be extra careful.

"Nah, I ain't talked to him yet, and you know Ma gon' go with whatever he says," he scoffed and I laughed. As we started getting closer to my car, I saw that nigga Brice mean mugging me. "Fuck this nigga looking at?" my brother gestured towards Brice.

"Go get in the car," I told him and put my keys into his hand. He hesitated but then finally went and did what he was told. "Can I help you, homie?" I asked Brice.

"Yeah, you can leave Aysia alone, and stop having your people check up on me!" he screamed. What the fuck was he talking about?

"Man, I ain't gone even waste my time on your bitch ass," I waved him off and started towards my car.

"You know I'm still hitting that right?" he called after me.

"Oh word?" I turned to him smiling.

"Word, pussy is still nice and tight too so you must not be hitting the way I am," he cracked and then laughed. I walked back over to him and he backed up a few inches. "Aye, stay back nigga," he frowned and then looked around as if he was scared someone was gonna run up.

"The next time I see you, you're getting murked. There won't be any talking, tussling, or nothing. I put that on everything I love," I told him calmly. He just stared into my eyes with his deranged ones, and after a couple moments, I walked over to my car.

"What was that about?" Kendall quizzed.

"Nothing man," I responded and backed out of the parking space. Something was strange about that nigga. The look in his eyes wasn't right, and the fact that he said I had people checking on him was weird too.

I immediately took Kendall home, and then called Aysia on the phone to tell her to meet me at my crib. When I got there, she was sitting outside on my steps, looking so beautiful as usual.

"Sup shorty," I smirked and helped her stand up.

"Hey baby," she smiled and jumped into my arms excitedly. After a few kisses, I stuck my key into the door and let her in first. "So what you rush me over here for? You missed me?" she questioned and then lightly pushed me onto the couch before straddling me.

"I always miss your pretty ass, but nah, I wanted to ask you something and I want you to be honest with me," I responded.

"Shoot," she half smiled and stared down into my face.

"When was the last time you talked to Brice?" I inquired.

"Well... at the movies that night," she replied while playing with one of my dreads.

"And he hasn't hit you up or nothing?" I cocked my head.

"I mean, yeah, he texts me and shit but I don't respond," she shrugged.

"Why the fuck you ain't tell me he was messaging you, Aysia?" I frowned.

"I didn't think it was a big deal, Kaleeini. I mean it's not like I say anything back!" She turned her lip up.

"Well it is a big deal when another nigga is texting my fucking girl!" I barked.

"I'm sorry baby, I didn't know," she caressed my face and adjusted herself in my lap.

"You fucking him?" I blurted out. She stared into my eyes for a couple seconds before speaking.

"For real?" she scoffed.

"I'm just asking, and I need you to answer," I huffed.

"Why are you asking me this? Do you think I'm fucking him? Can't you tell when a bitch is giving pussy away?" She rolled her neck and then climbed out of my lap.

"All of that is bullshit, just answer the question, Aysia," I sighed.

"No, I ain't fucking him, Kaleeini. The only nigga I'm fucking is you, and clearly I shouldn't be doing that either," she said before standing up to leave.

"Shut up," I said and yanked her back down onto the couch. I pulled her fine ass close to me, and ran my finger down her full lips. "Don't you ever say that again," I pecked her.

"Don't ever ask me that again," she replied in a low tone. "You know I've been all about you Kaleeini, even when I was with him. So why would I cheat on you when I finally got you?" she said and kissed me.

"I'm just making sure you realize what you got," I smiled.

"You need to realize what you got too nigga!" she rolled her eyes.

"I know what I got shorty, and quit all the attitude before I have to discipline your ass," I pressed my lips against hers softly.

"I think I may like that," she whispered before tonguing me down.

I reached down to unbutton her jeans, and she did the same to me. I pulled her shirt over her head, and then promptly unhooked her bra. I cupped her perky breasts and devoured her nipples.

"Mm," she purred as I went to town on them.

I sat back up, and then she pulled my dick from my pants. She stood up, and then let her jeans fall down, before sitting on my dick backwards.

"Fuck," I moaned as soon as I entered her tight walls. Her pussy fit my dick like a glove, and I was mad I even let that nigga convince me that he was still fucking her.

She gripped my knees, and then began bouncing slowly. Her pussy was damn near strangling my dick, and dripping wet at the same time; perfect combination.

"You gon' make me nut fast shorty," I frowned as I watched her ass bounce in my lap. She looked over her shoulder at me, making the cutest sex face. I gripped her small waist, and then drilled into her making her cream.

"Damn Kaleeini," she panted out of breath. I pulled her closer to me, and she turned her face to the side so that I could kiss her full lips.

She wound her hips on me while going up and down, and my

dick got harder letting me know I was about to explode. She bounced faster, and a couple moments later I was releasing.

"Shit!" I called out as I attempted to catch my breath. She got up, letting my dick fall out of her, and then straddled me so we could kiss. Damn I think I loved this girl.

Aysia, Shannon, and Willow were in my room, chilling and listening to music. It was a Saturday, and since our men were working, or gone away in Shannon's case, we were just hanging out. I'd just cooked ravioli for everybody so we were stuffed.

Ahhh, I am so lit. Ahhh, pose bitch!

"Ooh this is my song!" Aysia said and turned up "Pose" by Rihanna.

We all wound our bodies to the beat, and then I got up to dance. I had on some short shorts and a red tube top. I started twerking my ass and my friends were laughing and cheering me on. I was flinging my hair and shit being extra, and then when I looked up in my doorway, KJ was standing there. I jumped back and Aysia turned the music off.

"KJ, what are you doing here?" I asked out of breath.

"Enjoying the show," he squinted his eyes. I didn't say anything, and just looked at my friends. "Come here and let me talk to you," he waved me over. I walked over and he took me into the bathroom, and then closed the door. "You barely got any clothes on and popping your ass like that with my baby inside you," he commented as his eyes scanned my body.

"I didn't think about it KJ, I was just playing around," I chuckled. He walked closer to me and I tensed up.

"You better be glad that shit turned me on," he said before pressing his lips against mine, and then tonguing me down nastily. He dropped down, and began unbuttoning my shorts.

"KJ, my friends can hear," I said and tried to move his hands away.

He continued removing my shorts, and then pulled one side of my thong down. He kissed the tattoo I had of his name right by my pussy, and then finished removing my bottoms. He stood up and then bent me over the sink gently, before releasing his dick and sliding inside.

"Damn Gigi, you always feel so good," he panted and kissed on my neck. His eleven inches filled me up, and I came only a couple minutes in. I gripped the sides of the sink as he beat it up from the back, and sucked on my neck.

"Aaah, uuuh," I called out because I couldn't hold it in any longer. My friends would just have to hear me getting fucked.

KJ bear hugged my torso using one arm, and then gave me four hard pumps, so I knew he was about to cum.

"Uuuggghh," he groaned. I loved the sound he made once he reached his peak. Once he caught his breath, he pulled out of me. I turned to face him, and we kissed for a little bit. "Get dressed so we can leave," he said.

"To where KJ?" I inquired as I pulled a washcloth out to clean myself up.

"Just do what I said, shorty," he chuckled as he cleaned his dick off.

"Yes daddy," I replied as I put my thong and shorts back on.

He pinched my ass when I was opening the door, and then he went to the living room while I went to tell my friends I was leaving. When I walked into my room, they were staring at me with half smiles.

"I know y'all bitches heard me," I smiled and unplugged my phone from the charger.

"Heard what?" Shannon played dumb while cheesing.

"Heard KJ putting a hurtin' on that pussy!" Willow's vulgar ass commented and everyone started laughing.

"Anyways, I'm leaving soooo..." I said as I grabbed my new Birkin that KJ had just bought for me.

They all stood up to leave, and then the four of us went into the living room where KJ was on the couch. He had on basketball shorts, a t-shirt, socks, a black snap back and Nike slide-ins. I loved how he was sexy no matter what he wore.

As soon as we got into his car, he sped down my street. I wondered where he was taking me, because you never knew with KJ; he was so random. I must say though, these last couple of months being his girl were pure bliss, just like I knew it would be. We'd always been best friends, but now our bond was stronger. It just solidified what I already knew, and that was the fact that Kendrick Dreaux King Jr. was my soul mate.

We pulled up to his house, and I rolled my eyes. I bet he pulled me from my friends just so he could fuck me all afternoon into the night. He opened my door for me, and then we walked up to the door. 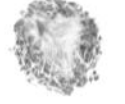

When I entered, the foyer was dimmed with a red light. I didn't know where he got the red tint from, but it was so cute. In the middle of the foyer was a small round table covered in a white tablecloth. There was a rose in the middle of it, and plenty of rose petals surrounding it. There was also a red slim candle on it, and KJ rushed over to light it. He then slid the chair out for me, and I walked over to sit in it. He walked away, and then brought back a pan of cake slices it looked like.

"A variety of cheesecake flavors," he said. Cheesecake was my favorite food, especially from the Cheesecake Factory.

"Thank you baby," I beamed and took the fork to take a bite of the cookie dough flavor. I'd just eaten, but I was never too full for cheesecake.

He walked away as I ate my cheesecake, and about ten minutes later, he came back smiling. I put the pan of cheesecakes down, and looked up at him.

"What is all this for, Kendrick?" I quizzed and covered my mouth since it was full.

"Because I want you to know that I love you," he said.

"I know you love me," I half smiled.

"Yes, but we got off on a bad start when we got together, and I want you to know that our feelings are very mutual, shorty. I don't want you to think that you're the only one who wants this right here," he replied.

"I don't think that anymore," I shrugged.

"See, but you did, and I need you to forget that."

"Forgotten," I snapped my fingers in the air and smiled. He pulled a chair up to be next to me, and then reached into his pocket and pulled out a velvet box. He opened it and there was a heart shaped yellow diamond ring.

"KJ!" I squealed. I had never seen anything so beautiful in person.

"This is eighteen karat gold baby, cost me one hundred grand," he grinned making his dimples appear. His jade green eyes were sparkling, signaling his happiness. "This isn't an engagement ring, especially because my mama said colored engagement rings are tacky," he chuckled. "But it's just something I wanted to get for you to express how I feel for you," he finished. He slid it onto my finger, and then I held my hand out in front of me, and blushed at the sight of it. "You like it?" He questioned.

"Of course, and even if it was an engagement ring I wouldn't think it was tacky," I responded before kissing him.

"I'm gonna propose to you one of these days though, I promise," he cheesed.

"I know," I said before kissing him passionately.

"Oh, and I got you this too." He pulled out another box containing a platinum diamond bracelet, with a yellow gold heart hanging from it. Engraved on it was *Kendrick loves Gianna.*

"Baby," I whined as he fastened it on my wrist. Tears were coming from my eyes because I was so happy.

"I love you, Gigi," he stared into my eyes once the bracelet was on. I kissed him so hard with my eyes closed.

"Can we get tattoos on our ring fingers then?" I raised a brow. I hoped he said yes because I really wanted to do it.

"Fine, only because I love your ass," he responded and I kissed all over his sexy face. I ate a couple more bites of my cheesecake, and then we left to go get our tattoos.

Before we got together, people would always tell me to stop hoping he would change and make me his girl, but I just couldn't give up. I was glad that I didn't.

It was Friday night and this girl from high school named Tasha was throwing a party for her birthday. We all were pretty cordial with her so we decided to attend.

"Girl, KJ is gon' have a fit if he sees you wearing that hoochie shit," I smirked at Gianna.

"He won't know," she giggled and looked at herself in the mirror.

She was wearing a black bandeau top that had her whole stomach out, and a long black skirt with a high split. Her hair was straightened and hanging down her back.

"I see you tryna get all you can out of your body before that stomach starts poking out," I said as I put mascara on my lashes.

"I sure am," she said and then her phone rang. She put her finger up to her mouth to tell me to be quiet. "Yeah, I'm just chilling with my mom tonight, I can come by later," she said. "Okay, bye baby," she chuckled and then hung up.

"You know KJ ain't no dumb nigga, you gon' get caught Gigi," I laughed.

"And, he ain't gon' do shit to me," she smacked her lips and smiled.

Once Shannon and Willow texted us that they were outside, we hopped into my car and headed out to the party. When we walked up to the front, "All Right" by Future was playing so fucking loud that I felt it in my chest.

"I hate house parties," Shannon turned her lip up.

We walked into the front, and we were clearly overdressed. There were a couple of chicks dressed good like us, but the majority had on tights, chucks, and tube tops for the night.

"Hey y'all, thanks for coming," Tasha smiled and hugged us lightly. She had on a white dress and a gold birthday crown on her head.

As for me, I was wearing a red skirt and a matching red frilly top. Willow had her two French braids, and they were hanging long down her back as usual. She wore a simple black dress because she said she only dressed up when Kendrin was around. Shannon had on a camel colored tube dress, with her long hair in a huge bun on her head.

"It stinks in here," Gianna frowned and checked the time on her watch. I smiled when I spotted her big diamond ring she'd just gotten from KJ.

"It is a little stale and musty," Willow shook her head. We were standing there like four prissy ass bitches, but you would be too if you seen this ratchet shit.

"There goes some seats," Shannon pointed to a couch. As we were walking through the party, some guy grabbed Gianna by the waist.

"Aye shorty, dance with me," he smiled down into her face.

"I'm good," Gianna replied and moved his hands off of her.

"Damn, pretty bitches are always stuck up," he sucked his teeth and shook his head. We rushed to the couch hoping not to bump into anymore bucket heads on the way.

"Would you ladies like a drink? We have Vodka, Tequila, and pretty much any kind of juice you want," some girl smiled. She was holding a tray with clear cups all over it. I loved these house parties because you could get a drink at any age.

"Can we get three cranberry and Vodka's, and then one regular cranberry," Shannon ordered for us. The girl nodded and wrote it down before walking away.

"I'm mad she tryna have some VIP drink service in this ratchet shit," Willow rolled her eyes and we laughed.

"No Way" by Adrian Marcel came on, and we started rocking a little and singing along, as people slow freaked on each other. The level of funk went from five to ten during that time, but at least we had our drinks by now.

Just then, we heard a lot of ruckus by the front door. The four of us were stretching our necks to look at what was happening, and low and behold it was KJ walking in with his brother Kendrin, and best friend Lenny. People were acting like celebrities were in the house.

I looked at Gianna and smiled, and she sunk low into the couch. Lucky for her, KJ didn't see her, probably because the lights were low. I could smell their colognes as they walked by us. They all went to this little island in the house, and he, Lenny, and Kendrin sat on the bar stools. We all watched, especially Gianna and Willow, as a couple guys and girls approached them.

Suddenly, "Saved" by Ty Dolla $ign came on, and some girls started trying to dance on KJ, Kendrin, and Lenny, to which they did not protest. Gianna hopped up so fast and booked it over there. She burst through the crowd, and KJ hopped up off the barstool. He grabbed her arm, and pulled her to the corner. He leaned her up against the wall, and she folded her arms across her chest while rolling her neck, clearly going off. KJ was smirking down into her face, and then she pushed him back lightly. He yanked her closer to him, and then their crazy asses started tonguing it up. I looked over at Willow, and she was fuming as she watched some random girl freak Kendrin. Shannon just rubbed her back to hopefully calm her.

"Are you guys ready to leave?" I asked them.

"I don't care, it's up to y'all," Willow replied trying to save face.

"Okay, let me go get the car. I will text when I'm out front," I said and got up. I shook my head and laughed at Gianna and KJ still sucking face like they didn't already have a baby on the way.

As I was walking down the dark street to my car, I felt someone grab my arm and turn me around. Brice grabbed my face and tried to force me to kiss him.

"Move nigga!" I shouted and shoved his face. After tussling a bit, he finally gave up and stared at me panting. "What the hell is wrong with you, Brice?" I screamed.

"What the fuck you doing, Aysia? You for real about this nigga?" He stared down into my eyes.

"Who, Kaleeini? You're asking if I'm serious about Kaleeini?" I squinted my eyes in confusion.

"Yes! Unless you fucking someone new already! My cousin told me you're selling pussy!" he barked.

"Wow. But yes, I am serious about Kaleeini, Brice. That's my man. Look, our relationship had run its course, and our break up was long overdue babe, be honest," I said in a calmer tone. I could tell he was slipping into an episode.

"You didn't have no problems with me until you started checking for this nigga. Oh you like him just because he got money and shit?" he scowled. "Ooooh, I see. You've been fucking him all along. You're pregnant! I know it! You've been fucking him since I met you! It's because he has money!" he screamed.

"It has nothing to do with that! And for your information, I've liked Kaleeini since high school, so this wasn't no random thing—"

WHAM! He slapped the shit out of me with a closed fist. My eye was immediately feeling sore, and I couldn't open it.

"Let me tell you something Aysia, you gon' always be my bitch, and that pussy gon' always be mine. I know people in high places too, and I will have you and that nigga killed," he gritted with his hand around my neck. "I don't care if you're pregnant!"

Tears were running down my face because of the pain in my eye and because I was scared. In this state, I had no idea if he was gonna kill me or let me go.

"Now I'll let you sleep on it," he added and lightly hit my head against the concrete wall. "Oh and by the way, I killed that nigga that you sent to rob me," he whispered before running off.

I stood there panting for a little bit, and then rushed to my car. I cranked it up, and then texted my friends to have KJ take them home. I heard them text back but I ignored it. I rushed home, and quickly darted back to my room before my mother began questioning me.

I didn't know what the fuck to do. Brice was crazy as fuck, and I knew for sure Kaleeini was too. The whole King family were not the people you wanted to play with. I didn't want this shit getting out of hand, and have Kaleeini's family looking at me like a troublemaker. Also, I knew Brice's family would start to believe his delusional claims about me. I didn't want a war to start over me, I just wanted to live my life in peace. I felt so trapped, and it was nothing I could do about it.

I shook my head at my thoughts, and then gathered my things for the shower. This winter was gonna be cold and brittle. I could feel it.

As I was getting my lap dance, I saw Willow and Shannon get up and go over to my brother. I was surprised and relieved that Willow didn't act a fool over this girl dancing on me. It looked like she finally understood that I wasn't her nigga anymore. I stared down at the girl's ass as it bounced in my lap, and my dick got hard as hell. The song switched and she turned around to dance for me facing me.

"What's your name?" I asked her. She was fine as fuck, and I was definitely looking to hit.

"Rosalind," she smirked and put her hand out for me to shake it.

"Rosalind, you're sexy as hell shorty," I nodded and pursed my lips.

"Aye y'all, let's go so I can take them home," my brother told us, while holding hands with Gianna.

"Alright, I'll be out there in a little bit," I said as Lenny got up to go with them. Willow stared at me but then looked away when we made eye contact. "Let me get your number, I don't have my car," I told Rosalind. I was looking to fuck tonight, and tonight only. Since breaking up with Willow, I'd been horny as hell.

"Okay," she giggled and then read it off to me.

"Aight, I'm gone hit you in like thirty and you better pick up," I raised a brow and she nodded with a smile. I walked outside and Rosalind was right on my heels.

"I don't get a hug before you go?" she quizzed.

"Hell yeah you can get a hug," I said and pulled her towards me. I squeezed her round ass, and she chuckled.

"See you in a bit papi," she licked her full lips and then flung her hair behind her shoulder.

Just then, KJ pulled up and honked his horn. I jogged over and opened the backdoor. The only seat available was the one next to Willow, but I wasn't gonna be petty. I just scoffed and then sat next to her. She didn't look at me; she just stared out the window as KJ pulled off. She wasn't too dressed up, but she looked good and smelled good too. I looked down at her smooth thighs, and reminisced about being in between them. She was too fucking crazy though, so I shook the thoughts from my head. Her phone chimed, and she pulled it from her purse to check it.

"Who the fuck is hitting you up at this time of night shorty?" I frowned. The thought of her fucking with someone else angered me.

"My mother, and it's none of your business anyway. Worry about that bitch at the party's phone," she spat and I laughed. I couldn't help myself, so I reached over and squeezed her warm thigh. It was so supple, and I missed sitting them on my shoulders to eat that pussy. "Move," she smacked my hand away and I chuckled lightly.

KJ dropped Shannon and Willow off at Willow's house, and then he took me and Lenny home, before retiring to his own crib with Gianna.

I went into my house and texted Rosalind. I didn't wanna text her my address though, so I sent her a message asking for hers instead. I just wanted some pussy and nothing else. Once I got the info, I hopped into my car and drove over there.

"I'm glad you didn't forget about me, papi," she bit her lip and closed the door behind me. She had changed into a skirt and top.

I yanked her over to me, and started kissing on her neck while raising her dress. She didn't protest and I was happy about that. I pushed her panties down, and she promptly stepped out of them. I bent her over the couch, and then went into my pocket to grab a condom. I released my dick to roll it down, and the sight of her pussy from the back had my dick brick hard.

"Ooooh," she purred once I slipped into her. I could tell early on that she had some good pussy. I grabbed her waist, and then pounded her like my life depended on it. "Work that shit baby," she called out and it turned me on. I grabbed her hair in my hand, and then went even harder in the paint. Her pussy was wet as hell, and her ass was jiggling all over the place. I threw my head back to enjoy the feeling, and she gushed on my rod. She was now sopping wet from cumming, which in turn made me bust hard.

"Fuck shorty," I panted as I slid out of her.

"Mmmm, you didn't even tell me your name," she smirked.

"David," I lied and chuckled on the inside.

"Well, we should do this again, David," she smiled at me and then stood up slowly. She looked into my face, and then made a weird expression. "I've only seen that eye color on one other person," she said.

"Oh word?" I smirked and wiped my dick off with the wipes she had on the stand.

"Yeah," she said in a low tone.

"Well I will hit you later shorty," I stood up and kissed her cheek.

She nodded slowly, and I could tell she was thinking about something. I didn't really care, I'd gotten my nut and I just wanted to go home, shower, and chill. I wished Willow could cook me something to eat, but oh well. I would just go to my parents' home to eat whatever my mom had cooked. On the way to my parents' home, I shot Willow a text.

Me: *Goodnight shorty, I love you.*

She texted back a couple minutes later. I knew it was wrong to text her that after fucking another bitch, but it was the truth.

Willow Love: *Well you need to act like it. Night.* I laughed and shook my head.

I walked into my parents' house and went straight to the kitchen. I turned the light on, and then went into the fridge. I saw my mother had made spicy fried chicken, red beans and rice, and string beans. I made myself a plate, and then grabbed a bottle of water. Once I finished, I was too tired to go home, so I decided to sleep in my old room.

"Aaahh, Kendrick," I heard my mom moan and I shook my head.

My parents would be on breathing machines and still fucking. I'm surprised they only had four kids. I cackled at my thoughts and then retired to my room. Tonight was pretty cool.

ROSALIND WAS SUPPOSED to come to visit me this weekend, but she said she was too sick. I wasn't really tripping though, because I really wanted to see Shannon. Like always, my baby cleared her schedule to accommodate me. It made me feel bad about fucking around on her even more.

While being away I'd done a lot of thinking, and I'd made up my mind that I was gonna end things with Rosalind. I loved Shannon, and although I was with Rosalind first, my love for her wasn't as strong. She wasn't down for me and shit like Shannon was. Shannon would do anything for me, and vice versa. I loved that girl more than anything, and that's ultimately where I wanted to be. Plus, my family knew and liked Shannon a lot, and they had reason to.

I drove to the hotel that I had paid for Shannon to stay in. I couldn't wait to see her and touch her, and do all kinds of shit to her. On the way there, I stopped and got some flowers for her because she loved flowers. I know most women did, but Shannon really loved them. Flowers could make a bad day good for her, and she didn't care what kind.

Once I got the flowers, I continued on my route to see my shorty. I got to the hotel, and then headed on up since I'd gotten a key already. I knocked lightly, and then entered wearing a big ass smile. I walked all the way in, and there Shannon was, sitting on the bed wearing a white lace lingerie outfit.

"Damn baby," I smiled and handed the flowers over.

"I'm guessing you like this," she giggled with her pretty ass. Damn, I was feeling even worse about being with another girl.

"Hell yeah I like it, I like everything you do," I kissed her soft lips. Her smooth brown skin was blemish free, and looking freshly moisturized. She smelled like fresh strawberries and looked good enough to eat.

"I brought some champagne," she held up the bottle.

"How did you get that?" I frowned and laughed.

"You know Lauryn is twenty-one," she said referring to her older home girl. I just nodded to say I remembered. "Here, you open it baby, it's too hard," she pouted and handed it to me. I cracked it open and then she held up some glasses for me to fill up. "I brought you some cornbread too." She lifted a pan of the dish. Cornbread was my favorite food, especially Shannon's or my mom's version.

"I love your ass Shan, you always going above and beyond for a nigga," I spoke honestly.

"It's because I love you," she half smiled.

"I know and I love you even more because of how much you love me," I replied.

"You better love me," she taunted and sipped the champagne.

"I do, no matter what, just know that I love the fuck outta your pretty ass," I said.

"Why do you keep saying no matter what Kenzie? I'm starting to think you did some shit," she furrowed her brows.

"Nah, I'm just letting you know. All relationships go through things, and no matter what we go through I want you to know that I love you," I responded.

"Oh okay, well same here. I love you no matter what," she smirked.

"So how is life in Maryland without me?" I asked, trying to change the subject. I didn't want her to start getting paranoid, and then start trying to snoop on me and shit.

"It's miserable, but my friends make it a little better. You know your cousin broke up with Willow," she scoffed and shook her head.

"Yeah, because she's wild as fuck. He had no choice," I shrugged.

"I know Willow is a handful, but won't no other girl love Kendrin the way that she does," she explained.

"I agree, she just needs to tone down her behavior, that's all," I said, tired of talking about them.

"So how much do you miss me while you're out here?" she questioned and then stood up in front of me.

"This much," I answered as I started to push her panties down. I then laid her back on the bed, and spread her legs open. I licked slowly between the slit, and then took her clit into my mouth.

"Kenziiieee," she cooed as I sucked on her button. Shannon was the only one I ate out. For some reason Rosalind didn't get that treatment. I slipped a finger inside of her, and began plunging it in and out as I fucked her with my mouth. "I'm cumming, shit," she panted and gripped the comforter.

Once she released, I stood up to undress. She sat up on the edge of the bed, and took my dick into her mouth. She moved her mouth up and down my shaft, letting my head bump her tonsils.

"Damn," I moaned softly as my baby worked her jaws. I massaged her scalp as she played with my balls. I felt myself about to nut, so I started to hump her face in a circular motion. "Aargh," I called out as I busted in her mouth. She took it down with ease, and I pushed her on her back.

I climbed in between her legs, and then unhooked her bra since the clasp was in the front. Once her titties were free, I devoured her nipples. I then pinned her hands above her head, and bit my lip while staring into her pretty ass face. I pushed the head of my dick into her tight pussy, and almost nutted on contact.

When I first started dating Shannon, I felt bad that I was eating her out and raw dogging her, basically doing shit that I wasn't even doing with Rosalind. But now it was like second nature. I was the only nigga to ever touch Shannon, and I was gonna be the last too.

"Uuuh, uuuh," she whimpered as I worked in between her hips. I could hear her gushing every time I slammed into her walls.

"Damn baby," I whispered into her mouth as we kissed. I'd forgotten how much I missed this pussy.

"Uuuh, uuuh," she cried out as she released on me.

"Mm," I commented at the feeling of her nectar coating my pole.

"I love you so much, Kenzie," she purred and caressed my face as our tongues danced.

"I love you too baby girl," I replied before starting to beat it up. I propped myself up a little, and then proceeded to go ham. "Uuggghhh," I grunted loudly as hell as I shot what seemed like everything inside of me into her. I bear hugged her slim body, and then kissed her like it was the last time.

Yep, as soon as I got back, I was gonna have to give Rosalind the heave-ho. Hopefully she took the news well, because I didn't want anything coming in between Shannon and I.

I WAS SITTING outside on the porch of my mother's condo, just watching people go on about their lives. It was Friday afternoon, and all kinds of shit was going on even though it was freezing. People watching calmed me, and I loved doing it when I had a lot on my mind.

Currently, all I could think about was Kendrin, and him fucking on all kinds of bitches. We'd been broken up for about a month now, and it wasn't getting any easier. I had loss of appetite, and I never wanted to really go anywhere unless my friends forced me to. I hated that he had that much control over me, but it was what it was. I wasn't gonna chase him though.

As I was relaxing, I saw Kendrin's black truck pull up. I tightened my scarf around my neck, and pretended not to notice. He exited the car and started walking over, looking good as hell. I could tell he'd just gotten a fresh cut although he had a beanie on.

"What's up, shorty," he said as he sat down next to me on the steps.

"Hey," I replied dryly. For some reason I wanted to cry, but the cold was helping me keep the tears at bay.

"Why are you out here in the cold like this?" he questioned.

"Because I like it," I responded being short.

"Come take a ride with me, I know you're hungry," he offered and nudged me.

"Actually I'm good, but thanks," I scoffed. His cologne became stronger, letting me know he was scooting closer to me.

"How you gon' be mad shorty? You're the one that fucked up," he said and kissed my cheek. Although cold outside, his lips were warm.

"You know I don't like seeing you with other girls, and then you flaunt it in front of my face? Everybody knows you were my man, and you hitting on girls right in front of a party of neighborhood people," I shook my head and sniffled because of the cold air.

"So you're saying I embarrassed you?" he quizzed and I looked into his green eyes before nodding.

"And hurt my feelings," I said before looking down at my UGG boots.

"Just like you be embarrassing me when you be fucking people up for no reason," he laughed.

"I have a reason. I'm jealous as fuck," I shrugged.

"But why shorty?" he inquired.

"Because Kendrin, bitches are always trying to get at you, your brother, and your cousins, so I need to make sure nobody is coming for mine," I replied.

"Willow, there is no need for that baby. You know you're the only one I'm fucking with, so why even do all that? They want what you have. There are plenty of niggas that check for you, but I don't sweat it because I know you're mine," he kissed the corner of my mouth. "Everything about you is mine, so I ain't gon' trip off no niggas checking for you," he said.

"So if a guy came up right now and started flirting with me, you wouldn't care?" I raised a brow because he was fronting right now.

Kendrin had gotten into a couple of altercations when niggas had flirted with me. I remember one guy pulled me into a tight hug at a party, and Kendrin broke his jaw. He swore he saw him touching the small of my back, leading down to squeeze my ass.

"Of course I would care, but I would tell his ass to back off, man to man. I ain't gon' haul off and beat his ass unless he tries to touch you or some shit," he responded.

"I'm sorry Kendrin, I'm just overprotective of what's mine," I looked at him.

"And that's fine, but just tone it down, shorty. You're above these hood rats. You're my girl, my baby, my shorty, and they know that so they try to bring you to their level. Don't give in to them," he rubbed my back.

"So I'm your girl, your shorty, and your baby again?" I rolled my eyes playfully.

"You gon' always be mine Willow. Even if you were crazy enough to get with another nigga, you'd still be mine," he kissed my lips gently.

"And you know you gon' always be my nigga," I smacked my lips and cocked my head.

"I know, I got your ass sprung," he taunted with his fine ass. I rubbed his toffee colored cheek, and kissed his lips.

"You're pussy-whipped too," I grinned.

"How could I not be, that shit is fire," he said in a low sexy tone before slipping his tongue into my mouth.

We sat there kissing for a little bit, and then he finally pulled away. I wiped some of my colored gloss off of his mouth, and then planted one more quick kiss on him.

"I missed kissing and fucking your crazy ass," he smiled making his dimples appear.

"I knew you would. I missed riding your dick for you," I raised a brow.

"I wanted to go get food, but now I wanna eat something else," he stared at me lustfully with his dark green eyes.

"No, I'm hungry. You got your own place now so we can do that all day after we eat," I chuckled.

"Speaking of my own place, my house is almost complete. I can't wait for you to see it shorty," he said and stood up. He put his hand out to help me up as well.

"Ooh, can I leave some stuff there?" I asked as he opened his car door for me to get in.

"Don't you always? You left your earrings at my parents' house once and had my mom going nine thousand on me," he laughed and closed the door.

"I want a drawer, baby," I said once he got in on his side.

"You may get a side of the bed if you act right," he winked.

"For real?" I beamed.

"Yes, but you need to show and prove first," he raised a brow and cranked the car. The heat came through the vents and began to defrost my nose.

"I love you, Kendrin King," I giggled and kissed him. "Now let's go to IHOP, I want their hot chocolate," I demanded and he shook his head at me.

My baby would be back in Maryland tonight, and I couldn't be more excited. I missed him so much, even though I'd been visiting him a lot. I'd thought about popping up and surprising him a couple times, but he'd made it clear beforehand not to. If it was any other nigga I would've been suspicious, but I knew Kenzie wasn't the type to fuck around on me.

Today, I was gonna get his name tatted as a little surprise for when we saw each other tonight. He would be home around 7pm, and we would eat dinner with his parents and sisters.

"Are you excited?" Gianna asked as she got into my front seat.

"You should be," KJ's little sister Kendria commented as she got into the back.

"I'm excited but I'm scared. Is it gonna hurt?" I looked over at Gianna since she had KJ's name on her, as well as a couple other small tattoos in other places.

"Mine didn't hurt too bad, but it was kind of uncomfortable because I had to take off my panties for him to do the tattoo," she chuckled and so did I.

"Ugh, I can't believe you love my brother that much," Kendria chuckled. She was so grown and mature for fifteen. "I want to get a tattoo," she added.

"Girl, your brothers and dad would kill us!" Gianna yelled and looked in the backseat at her.

"I'll just get one with some bitches who are less scary," she joked.

"That's fine with me," I replied as we laughed.

"Gigi did you tell Shannon what I told you yesterday?" Kendria asked.

"No, I wanted to wait until I saw her. But since you're here, you tell her," Gianna responded.

We were pulling into the parking lot of the tattoo shop, so I quickly chose the first park I saw and shut my engine off. I wanted to hear what they had to tell me.

"Spill, Dria," I said to Kendria.

"Well, I was at a kickback with my cousin Kaylie, and this chick named Brooke was saying that her sister's boyfriend's name was Kenzie. Now it could be another Kenzie, but I've never met another guy named Kenzie in Baltimore," she explained and a lump formed in my throat. "She knows he's my cousin, but I don't think she knew I heard."

"Did y'all ask her if it was Kenzie King? Or y'all were just eavesdropping?" I questioned.

"We were just eavesdropping, but she was bragging about it, which makes me believe it's my cousin she's talking about," she said. I looked over at Gianna and she had a sympathetic look on her face.

"What's her sister's name?" I quizzed.

"Girl, I don't know! All I heard was that Kenzie was her sister's man, and Kaylie and I were looking like what the fuck," Kendria smacked her lips. "I just wanted you to know, especially before you get the tattoo," she added.

"Ugh! This is so fucking annoying!" I shouted and banged on my steering wheel.

"What are you gonna do if it is true?" Gianna inquired.

"I don't even know, Gigi. That would be a big fucking blow if I found out that not only has he cheated on me, but another girlfriend? Ugh," I turned up my lip.

"Don't jump to conclusions just yet, Shan," Gianna rubbed my back.

"Girl, if this was KJ you would've been swinging on his ass by now," I chuckled although I was bothered by the situation.

"So we going in or what shorty?" Kendria asked and popped her gum. She was such a tomboy because she had three brothers, but she stayed with a fresh manicure and pedicure nowadays.

"Why? You got somewhere to be, or better yet someone to see?" Gianna asked.

"Hell nah, once niggas find out that I'm Kendrick King's baby girl, they don't even want to talk to me. I'm gon' start lying and saying my name is Keisha Brown," she turned her lip up and then laughed, flashing her pretty smile.

She looked just like her mama, but had jade green eyes. She was caramel, had long dark hair to her butt, a small frame, and full lips. I knew niggas checked for her constantly, and I felt bad for them because of all the niggas she had in her family protecting her. Even her cousins were overprotective of her. I remember one time her dad got pissed as fuck because she wore an off the shoulder top and shorts to the mall. Kendrick King did not play when it came to his little girl. He was lucky though, because Kendria was a good girl and she loved her daddy too much to disappoint him.

"Girl, you look like your mother and the green eyes are a dead giveaway that you're a King," I responded to Kendria. A couple moments went by before anyone spoke. "I'm gon' wait on it," I sighed and cranked the car back up. I felt bad for believing the worst in Kenzie, but I just couldn't get that tattoo.

"And if he wonders who told you, you can tell him it was me. He ain't gon' do shit," Kendria commented and we all started laughing.

I dropped the two of them off at KJ's parents' house, and then went home so I could get ready to go to Kenzie's parents' home for dinner. During my shower, and whole get ready process, I couldn't stop thinking about what Kendria told me. I prayed like hell that the girl at the kickback was just blowing smoke.

I decided on a yellow dress with beige sandals. I put on my gold jewelry, my cappuccino lipstick, and then brushed my hair back into a ponytail. "Relax Shannon, you have no proof yet," I told myself as I looked into my mirror.

I got to Kenzie's parents' home, and texted him so that he could buzz me in. "Hey cutie," his mother Jessica answered the door. "I see you took the occasion seriously," she chuckled. She was wearing skinny jeans and a cute layered top.

"Yeah, I guess I'm overdressed," I replied as I walked in.

"It's cool, mami," she said and closed the door behind me before giving me a hug. Her long brown hair was in a bun on her head, and fuzzy slippers were on her feet. His mom seemed like she was wild back in the day, and I really liked her. I followed her to the kitchen, and then sat at the island.

"Actually, if you wanna help you can take these plates. I don't know where my daughters are who agreed to help me earlier," she shook her head with a smile.

"Sure Mrs. King," I nodded and hopped up to collect the plates she'd set out on the counter.

After setting the table, Kenzie's sisters Kennedy and Kendlie started bringing the food dishes into the dining room. I hugged them both, and we sat at the table having girl talk until Kenzie, and Mr. and Mrs. King entered the room.

"Shannon, hi beautiful," Mr. King greeted me and we hugged. Kenzie and I made eye contact, and then he slowly slid his arms around my waist and pecked me lightly.

"You smell good," I commented and then stared up into his green eyes.

His dark toffee skin was so beautiful, accompanied by his short curly fro. He looked just like his father, only lighter, so his features were perfectly chiseled into his face. I kissed him again and then we sat down at the table.

The dinner was nice, and funny enough, it helped me to temporarily forget about the whole other girlfriend situation. I loved his family, because it was always jokes and shit flying around.

After helping Mrs. King clean the dishes, I went into the den where Kenzie and Mr. King were.

"I'm gonna go chill with your mama," his father smirked and got up. I plopped down next to Kenzie, and he looked at me with a closed mouth smile.

"What are you thinking about?" he asked.

"If I ask you something, can you promise to be honest with me, no matter how bad the truth is?" I prepped him.

"Umm, yeah, I'm always honest with you," he tittered.

"Someone overheard a girl named Brooke saying you were her sister's boyfriend, what's up with that?" I raised a brow.

"Wait, whoa, this Brooke girl said *my sister's boyfriend is Kenzie King*?" he quizzed to clarify, and I nodded even though that wasn't true. Kendria specifically said the girl didn't say his last name.

"And why didn't you correct her ass?" he inquired and squinted his eyes.

"I wasn't there, Kenzie," I sighed because I wanted him to think that I in fact was there.

"So this is some hear-say shit?" He grinned looking so sexy. I stared at him because I felt dumb. "Baby for one, ain't no telling what was really said, and secondly that's where we at now? We going off of hear-say?" He frowned.

"Kendria heard it Kenzie, your little cousin," I told him.

"Her fifteen going on thirty, ass? People know that's my cousin, Shan, they could've just been saying it just because she was around," he shrugged and then rubbed my back.

I felt stupid as fuck. Kenzie was famous around Baltimore because he was a phenomenal basketball player, destined to make it to the NBA, and because he was the son of one of the King brothers. Everybody knew everyone in the King family, and anyone associated with them. Girls dreamed of becoming a wife or girlfriend to one of them. Shit, even a one-night stand with a King brother would do, and that was regardless of the generation, so I don't know why I let that shit get to me.

"I'm sorry, baby," I scooted closer to him, and then draped my arms over his shoulders.

"I need a better apology than that, shorty," he bit his lip.

"How about this," I crushed my lips against his, and then slid my tongue into his mouth. Brooke and her sister could suck a fat one.

My DAD OWNED a strip club named King Brothers, and it was only right that I opened my own establishment of course. That's what I loved about my father. Regardless of us growing up rich as fuck, he still wanted us to work. He could've easily passed down KB's, but he didn't; he made me get my own shit.

Kendrin, Kaleeini, and I owned a triple level club named Kingin'. The bottom floor was a strip club, and the middle floor was reserved for private dances. The top floor was the club area, because it was the closest to the rooftop where we held events and shit sometimes. I thought of opening another business, just as an extra cover up for my drug money, but with my club alone I was bringing in a nice amount of money. It was way more than I thought, so I was able to put off opening a secondary business for now.

I used to love owning a strip club, because I could have a different bitch every night. Sometimes it was a stripper, a waitress, or sometimes it was the girls who just came to watch. But now that I had Gianna, I couldn't really dabble like I used to. Ha.

I walked through the back area of my club so that I could ride the elevator up to my office. Gianna, Aysia, and Kaleeini were coming through to the strip club part so we could all chill on some double date shit I guess. I walked into my office and powered on my computer. After working for about an hour, I heard a knock on my office door.

"Come in," I called out.

The supervisor on duty, Diana, walked into my office. If you're wondering, yes I definitely smashed because she was sexy as fuck, but she knew it was nothing more, so she was still cool.

"Someone is asking to speak with you," she said and then smiled.

"Did they give you a name?" I quizzed.

"He just said TJ," she shrugged.

"Tell them I will be down in a couple minutes," I told her and she nodded.

"You want me to bring you up a drink?" she offered.

"Nah, I'm good shorty, but thank you," I cheesed and she blushed.

Once she left, I finished up what I was doing and then locked everything up. I went down and found Diana, and then she pointed me in the direction of the guy.

"You've been looking for me?" I questioned and raised a brow.

"Yeah, Kendrick, right?" he asked to be sure.

"Junior, yeah, what's up?" I inquired. He needed to hurry the fuck up, because my girl and peoples would be here soon. And after a hard ass workweek, I was looking to chill.

"I wanted to speak with you about some work," he smirked.

"Some work? What kind of work?" I inquired.

"I know who you are Kendrick, and I'm tryna be down. I've just moved here from Florida, and I'm trying to get my bread up. I heard you the man out here," he replied.

"I see. Well, I don't speak about work in times and places like these. Leave your information with the young lady you spoke to earlier and I will holla at you," I said and started to turn around.

"See man, I'm needing to get shit started ASAP. I know how you niggas in high places work. You ain't gon' call me for months, if you even call at all," he scoffed.

"TJ, right?" I frowned and he nodded. "You not starting off on the right foot with me, which may not be the best thing to do. Give your info to the young lady, and like I said, I may call you," I fake smiled and then walked away. You see that shit went from 'I *will* call' to 'I *may* call' quickly.

I went to the section that was roped off for my family and I whenever we came, and waited for Gianna, Aysia, and Kaleeini to arrive.

"Drink for you boss," Diana smiled and set down a napkin and then my drink on top of it.

"Thank you," I replied and she switched out of the booth.

As I was texting on my phone, I felt someone come stand at the rope. I looked up to see Zaria. She had an obvious attitude, and her arms were folded across her D cups.

"What's up shorty?" I chuckled and sipped my drink. These bitches really be having attitudes for no fucking reason.

"Can you tell him to let me by?" she raised a brow and pointed to Bolo.

"Nah shorty, I'll get at you later," I shook my head. She nodded slowly, paused, and then walked away through the crowd of people.

I stretched my neck to look for my baby girl, because the strip club was starting to get packed. I didn't want her trying to get through the rowdy crowd while carrying my baby. A few moments later, I saw my shorty emerge, followed by Aysia and Kaleeini. Gianna was wearing a tight ass red dress, with a diamond cut out in the middle. I could see her little two-pack she kept. Her brownish red hair was down, and had a part on the side like Aaliyah. Bolo moved the rope, and the three of them walked in.

"Shouldn't you take that out?" I asked referring to her belly button piercing.

"No, I'm not even showing, KJ," Gianna grinned and then poked her lips out to kiss me. Her dress' neckline was slightly plunging, and her breasts caught my eye.

"I see these are starting to show," I licked my lips and squeezed one.

"Stop KJ, they're sore," she whined and slapped my hand before sitting down on the velvet couch.

"Sup man," Kaleeini slapped my hand and then I hugged Aysia, who appeared to be somber as fuck. She sat down in Kaleeini's lap, and he kissed her lips.

I turned my attention back to Gianna, and then cornered her in the seat booth. She smiled and then started to suck my lips. While we were kissing, I ran my hand up her dress, and pushed her legs apart a little.

"KJ, not here," she whispered in between kisses, as one of the strippers danced to "Antidote" by Travis Scott.

I ignored her and pulled her panties to the side. I slipped one finger into her and started plunging in and out. I then added one more finger, and her pussy was gripping them tough.

"Aaahh," she moaned softly under the loud music, and it sounded so good.

I pulled on her bottom lip with my mouth, and continued finger fucking her until I felt her juices spill and her leg tremble a bit. I slid my fingers out, and then fixed her underwear back.

"I'm glad I didn't start fucking you when I met you, because I wouldn't have gotten any work done," I joked and she chuckled. I licked her juices off of my fingers, and then went to look down her dress.

"Stop boy!" she laughed and pushed my hand.

"Just let me see one," I smiled referring to her titties. They had been plumping up recently, making me become an even bigger horn dog.

"You saw them both this morning, and you can see later tonight," she bucked her eyes and then pecked me.

We then rushed off through the crowd so we could pee and wash our hands. Soon after we returned, a waiter came in and brought bottles with a bucket of ice and juices, along with some fries and wings. We made ourselves a drink, and I poured Gianna some juice while she and Aysia stuffed their faces.

"Focused On You" by Eric Bellinger came on, as this one stripper named Candy came on to dance. Gianna got into my lap, and then started giving me a lap dance. I let my hands rub all on her ass and body as I enjoyed the view. Some days I thought the only woman I would ever love would be my mama, but Gianna had changed all that.

"So this is what you been up to!" I heard Zaria scream even though the music was loud as fuck. Gianna stopped moving and stared at her. "This the little bitch you been posting all on the gram?" she laughed and tried to get past Bolo but he stopped her.

"Watch who you calling a bitch," Gianna stood up.

"Sit down, you're pregnant," I told her and sat her feisty ass down. "Don't think you about to pull her to the side for a talk like that last bitch, Kendrick!" Gianna yelled and frowned at me.

"KJ, bring yo ass out here and talk to me!" Zaria screamed.

"You getting real disrespectful hoe," Aysia got off of Kaleeini's lap.

"And who the fuck are you?" Zaria frowned at Aysia.

"I'm about to be your worst fucking nightmare if you don't get your thirsty ass from over here." Aysia folded her arms and poked her hip out. Kaleeini grabbed her and locked her in his lap.

Just as I stood up, so did Gianna. "Get her ass away from here, KJ," she pointed and then tossed her long hair behind her shoulder. She looked so sexy when she was mad. I nodded my head to my boy Reaper who was off to the side, and he snatched Zaria up to put her ass out. She was screaming and shit but the music was loud enough to mask it.

"You better had cut all these bitches. They better be mad because you're *not* fucking with them no more, and not because you *are!*" Gianna pointed up in my face with her fresh nail.

"Or what? Fuck you gon' do?" I smirked and got in her face.

"I'm gon' leave your stupid ass," she chuckled because I had started kissing on her neck.

"You gon' leave your baby daddy?" I grinned and squeezed her ass.

"Yep nigga, you better be careful," she raised a brow.

"You ain't going nowhere, because you know I'm being a good boy," I laughed and she smiled. She cupped my face, and planted a kiss on me.

"I love you, stupid," she played with my chin hairs.

"I love you, crazy," I replied.

ONE HOUR LATER...

"You good?" I asked Aysia as I kissed down the side of her face. For the past couple of weeks, she'd been acting all weird and shit.

"Yeah, I'm okay," she replied in a low tone.

"Come on, let's go," I said and tapped her so that she would get up from my lap.

"What, why?" she questioned.

"Because we about to go to my crib and talk," I answered and moved her. We'd been there for two hours now and she hadn't changed her mood, so I was ready for some answers.

"We're gonna go," KJ stood up. Gianna was behind him and they were holding hands.

"Same," I replied.

The four of us made our way to the back of the club to exit, and I opened my passenger door so that Aysia could get inside.

"Talk to me," I said once we got on the road. I reached for the air conditioning knob so that I could crank up the heat.

"Nothing is wrong, Kaleeini," she chuckled and then pulled the visor mirror down. She checked herself out, and then reached into her purse to pull out some makeup.

"And what's up with you wearing that shit all the fucking time now?" I frowned. Aysia only wore make up when we went out, but nowadays she was rocking it even when we were just chilling at the crib.

"If you have so many problems with what I do, maybe you shouldn't be with me," she replied dryly and then put the visor up.

"Oh word? That's how you feel?" I chuckled as I pulled into my parking spot at my condo.

"The question is that how you feel? You're the one complaining about my behavior and the way I look!" She screamed so loud I thought my windows would break.

"Aysia, what the fuck, shorty? Calm down," I said and reached to touch her.

"Don't tell me to calm down," she spat. "Take me home please," she added and sniffled.

"I ain't taking you no fucking where," I scoffed and threw my hood over my dreads.

"Fine then," she grabbed her purse and then exited the car. I hopped out after her, and hit the alarm to lock my car. She was wearing a tight ass dress with really high heels, and switching her little ass off.

"Get your crazy ass back over here before you get arrested for prostitution," I yanked her arm back towards me.

"Move Kaleeini, leave me alone," she started to cry. I grabbed her hand and then led her inside my place.

"Aysia, what's up?" I folded my arms once we got inside my crib. I didn't bother to turn the lights on, so it was still dim.

"Kaleeini, maybe we..." she paused.

"Maybe we what?" I quizzed and hung my keys on the wall.

"Maybe we should take a break for a little while," she sniffled.

"That's what you want?" I raised a brow.

"Yeah," she whispered.

"Cool," I nodded and then went to my kitchen to get some water. When I came back, she was still on my couch. "Ain't you gon' leave?" I questioned.

"You want me to go?" she sniffled as tears ran down her caramel cheeks. I didn't know what the fuck was wrong with her, but I wasn't gone keep asking. She clearly didn't want to talk, or for me to make her feel better.

"We're broken up, right? I mean I guess you can stay the night but I didn't think you would want to," I shrugged and sipped my water.

She dabbed the tears on her face and then looked around for a little bit. "Can I sleep on your couch? It's too cold to walk home, and my mama is sleep," she looked up at me.

"Covers and pillows are in the linen closet," I responded and went to my room after cutting on the heater.

I was angry and irritated but I wasn't gon' show that shit. I wasn't the type to wild out unless needed, and it clearly wasn't needed here. Aysia was on some bullshit, and until she could trust me as her man, she was gon' be on that bullshit forever.

I polished off my water, and then went to take a hot shower to calm my nerves. When I got out, I saw she was on the couch, fully clothed and knocked out. I shook my head and went to my room to lie down. KJ and I had an early money count in the morning, and I needed to be alert for that shit.

In the middle of the night, I felt my bed moving as if someone was getting in it. I looked to my right to see Aysia getting in, wearing one of my shirts. Her face was stained with makeup, and I saw a small bruise under her eye. As soon as she got near me, I pulled her into my arms and kissed her soft lips. I couldn't be mad anymore seeing her like this. I loved her and I wanted her to understand that.

"I'm sorry, Kaleeini," she sobbed.

"Baby, what's wrong with you?" I questioned and caressed her soft face.

"Nothing," she half smiled and then pulled the shirt over her head to expose her naked body.

"What happened to your eye?" I quizzed.

"I was reaching up into my closet and my hair straightener hit me," she chuckled lightly. She then climbed on top of me, resting her pussy on my dick. She started to kiss my lips gently, making my dick brick up. I reached down to position it at her opening, and she lifted upward a little, before sliding down on it.

"Aaah, uuh," she whimpered as she adjusted to my size.

She leaned down, pressing her body against mine, and we began to make love with our mouths too. After a couple moments, I flipped her onto her back so that I could be in control.

I didn't know what the fuck was going on with her, but I was gonna find out and end it before it got worse. As her man, it was my responsibility to make sure she was good at all times.

I'D GOTTEN a styling job for the photo shoot of this new boutique, and I was so excited. The pay wasn't too much, but I just wanted to build my resume more. I wasn't feeling too hot today because I'd been throwing up since 5am, but I still needed to get the job done.

I put on some thick black tights, a loose fitting gray crop top, and some all black Nike Huaraches KJ gifted to me. I slicked my long hair into a ponytail with a deep side part, and slicked my edges down. I was really getting annoyed by my hair because it was way too long, and my arms were starting to hurt whenever I had to do it.

I walked out of my vanity room, and grabbed my duffle bag to leave. Yes, I had a vanity room now that I had moved in with KJ. Living with him was like a fucking dream come true. When he wasn't out working, we would stay up all night talking, watching movies, eating, and fucking all over the house. Every time I thought I couldn't be more in love with him, I proved myself wrong. It was like living with my fine ass best friend.

I took my phone off of the charger and left out to my job. When I got to the set, there were about seven girls there getting their makeup done.

"Hi Gianna, the clothes are over there. There are plenty of pieces and accessories for you to piece together. There are size cards with each model's name on it also. We need three outfits for each," the creator Cynthia smiled at me and led me to my area.

"Alright, sounds good," I nodded. I was excited because I loved styling, and this would be fun. I drank a couple sips of my club soda to calm my stomach, and then I got to work.

After setting out three outfits for the models, with the right sizes and accessories, I had Cynthia come take a look for approval.

"Oh my gosh Gianna, this looks dope. And I know if it looks this good on the table, it will look even better on," she nodded and hugged me tightly. I almost threw up on her because she was squeezing me.

"So whenever a model is ready, you can send them over for me to start dressing," I said and took another sip of my club soda once she let me go.

"Great, because Wendy is ready," she smiled.

Wendy was really nice and super easy to work with. I dressed her in her three outfits, and took pictures for my portfolio before sending her off to do her photo shoot. I did the same with the next girl named Fantasia, and then it was time for the third, Zaria. I ate a couple Fig Newtons because I was hungry, and one almost got caught in my throat when I saw Zaria's face. She was the girl acting a fool at Kingin' that night. I washed the Fig Newton down with my club soda, and then put on some hand sanitizer so that I could dress her.

"Okay, so these jean shorts, this top, and then the belly chain and wedges," I set it up for her to go put on behind the divider. She smacked her lips at me and snatched up the outfit.

I waited patiently as she tried on the clothes and then finally she peeked out and said, "Excuse me."

I looked over in her direction and she waved me over. "What size are these shorts?" she pointed down to them. They were barely around her hips, and clearly weren't gonna be able to close. "They're a size one. That's the size you had on your card for jeans," I replied.

"Well then get me a size one because these don't fit," she spat.

"Zaria, that is a size one, let me get the three for you," I said and started to turn.

"I don't wear a fucking three, I wear a one! This must be a zero!" she yelled loudly.

"Is everything okay?" Cynthia rushed over.

"Your stylist here gave me the wrong size pants!" Zaria spat.

"Okay, so let's get the right size then," Cynthia looked to me.

"Her size card says a one, which is what I gave her. I offered to get a size three but she doesn't want that," I explained to Cynthia.

"This ain't no damn one," Zaria chimed in. Cynthia walked around the back of Zaria, and tugged on the waistline to check the size.

"This is a one, hmm—"

"Well your shit must run small!" Zaria rolled her eyes. She was so unprofessional. I couldn't believe KJ stuck his dick in this hoe.

"Maybe, let me see. Are any of the other models a one?" Cynthia asked me.

"No, they're only double zeros, fives, and threes," I replied and shifted my weight to my other hip. Cynthia sighed and then looked me up and down.

"What size do you wear?" she questioned.

"I'm usually a one, but I'm pregnant so no telling," I chuckled and stared into Zaria's eyes. She was dumbfounded at the fact that I was pregnant by KJ.

"Try on these shorts for me so I can see if my stuff runs small. You don't look pregnant," she smiled.

I walked away to grab the sizes, and then went to try it on. The size one fit me perfectly, and I walked out to show it to Cynthia.

"Your clothes don't run small Cyn, she wears a three," I said and twirled around in the shorts to model them fully.

I didn't know why Zaria was tripping, it's not like the size three was huge, because it wasn't. Zaria growled loudly as I went back into the bathroom and put my tights back on. I came back out and brought her pants sizes in three and she didn't fit those either. I brought her a size five, which fit great, and she was furious. She wasn't even modeling right because she was so angry. The photographer had to keep guiding her, and she took way longer than the other girls.

I was unbothered as I munched on my Fig Newtons, and then proceeded to style the other chicks before collecting my coins. As I was walking to my car, I heard some heels clicking behind me. I looked over my shoulder and she was following me.

"What!" I shouted. I was sick, hungry, and I wanted some dick. I didn't have time to be fussing with some thirsty bitch who wanted more than a wet pussy from my nigga.

"I hope you don't think just because you trapped him with a baby that you gon' have him," she smirked and folded her arms.

"Girl bye!" I threw my hand in her face and then hit my alarm to open my trunk. "You know as well as I do that Kendrick is *my* nigga. We're gonna be a family soon," I winked at her and then turned to my car.

"Bitch!" she screamed and charged me. I turned around and kicked her ass in the stomach before she could touch me, and she flew back onto the ground after almost breaking her ankle in the heels she had on.

"Stupid bitch! And move from behind my car before I run your ass over!" I hollered as I got into my whip.

She thought I was kidding until I started reversing like her ass wasn't there. She scrambled to get out of the way, and then banged on my hood as I passed her. I slammed on my brakes and threw the cup of passion tea latte I'd had this morning at her. It hit her in her large breasts, and then splashed all over her white halter-top. She screamed at the top of her lungs as I sped out of the parking lot. Dumb ass bitch.

Kaleeini and I had been doing pretty great since that little stint after the club that night. I'd been worried sick prior to that, thinking that Brice was about to kill him or me. I knew I should've told him, so that's why I was finally going to tonight. I wanted him to be in a good mood so that he wouldn't react badly, which is why I chose a night that we went out on a date.

"I'm stuffed baby," I clutched onto Kaleeini's arm as we walked down the sidewalk coming from Pazo.

"Me too, that shit was bomb," he chuckled.

My teeth chattered slightly because it was so damn cold outside. December was slowly approaching and I knew it was only gonna get colder. At least I had Kaleeini to keep me warm this winter though. Brice was cold ass ice from the inside out, so it felt great being in an actual healthy relationship again. Kaleeini was everything.

We finally made it to the car, and before Kaleeini got in and cranked up, I twisted the heater knob on. As soon as he turned the car on, I wanted that hot ass air to blow through on me.

"I told your ass not to wear a fucking dress," Kaleeini smacked his lips. He tightened his hood around his dreads, and then reached for his seatbelt.

"Pain is beauty," I smirked and then leaned over to kiss his cold full lips.

"Mmmm, do that again," he nibbled on his lip while his green eyes glistened. I pressed my lips against his, and held it there for a couple seconds. "Let's hurry up and get home," he grinned and finished fastening his seatbelt. I did the same, and then we pulled off.

We drove a couple blocks, and the streets were pretty empty along the way.

POP!

POP!

POP!

"Aahhhh!" I screamed as three gunshots were fired at us. Strangely, I saw no holes in the windows or car. I kept looking around frantically as Kaleeini sped off taking back streets.

"What the fuck!" he yelled as he drove. He was going one hundred miles per hour it seemed, and I was scared as fuck. So many thoughts were jumping around in my head, and I was hoping this was a dream.

"What just happened?" I screamed.

"Somebody fucking shot at us and drove off," he shook his head and exhaled. He didn't seem to be half as scared as I was though. "I got their fucking plate number though, dummies." He shook his head angrily as he continued to drive as if we were on a wild speed chase.

"Are these bullet proof windows and doors or something?" I frowned in confusion while panting still.

"Hell yeah, a nigga like me can't drive in anything else. I'm getting you a new car that's bulletproof too tomorrow," he said. I didn't respond and just prayed that we made it to his home before we got shot at again. There was no way I could go to my own home; I needed to have him with me.

Ten minutes later, we were pulling into the driveway of his new house. He'd finally moved from his condo, and his new shit was decked the fuck out. He said his condo location was too well known, and it was only temporary until his real estate agent found a house in the area he preferred. I liked it because it was big as fuck, and because he was near KJ and Gianna. I hoped he asked me to move in one day, especially because I spent most of my days here with him anyway.

He pulled into his huge garage, and shut off the engine. He took a couple deep breaths and then pulled out his iPhone.

"What are you doing?" I asked.

"Putting that license number in my notes before I forget," he replied while typing.

"How do you even remember?" I wondered.

"Photographic memory, shorty," he said and then climbed out of the car. He came around to let me out, and then gently crushed his lips against mine, which calmed me.

As we entered the house through his garage, I came to the decision to tell him about Brice's threats. I'm pretty sure that it was Brice who either set this up or did it, and even if it wasn't, Kaleeini and his cousins needed to know. If Brice didn't strike tonight, he may do it soon. I would feel like shit if he were able to touch Kaleeini, all because I didn't speak up.

We walked through the foyer and up the stairs to his bedroom. As he undressed down to nothing for a shower, I watched him while staying fully clothed.

"Babe, I have to tell you something," I sighed.

"What's up?" He leaned against the dresser and folded his arms. He was butt naked with his dick swinging. His sexy light complexion seemed to be glistening under the dim light.

"Can you cover up, you're distracting me!" I chuckled as I looked at his eight pack and pecks.

I saw Morgan tatted on his arm, and smiled at the thought of the love he had for his mother. As my mom always said, a man who hates his mother is no good. I think he and KJ got them at the same time because he had Nic on his arm in the same place. I remember Gianna and I thought it was a guy's name, and KJ damn near cursed us out about his mama.

"Aight, go," he said after wrapping a towel around his waist, and tying up his dreads.

"About a month ago, Brice threatened me. He actually threatened me *and* you. He said he would kill us both if I didn't come back to him. I think he was behind what happened tonight," I finished and stared up at him from across the room.

"And what possessed you to keep that from me?" He squinted his eyes and adjusted his folded arms.

"I-I-" I just shrugged and stuttered. He shook his head, and then walked over to me. He kneeled down in front of me because I was sitting on the loveseat in his room.

"Aysia, do you know who I am?" he questioned.

"Kaleeini Drake King?" I chuckled nervously because I had no idea where this was going.

"Yes, but I'm a part of a humongous crime family. If someone threatens me, or you, you need to tell me shorty. Being me, and being with me is dangerous, and when shit like that happens I need to be the first person you tell, even if you have to borrow someone's phone. If I had been in some non bulletproof car we would've been dead, you get that right?" He furrowed his brows and I nodded. "We a team right?" he quizzed.

"Of course we are," I responded with a half smile.

"Then act like it. You have to have my back if you gon' be my girl. Keeping secrets from me ain't cool, especially if someone is threatening me, or you especially. What you thought, I couldn't defend myself?" He laughed at the thought.

"Of course, I know you can. I just didn't want you fighting for me, and have your people thinking I'm some troublemaker," I said.

"You're my woman, and a part of showing my love for you is fighting for you. If I didn't fight for you, or if I wasn't willing to, then you should be worried. And plus, my family knows that you're not a troublemaker, shorty," he rubbed my shoulders. "My mama is a good judge of character, and she had nothing but good things to say," he grinned.

"I know, I'm sorry, Kaleeini. I guess I was just paranoid," I played with one of his dreads.

"You good... this time. Promise me that you're gonna always be honest with me, especially when it's some dangerous shit?" he said.

"I promise, I love you," I said and then bucked my eyes because I didn't mean for that to come out.

"I love you too, shorty. Now let's go take a hot ass shower, I'm still cold as fuck." He helped me up and then unzipped my dress. I was happy that he responded the way he did. He didn't even seem to notice. "Only thing my mom did say is that you wear too many short dresses," he laughed and I turned to look at him with my jaw on the floor. "Aye, but your man likes them and that's all that matters," he smiled down at me, before pecking me.

I knew shit was about to get crazy, and I just prayed that we made it out alive and together.

As SUSPECTED, fucking that Rosalind bitch was a huge ass mistake. She stayed texting and calling my fucking phone, and didn't care that I never responded. She was liking every picture that I posted of Willow, or of me and Willow, and was just being petty and jealous. I only fucked once! She couldn't possibly be this attached to a nigga. But I knew when I looked into her eyes that she was gonna be trouble. The scariest part of this all was that she somehow found out my name was not David.

I was on edge every day thinking that she was gonna show up or pop up somewhere and tell Willow I fucked her. Yeah, Willow and I were broken up, but let's be honest; Willow and I were never really broken up. We may say we're not together, but we never really mean the shit. There was no way either of us would move on and be with other people. That girl was gonna be my wife, and there was no way some random one-night stand was gonna get in the way of that.

Willow always worried that I would cheat on her or some shit, ever since I did that one fucking time in the beginning of our relationship. I knew if she found this out, her paranoia would elevate. It would take me one hundred steps back, and I had only moved about three steps forward. This whole time I'd been trying to prove to her that I was all about her, and shit I am, but Rosalind was trying to destroy all the shit I had instilled in my shorty.

I was leaving the movies with Willow, and I felt my phone going crazy in my pocket.

"Who the fuck is that Ken? They were calling you during the whole movie?" Willow pouted as we got into the car.

"Wrong number," I lied badly.

"It better be," she retorted.

"What the fuck is that supposed to mean?" I asked. See, she was already starting to accuse me of shit again.

"It means it better not be no bitch blowing you up like you her nigga! Only girl that should be blowing you up is me, Kendria, or your mama!" Willow hollered.

"Here we go," I huffed.

"Yeah, we gon' be going somewhere alright! One of us is going to heaven and the other a jail cell if I find out some bitch thinks she needs to call you that much." She shook her head with her full lips twisted up. "And let me give you a hint, I won't be the one going to the hospital! That hoe will!" She pushed one of her French braids behind her back and then pulled her phone out.

"Calm your ass down, didn't we just have a talk about this?" I frowned. I felt like Willow's ass would never learn or grow the fuck up.

"Yes, I'm sorry," she replied but it didn't sound sincere, of course.

"You will never learn, Lo," I shook my head and pulled into the parking lot of the restaurant.

"Let me see who's calling you, Kendrin. If I'm wrong, I will apologize and from this night forward I will have my act together," she put her hand out. Her long nails were damn near about to stab my shoulder.

"What? No, you should already have your act together like we discussed. That's the only reason that we even got back together, Willow," I turned my lip up. She had the game fucked up tryna do deals and shit.

"I know daddy, but just prove me wrong," she smirked with her pretty ass. I knew what she was trying to do.

"Daddy ain't doing shit," I chuckled and so did she.

She ran her hand across my lap, and then unbuckled my jeans. She pulled my monster out, and then started to lubricate the tip.

"Shit," I mumbled as she worked the rest of my dick into her mouth. I looked down at her head bouncing up and down in my lap, and clenched my teeth at the feeling. "I'm about to bust babe," I panted and rubbed her smooth, cinnamon colored back.

I put my hand up her dress, squeezed her ass, and then pushed her thong to the side. She continued to go ham on my dick, and I slipped two fingers into her from behind.

"Aahh, aaah," she moaned, letting my dick fall out.

"Put that shit back in your mouth," I told her.

She took my dick back into her mouth, and started sucking the life out of me. The harder I fingered her, the harder she went at sucking my dick. "Aaah, aaah, uuuuh," we both called out as we enjoyed one another's work. We both exploded, and I slowly slid my fingers out of her. I licked her juices off, and then she plunged her tongue into my mouth.

"I'm gon' take you home, I wanna eat some pussy," I bit my lip and yanked her into my lap. She tasted so good. I caressed her ass cheeks under her dress, and kissed all over her neck.

"What about food though, Kendrin?" she whined as I groped her.

"We'll get something from the drive thru," I replied.

"Okay," she smacked her lips and then climbed back over into the passenger seat.

"You better do that shit good since I can't have a nice sit down dinner," she bantered and smiled as I fixed my pants.

"Shorty, shut your mouth. Every time I eat that pussy you be climbing up the walls and begging me to stop. You couldn't even get on top last night because your legs were too weak," I shut her ass down.

"Shut up, nigga," she laughed.

"Oh, oh, Kendrin I can't do iiiittt, my legs feel like jelly," I mocked her and she lightly punched my arm as I backed the car out.

We stopped at Burger King, and then went home so I could fuck her into a coma. After we finished eating, Willow went to run us a bath.

BZZZ

+1 (410) 555-3611: *Hello? I miss you.* I shook my head at the text from Rosalind.

I went to her number, and then quickly added it to the block list. I didn't wanna have to kill her ass, but maybe it was the only way.

"Bath time, daddy," Willow appeared naked.

I scanned her from head to toe and just admired what was mine. She had a slim-thick frame, perfect C cups, and my name on her hip. She had her two French braids taken down, so her hair was hanging loosely to the middle of her back.

I got up and walked over to her, then stared down into her eyes. "You know you gon' always be my shorty, right?" I raised a brow.

"No, do you know you gon' always be my nigga?" she cocked her head. "You already know I'm yours forever," she added.

"Yeah, I know, crazy," I cupped her face and pressed my lips against hers.

For now, I was gonna continue my life like nothing happened. Shit, what all could Rosalind do? Nothing but get a hollow tip to the dome if she kept playing around.

I'D BEEN BACK for over a month now, and unfortunately, I hadn't done what I promised I would do. I was still stringing Rosalind along, because I felt bad as hell. She was my girl, and I went out and fell in love with someone else. It was fucked up but there was nothing I could do.

However, today, I'd finally gotten the courage to go and talk to her about our relationship. I hadn't decided if I was gonna tell her about Shannon or not, so I would think about it on the way there. I kind of wanted to break up with her and say I wanted to focus on school, but then again that wasn't fair to Shannon. I didn't see how niggas did it, because having two girlfriends was stressful as fuck.

I pulled up to her house, and waited for a couple moments to make sure this was what I wanted to do. Did I really wanna give Rosalind up now? Yes, I had to. I loved Shannon and I couldn't do this shit to her anymore.

I climbed out of the car, and walked up to Rosalind's door, as slow as I could. Before I could even knock, the door flew open.

"Baby!" she squealed and draped her arms around my neck. How could I break such bad news to a person who was this happy to see me?

"Sup shorty, you look good," I commented. She had on a little ass dress like always, despite it being freezing outside, and for some reason she looked especially good.

"Thank you. I'm hungry let's go eat," she smiled.

Why did my intentions always change when I got in her presence? I was so sure of what I was gonna do, but now that she was here in the flesh, I was slightly conflicted. *Do the right thing, Kenzie*, I told myself so that I wouldn't backpedal.

"Ros, sit down shorty and let me talk to you," I sighed and walked around her. We made it to the couch at the same time and sat down.

"I'm listening, what's on my man's mind?" she cheesed. Damn she was beautiful. *Don't get caught up in that Kenzie*, I told myself.

"Look baby, you know I got love for you right?" I started.

"Love *for* me? I thought you were in love with me," she raised a brow.

"Regardless, you know I care, right?" I reiterated and she nodded slowly like she was suspicious. "Well, I-I need some time apart from you—"

"Why?" she hollered.

"I need to focus on school and basketball right now. It's kind of hard juggling both, and I hate having to neglect you. I think we should take a break, and you know if we find our way back to each other then great," I smiled. I just couldn't tell her about Shannon yet. She stared at me with a blank expression, so I didn't know how to read her.

"So you don't wanna be with me anymore," she nodded. "Is there someone else?" she questioned and folded her arms.

"Nah, I told you I need to focus on school and basketball, shorty. Ain't nobody else," I half lied.

Shit it *was* hard juggling basketball, school, and two fucking girlfriends. Cutting Rosalind would be one hell of a fucking load off.

"Well, I have something to tell you, too," she twisted her mouth up.

"What's up?" I frowned. I wasn't expecting for her to have a secret, and I was hoping it didn't piss me off.

"I'm pregnant, Kenzie," she blurted and my stomach started churning like butter.

"Pregnant? How?" I frowned.

"How? Because you've been fucking me!" she yelled.

"No, I know how. But we're always safe, Ros, I'm confused," I shook my head. My mama was gon' murder my ass.

"I don't know Kenzie, maybe the condom broke and we didn't know. All I know is that I'm having your baby," she replied.

"Fuck, so how are you feeling? You gon' keep it?" I quizzed hoping she said no.

I made sure to be extra careful with Rosalind, so I didn't know how I still slipped up. This baby would definitely throw a wrench in my relationship with Shannon. Fuck!

"Yeah I'm gonna keep it. You know my family doesn't believe in abortions, it's part of my religion as well," she said calmly.

"A baby, hunh," I covered my face with my hands.

Not only did I have to worry about Shannon going crazy, but my fucking mom was gonna have a heart attack. She was forever saying somebody was gon' trap me because I was going to the NBA. I didn't feel like Rosalind trapped me, but the fact that my family had no idea about her, would make them believe she did.

"Yes, a baby, Kenzie. I know you said we need a break but this isn't the right time for us to go on a break. We have a baby coming and I'm gonna need your help," she rubbed my back.

"I still think we need that break, Rosalind," I huffed. This could not be happening right now.

"Fine, we're still gonna be spending time together. And I think it's best I finally meet your mom, didn't you say she's Cuban too?" she grinned like this was a happy occasion.

"She's Afro-Cuban, yes. Look Rosalind, I need time to think so I'm gonna hit you later," I said and got up off her couch.

"Okay, I will be waiting. I love you," she called after me once I walked out the door. I didn't bother to respond or look back.

I drove straight to Kingin', because I knew my older cousins KJ and Kaleeini would be there working around this time. It was around 1pm when I walked in the back area and texted my cousin to buzz me in. I needed some advice, and right now they were the only ones I could talk to.

"What's up, player?" KJ grinned and stood up to greet me.

"A bunch of bullshit," I sighed and plopped down on the couch in his office.

"How so nigga? You got a basketball scholarship, a beautiful girl-friend, and you getting your education," he smiled.

"Where is Kaleeini?" I asked before getting ready to tell him everything.

"He's handling something for the team right now," KJ replied.

"Oh, aight. Well I'm just gon' get straight to it. I got another bitch pregnant," I said and looked into his matching green eyes.

"Nigga, what? What the fuck is wrong with you?" he squinted his eyes in confusion.

"Kendrick, man, it ain't even what you're thinking. I strapped up every single time, and the condom never broke," I explained.

"Then how the fuck is she pregnant?" he frowned in confusion.

"Shit, I don't know. Maybe some shit leaked, or fuck—I don't know!" I exclaimed.

"Did you maybe fuck raw for a couple pumps and then strap up?"

"No, I have never put my raw dick into her, not even for a second," I put my hands up in mock surrender.

"Good, I was about to go in on your ass. That probably ain't even your baby man," he shook his head.

"Yeah it is," I nodded.

"How the hell do you know? Ain't like she's your shorty," he responded.

"That's the thing... she *is* my shorty. She was before Shannon," I stared at him intently. He stared back, and then started laughing.

"Wait, so you're saying you had two girlfriends this whole time?" he questioned.

"Yeah man, I ain't even want to but it happened. I couldn't resist Shannon," I shrugged.

"I don't know who gon' kill you first, Shannon or Aunt Jessica," he cheesed because my problems were obviously amusing.

"Man, this shit ain't funny! What the fuck should I do? Should I tell Shan and my mom or just wait it out?" I asked.

"Kenzie, I know you said that was your girl but I don't think that baby is yours. If you say you always strapped up, and didn't slip up one time, how is it that she's pregnant by you? I would wait until I got a paternity test," he said.

"I don't want her running into Shannon with a big ass belly though," I frowned.

"You have two options Kenzie, lose Shannon now or lose her in nine months, it's up to you. I say tell her now and spend the rest of your days trying to get her back," he shrugged and I nodded. "It's gonna hurt her way more if she hears it from someone else."

I knew he was telling me the best thing to do, but I was gonna savor the moment with Shannon. I knew once she found out she would never look back.

"SHOULD you even be working out, Gigi?" I asked. We went to the gym every Monday and Wednesday, but now her two-pack had turned into a small bulge.

"Yes, my doctor said I could, just nothing strenuous," she chuckled.

"Girl, you're like the only pregnant bitch I know that be in the gym. I know when I get pregnant, I'm gon' be on that couch eating moon pies and cheesesteaks from Legends," I giggled and so did she.

"Ooh Legends, let's go there after this," she rubbed her semi bulging stomach. I just rolled my eyes playfully at her ass.

We both got onto the treadmills and started walking at a medium pace. After about ten minutes, I saw a girl walk onto the row in front of us. She mean mugged me, and then got onto a treadmill herself.

"She mad," I snickered.

"Clearly." Gianna shook her head and looked the girl up and down from behind.

After a good forty-five minutes, Gianna was ready to go get a burger from Legends, so we walked off to go to the locker room.

"Here," Gianna handed me a couple wipes to get the sweat off of our foreheads, and then we grabbed our big jackets to put on. It was super cold out, so we still dressed warm for the gym.

BAM!

I looked over my shoulder to see the girl from earlier, slamming her shoes onto the bench. I turned back around to face Gianna, and we just shook our heads and laughed.

"Is there something funny?" the girl called out.

"Yeah bitch, you," Gianna snapped.

"Gigi, calm down," I smiled and put my hand in front of her. Gianna rolled her eyes and sipped her water.

"Y'all don't even know me, so what the fuck is the problem?" the girl cocked her head.

"Look, ain't no problems, aight?" I rolled my eyes and turned back around. I was trying to turn over a new leaf like Kendrin had been begging me to, but damn were people making it hard for me!

The chick didn't say another word as Gianna and I gathered our things so that we could leave. We walked through the gym, and then so did the girl, but she was a little ways behind us.

"Watch this bitch," I said to Gianna as we made our way to the exit of the gym.

We braced ourselves before opening the door because it was so cold it was painful. We rushed to the car, and cut the heater on blast. As I was about to back out, I saw that stupid bitch standing behind my car. I slammed on my brakes, causing Gianna to scream, and then threw my shit into park.

"What the fuck is wrong with you?" I shouted over the parking lot after hopping out of the car.

"You tell Kendrin to return my calls so we can talk about our baby!" she screamed and rubbed her midsection.

She was wearing a big puff jacket in the color purple, but I did remember seeing a slight bulge while in the locker room of the gym. As soon as she brought up Kendrin, I recognized her from that party. She was the one he was talking to before he got into the car with us. I knew he fucked her, but I had no concrete proof. The saying igno-rance is bliss was all too true.

"Cat got your tongue?" She raised a brow and then turned on her heels to leave.

"Willow!" I heard Gianna call my name. I stood there in the ice-cold parking lot, watching this girl switch off to her car. I couldn't move. My hands were sweating despite the cold weather, and I could feel hot tears running down my cheeks. "Willow!" Gianna called me again. I slowly turned around and treaded back to the car.

"What happened?" she frowned once I closed my door.

"Nothing," I sniffled and quickly wiped my face.

"Nothing? You're crying, Lo," she replied.

"That bitch said she's having Kendrin's baby," I said and my stomach started to hurt. If she was telling the truth, there was no way I could be with Kendrin. As much as I loved him, this betrayal would be just too much to bear.

"Why are you crying already, Willow? You don't even know if it's true," she rubbed my back.

"Yeah," was all I said as I finished backing out.

We stopped at Legends to get our food, and then I drove her to KJ's home. Kendrin had recently moved to a mansion not far away, so I drove there right after. It was too cold to get out and knock or ring the doorbell, so I texted him to tell him I was here. Once I saw his sexy ass in the doorway, I got out and jogged up to him. He tried to hug me but I moved swiftly out of the way.

"Get yo' ass over here," he grabbed me back after he closed the door, and forced a kiss on my lips. "Fuck is wrong with you?" he grinned, showing his deep dimples.

"I just came to say congratulations," I sniffled and stared up at him.

"Congratulations for?" he raised a brow.

"You're gonna have a baby with that bitch from Tasha's party, nigga," I twisted my mouth up. "She told me today."

"I—"

"Don't even say you didn't fuck her because we both know that you did," I cut him off. He took a deep breath, and I turned on my heels so I could go collect the little shit I had here.

"Aye wait," he grabbed me from behind. "Yeah, I fucked her once, but we weren't together, Willow. Also, I highly doubt that's my baby. She ain't said shit to me and I strapped up." He held me tightly from behind. "I promise you it's not my kid, Lo," he kissed on my neck as tears flowed freely down my face.

"Why did you fuck her!" I sobbed loudly. I couldn't help but break down.

"It was only once, and never happened again," he said as he helped me out of my big jacket and beanie. He turned me to face him, and then pulled me close. I leaned my head back to look up into his face, and he pecked me softly. "I promise you shorty, it ain't mine," he said in a low tone.

I sat in the library at school editing my ten-page paper. I was so tired, yet so happy that this was my weekend day. After I turned this paper in, I would be free to go and chill with my friends, or watch Kenzie practice. Most likely I would do both.

As I was typing, a book slid over and bumped my arm. "Oh sorry," the girl smiled and grabbed her book.

"It's cool," I half smiled and then turned my attention back to my computer. I felt her looking at my screen, but I ignored it because it was natural for people to be nosey in here.

"I see you have English 101 with Dr. Sayers too," she cheesed.

"Oh yeah, he's an asshole sometimes but other than that, he's straight," I nodded and then went back to proofreading. I wasn't in the mood to talk; I was just trying to finish my paper.

"Tell me about it. I can't wait to finish his class," she rolled her eyes up in her head.

"I don't see you in my class," I frowned in confusion.

The class was a nice size, but it was only nine girls in there and she wasn't one of them. She did look familiar, but I just knew it wasn't from school.

"Oh, I have him on Mondays and Wednesdays," she replied.

"I didn't even know he had classes on those days," I said. I remembered looking for that schedule, but he only had Tuesdays and Thursdays available.

"Well it wasn't, but because there was such a high enrollment rate, they extended the class days," she said.

"Oh, I see. Damn, I wish I had registered late. I wanted those days," I chuckled and so did she.

"Who are you telling? I try every year not to have classes on Thursdays, but somehow it always happens. I got a history class today," she shook her head.

"This is my first year, but my older friends advised me to shoot for Mondays and Wednesdays so I did. What year are you?" I asked.

"I'm a junior, enjoy being a freshman while it lasts. Teachers are way more lenient when you're new," she sighed.

"Damn, thanks for the tip," I laughed.

"I'm Rosalind," she stuck her hand out for me to shake.

"Shannon, nice to meet you," I shook her hand and smiled. I was really trying to remember where I had seen her before but nothing was coming up.

"You know, if you ever need any tips or any help with studying, I can be a great help," she smirked.

She was a junior in a freshman level English class; I think I'll pass on her helping me with anything. How could I politely decline though?

"Oh wow, that would be great, Rosalind," I blurted. What the hell was I supposed to say? It's not like she could force her help down my throat.

"Put your number down," she slid her iPhone over to me. I contemplated putting a fake number, but what all could giving her my number do? I typed in the number, and then slid it back to her.

"Cool," she nodded and shot me a text so that I would have her number as well.

"Oh crap, I have to go, but enjoy Dr. Sayers' class," she grinned and then got up.

She didn't even log onto the computer or anything. It was almost like she strictly came here to meet me.

I finished editing my paper, and then took it to Dr. Sayers' mailbox. Gianna and Aysia were at the hair salon, and Willow was getting her nails done, so I decided to watch Kenzie practice until they were all ready to go the mall.

As I walked up to the gym, I saw that same girl outside fuming. I didn't know if I should speak or not, especially because she was obviously angry. I walked by, and we unfortunately made eye contact.

"Oh, hey Shannon," she beamed.

"Hey," I half smiled.

I wasn't trying to make conversation. I wanted to see Kenzie before the start of practice so I could get my kisses in. Thank God she grabbed her purse and rushed off somewhere.

I walked into the gym, and the guys were sitting down stretching in random areas, letting me know that practice hadn't started yet. I switched over to Kenzie, and he pulled me into his lap. He looked behind me, and then into my eyes as if he was trying to see if I was angry.

"What's wrong, Kenzie?" I questioned as I stared down into his face.

"Nothing, just making sure you're good," he chuckled nervously and then kissed my neck.

"Yeah, I'm good. I can't stay the whole time though, because me and my friends are gonna go eat and shop," I said.

"Alright, and aye, I love you Shan," he bit his lip.

"I love you too, Kenzie King," I blushed as I stared into his sparkling green eyes. I loved this nigga so much. So much so, that I'd finally gotten his name tattooed on the side of my hand.

So that stupid ass nigga Kenzie thought he was slick. And to think I actually believed him when he said that he wanted to break up because of his studies. I was more than willing to give him some space despite me being pregnant, but when I found out he was entertaining another bitch, I was pissed.

You see, it was sort of easy to get over on me because I kept to myself pretty much. I didn't watch too much TV unless it was the occasional Spanish soap operas. In addition to that, I wasn't one who got on social media either. The most I had was Facebook, but the last time I logged on was before I met Kenzie's lying ass.

This all started when I was at The Gallery mall with my little sister Brooke. We had just done a little shopping, because I needed to get my mind off of Kenzie's ass. It just so happened that I spotted my little fling "David" walking with some girl who looked no older than sixteen.

"There is the dude I told you I slept with," I pointed and tapped my sister with my elbow.

Now pause for a second. Yes, I did sleep with another man while Kenzie was away at basketball camp, but it was because I was lonely. Even when he was in Baltimore, he spent very little time with me.

David was sexy as hell, and so I decided to give him a taste. Lucky for me, the dick was phenomenal. Now back to the flashback...

"You slept with Kendrin King?" she bucked her eyes.

"What? His name is David," I frowned at her.

The first night I slept with him I'd had a bad feeling because his eyes were a very specific shade of green. It was a green that I'd only seen on Kenzie. I was still hoping my sister was mistaken.

"No, his name is Kendrin, boo, and that's his little sister Kendria. She and I have a lot of mutual friends," she chuckled like this was funny.

"Kendrin King? Who is he to Kenzie?" I questioned as we watched him interact with his sister by the food spot Krazi Kebob.

"His cousin, bitch, and that's not no second or third twice removed cousin, that's his first. Their dads are brothers," she raised a brow at me.

How did she know more about my man's family than me? That's what I get for only being worried about Kenzie and not his background and life.

"You have got to be joking right now B!" I massaged my temples because I didn't want my wrongs getting back to Kenzie.

"Girl, you need to get out more," she scoffed.

I tried to continue my day with my little sister, but the news about David, I mean Kendrin, had my mind blown. I was surprised he and Kenzie hadn't discussed me yet, but I was happy they hadn't.

I was lying in my bed, and 'Girl you need to get out more' kept circling my mind. I pulled my phone out and created an Instagram account; it was time to turn on my natural female detective skills. As soon as I finished creating my log in credentials, I clicked the search box and typed in Kendrin King. I then tried his little sister's name, but nothing came up for either.

Me: *What is Kendria's instagram? Or Kendrin's? I texted to my sister.*

Brookey: *Don't know if Kendrin has one, but Kendria's is Green-EyedMermaid... Why? She texted back.*

I ignored her question, and then pulled up Kendria's Instagram. I scrolled through her pictures, and she was a very pretty girl. I finally spotted a picture of her sitting between two guys, and one was Kendrin from what I could tell. The two men were pretty much identical, but Kendrin had less facial hair. The caption of the picture read 'Older brother's ain't nothin' but extra dad's' and she tagged them. I clicked the first username, and it was the other brother, so I backed out and went to Kendrin's. I dug deep into his and by the Grace of God, I spotted a picture of he and Kenzie. I prayed that he was tagged, and he was! I clicked Kenzie's profile, and my heart dropped to my stomach.

His profile was loaded with pictures of he and this girl. I felt my cheeks get wet, so I knew I was crying. I looked far into his profile, and she was there even forty-eight weeks in. I started sniffling because the tears were really starting to pour out. How could he do this to me? Yes, I slept around on him a few times, but he was in a serious relationship with someone else! This must've been why he didn't spend that much time with me. My heart shattered as I saw pictures of her with his family and cousins, people who I had never met myself. I was nonexistent it seemed, and that hurt.

I wiped my eyes, and then clicked this girl's profile to get a good look. Her name was Shannon and she went to Morgan State with Kenzie. I was gonna end their relationship ASAP. I followed her, and then went back so I could follow Kenzie, Kendrin, and his little ghetto girl whose name I didn't know. 'Lo Love ... Kendrin's Wifey' was the only thing in her bio. Shit, why not fuck their shit up too.

I stood up so I could go clean my face, but immediately had to throw up. Once I finished puking up all my lunch I'd eaten, I panted heavily to catch my breath. I remembered I was late a couple months back, and a smile spread across my face. I hadn't taken a pregnancy test, but I knew what was up. I was gonna knock out two niggas with one scandal.

So that's where my plan to fuck shit up began. These niggas thought they could just toss me to the wayside? No ma'am, if Rosalind was getting her heart broken then so was everyone else.

I had already planted the seed I needed into Ms. Lo Love's head when I followed her to the gym with her friend. I knew she probably wanted to kill herself thinking her man got another girl pregnant. As for Shannon and Kenzie, I had bigger plans for them, and it was gonna start with me befriending Shannon's man stealing ass. Stupid ass bitch.

"Aaah, uuuh, aaahh," Gianna cried out as I beat her shit up doggy style. I flipped her on her back, and placed her smooth legs onto my shoulders, while gripping her little waist. She put her hand up to my pelvis, but I shot her a look so she moved it. "Aauuuhh, Kendriiick," she whimpered.

I moved one of her legs off of my shoulder, and leaned down to kiss her sweaty face, while I humped her slowly in a circular motion. I pinned her wrists above her head using one of my hands, and then cupped her still small but plumper breasts in my other hand. I flicked my tongue over, and sucked her nipples hungrily as I felt my nut build up. I kissed her inner thigh, the one that was still on my shoulder, and then sat up to finish off.

"Gianna, shit," I groaned as I slammed into her sopping wet walls. She had cum about four times, and was drenching my dick. "Arrrgghh," I grunted as I shot my seeds up into her. I panted heavily as I looked down at her sexy ass. Her long ass hair was disheveled, and her light brown sugar skin was visibly damp. I slipped out of her and kissed her small bulge, before lying next to her.

"You can't be fucking me like that when I get bigger," she half smiled.

"I know, that's why I'm doing all that shit right now," I replied. We sat there in silence for a bit as we tried to catch our breath.

"KJ," she said.

"What's up, baby girl?" I answered as I checked the many messages on my phone. I hated having one hundred plus texts on my fucking phone, and every time I was close to clearing them, they piled back up.

"I ran into that girl from the club that night. She was a model for the styling job I did," she said and then looked to the side at me.

"Who?" I wondered and furrowed my brows.

"I don't know her fucking name... wait, it was Zaria," she replied and waited for my response.

"Okay, so," I shrugged. I didn't get why she was telling me she ran into her. Ain't like she followed her there; it was a job.

"She was acting all crazy and disrespectful to me. She even followed me out to the parking lot and tried to fight, knowing I was pregnant," she said. I chuckled because now I was irritated as fuck.

Zaria knew better, but for some reason she didn't like to act as if she did. She had the game twisted thinking she could approach my girl and try to fight her for no fucking reason.

"Hello!" Gianna shouted.

"Aye, lower your fucking voice shorty, I'm thinking," I frowned at her extra ass.

"I'm so tired of your hoes approaching me," she smacked her lips and folded her arms over the sheet.

"So what you gon' do about it?" I quizzed.

"What do you mean?" she raised a brow.

"You tired of them approaching you, so what you gon' do about it?" I reiterated.

"I don't know, but—"

"Exactly, you don't know. I'm gon' handle it. And quit acting like everyday you're getting approached by a different bitch because you know that ain't the fucking case, Gigi," I snapped. "You know how these hoes are, and you said you didn't care because it wouldn't bother you, so stop it," I added. I looked over at her and a tear was running down her face. I sighed because I remembered my mama telling me I had to be sensitive with her while she was pregnant. "What you crying for?" I tried to pull her close but she nudged me.

"No, move with your mean ass," she sniffled.

"I'm sorry baby, I wasn't trying to be mean to you," I said and kissed her cheek. She ignored me and stared up at the ceiling. "I love you, shorty," I pecked her lips and she continued to act like I wasn't there. "You want me to eat your pussy?" I grinned and I saw a smile tugging at the corner of her lips. "You wanna sit on my face?" I chuckled and she smirked and pushed me.

"Move stupid," she giggled while still trying to pout.

"Let's take a bath so you can cook me some food," I said. She smacked her lips, and then sat up. "Wait, I need a kiss first," I tugged on her arm. She rolled her eyes and then leaned down to give me the lightest kiss possible.

"Aahh!" she squealed when I hopped up to chase her ass. I caught her, scooped her up, and then took her into the bathroom within the room.

THE NEXT MORNING, I woke up bright and early because I had a long day ahead of me. "KJ," Gianna sat up and wiped her eyes.

"I'm gon' take you to dinner tonight," I said to her before dipping out. I knew she was gonna complain about me leaving her, and I didn't wanna give her the chance to.

It was around 5am, and I was headed straight to Zaria's crib. I sent off the texts I needed to send form my dummy phone, and then got out of the car. I went up her walkway, and beat on the door loudly and repeatedly.

"Fuck is you beating on my door like the police for!" she shouted and then flung the door open. "KJ," she gasped and then tried to close the door but I stopped her. I slipped in and shut it behind me.

"Fuck you doing trying to fight my pregnant girlfriend for?" I smiled at her.

"I-I didn't know she was pregnant—"

"You did, she told you at the shoot," I said and grabbed an apple from her fruit bowl. I bit into it and stared at her. I moved my hands in a winding motion to let her know to get a move on with this explanation.

"She umm, she stole you from me!" she finally responded. I bit the apple again, and shook my head at her as she tightened her robe.

"That was a bad idea, shorty. You know I was never your man. All the threesomes we had? Come on now," I chuckled and bit my apple again. "And I've gone weeks without speaking to you."

Maybe I had the wrong impression of what being someone's man was, because clearly her and London's definition differed from mine.

"I hate niggas like you! Act like my man but don't want me to call you my man," she scoffed and plopped down on the couch.

"Stand yo' ass back up, I ain't say sit down!" I barked. She shot back up and stared at me with her eyes bucked. "Now," I bit my apple again. This shit was bomb as fuck. "I would have you apologize to my girl, but she could give two fucks about an apology and so could I." I polished off the apple and put it into a Ziploc bag that I had. "Nice seeing you Zaria," I smirked and walked towards the backdoor.

"What does that mean KJ?" she chased after me.

I ignored her and as soon as I opened her back door, my masked men walked in to take care of her ass. I waited until I saw them leave out the back with trash bags and get into a van.

Once my cleanup crew had slipped in and out, I headed to my office building to meet with my team. I needed to let them know that I would be implementing a new system. From now on, I wanted immediate reports on the amount received at each trap from the trap worker and from the deliverer. That way if I had any discrepancies I would know who the fuck to knock off right away. Whatever amount they sent me had better match my records, and their amounts also better match each other's. I was gonna do the same with the money count as well. No one had crossed me since Ronald, but I wanted to keep it that way.

"Morning everybody," I smiled and adjusted my cap to the back. They all looked tired but I didn't give a fuck. This was a job just like any other, and sometimes you had to start bright and fucking early.

"Morning boss," they all said simultaneously.

I explained the new moves that would be made, and I saw a couple people become uneasy. "I hope this will result in less product loss, and less dumb niggas tryna cross me. Don't be that dumb nigga," I stated and then ended the meeting.

Once I was done, I headed to meet Kaleeini to do a money count, and plan how we were gonna get at this Brice character.

Tonight Brice was gonna expire. KJ and I had to make sure this was executed properly, because he was telling the truth when he told Aysia he knew people in high places. Not that they weren't still peasants to a nigga like me, but it was easy for him to hide out and maneuver around with so many people trying to protect him.

By now, he'd gotten comfortable and was taking less precautions. Right after he shot at me and Aysia, he was taking extra steps to protect his whereabouts, and just like I thought, he'd stopped doing that. I'm sure he thought the shit had blown over since there were no casualties, but he was sadly mistaken.

KJ and I sat in the car watching Brice as he picked up his order from Hip Hops. "I can't wait to blast this nigga," KJ smirked.

"Nigga, why?" I chuckled and looked over him.

"Didn't you say he put his hands on your shorty?" he quizzed and I nodded. Aysia couldn't possibly think I believed that hair straightener bullshit.

"Aight then, I can't stand niggas that hit females. Unless she's a low down dirty hoe," he said and we both laughed.

"Well my baby girl is nothing of the sort," I shook my head at KJ's crazy ass and laughed some more.

Brice finally stumbled out, obviously drunk off his ass, and then climbed into the passenger seat of a Nissan. He quickly got back out, and then fired some random gunshots into empty space. *What the fuck?* He got back into the car after securing his piece back in his waist.

"What the hell was that for? He could've killed an innocent bystander," I shook my head. "Something is off about this nigga," I added as KJ watched him closely.

I saw it was a bitch driving the car, and I hoped she was dropping him off; otherwise, she may get caught in the crossfire. She sped off just as Hip Hops was closing up, and after a couple moments, I peeled off after them.

The girl drove to these beat up ass apartments, deep in the hood of Baltimore, and parked against the curb. I shut my headlights off, and parked across the street but a little ways up. I saw him and the girl kissing, and then he hopped out.

"Let's go," I said and we got out of the car. We jogged across the street, and came from opposite ends to run up on Brice.

"Excuse me," he slurred as he tried to get by, obviously not recognizing me. He looked up at me when I didn't let him by, and then he turned around only to run into KJ. "Shit," he mumbled.

We sacked his ass and quickly carried him to the car, unbeknownst to his girlfriend. She was waiting for him to come back down, with Boosie blasting from her speakers. He was screaming but because he was sacked, it was very low. We saw him try to reach for his gun, so KJ clocked him upside the head and then we threw him into the car. We sped to the warehouse, trying to get there before his ass came to. Luckily, he was still out cold when we arrived, and even while we carried him inside. We threw him to the ground, and then I took some water to splash on his face. He slightly blinked, but was still laying there.

"Ugh!" he shouted when KJ kicked his ass in the stomach.

"Wake your bitch ass up, nigga," KJ sneered. Brice finally had his eyes open, and he just kept looking back and forth between KJ and I.

"Man, let me out of here, I don't have the packages," he slurred and looked around the huge empty warehouse. Here he was talking about some weird shit again.

"You ain't cuffed," KJ smiled. Brice rolled his eyes, and then slowly stood to his feet.

He tried to walk by KJ, but KJ stuck his arm out and clocked him in the neck. Once he flew to the ground, I pulled my gun from my waist.

"You had me shot at, bitch?" I questioned even though I knew.

"Nah man, I didn't," he shook his head, bitching up. "Wait, you fucked my girl!" he grimaced, finally recognizing me.

"She ain't your girl. And by the way, we had those plates ran and it came back to your brother," I replied.

"You killed my brother, nigga?" He squinted his eyes in anger, and then starting talking to himself.

"That would be me," KJ chimed in and grinned at him.

"I can't believe—"

"Sit your monkey ass down, nigga!" KJ got in Brice's face after he tried to hop up and get buck.

Brice cowered back, and I moved closer to him as I cocked my glock. He looked behind himself and tried to take off, but KJ tripped him.

"Aarrrggghhhh!" he screamed because he skinned his chin.

KJ pulled out a blunt, and then lit it using a match. I poured some gasoline on Brice's back, and he turned over panicking. Just as he did, KJ tossed the match on his mid section. He screamed so loud it was piercing. Once we started to see severe burn marks on his light skin, KJ dumped a bucket of water on him. Before he could even catch his breath, I blew his head open with three shots.

"I can't believe you did all that without losing your blunt," I laughed at KJ as the clean up crew took care of Brice.

"Nigga, I been getting high since I was fifteen, this shit is an art form," he responded.

After dropping my cousin off, I was finally able to go home and shower. I missed Aysia and wished her ass were in my bed waiting for me... naked. As I turned on my shower, I dialed her to see if she was up.

"Hello," she answered groggily.

"What are you doing shorty?" I quizzed.

"Dreaming about you," she giggled.

"Can I come get you in thirty or are you too tired?" I asked.

"Kaleeini, I hate you," she chuckled. "You know I can't turn down seeing you, even though I got work in the morning," she said and it sounded like she was getting up.

"Man, fuck that job, I got you baby," I laughed.

"We will see, be here in thirty Kaleeini. I don't wanna fall asleep unless it's after I've gotten some dick," she chuckled and so did I.

I promised her I would be there, and then got into the shower after tying up my dreads.

KJ and I had just come home from a nice little outing, and I was finally putting the new stuff I got into the dresser set I'd just gotten. We were finally adjusting to having two styles in one bedroom. He wanted everything to be so masculine, but you know I was not having that.

I sighed as I was putting my clothes up, because as usual, KJ had dipped out to handle some business. I loved when we could spend all day together, and *actually* spend all day. His definition of that was lunch or breakfast, a little shopping, and then leaving me to my lonesome. On rare occasions, we would come home and chill and fuck.

I finished putting all of my new clothes and shoes away, and when I stood up KJ walked in.

"Come outside," he beamed.

"For what? I'm hungry," I whined.

"You just ate, Gigi," he looked confused.

"We ate brunch, it's been two hours," I replied and walked over to him.

"Aight, well we can go get food in a little bit, come here," he grabbed my hand and we rushed down the staircase and through the foyer. When I walked outside, there was a beautiful navy blue BMW with tinted windows on rims.

"Kendrick, what is this?" I smiled and scanned the car.

I was standing in the doorway because it was too cold to be out there. The car was so pretty though, so I decided to walk out anyway. When I got outside, I saw there was a black G-Wagon too.

"KJ, what are you doing?" I giggled.

"These are for you, so you can stop driving that beat up ass Explorer," he responded.

"I like my little truck," I nudged him.

He pulled me close, and we began to kiss heavily. I pulled away to caress his face and stare up into his eyes.

"I love you, daddy," I pecked him and then sucked on his bottom lip.

"You better, shorty," he said before slipping his tongue into my mouth. Once we got our fix, I went and looked at both of the cars, and then we put them into the garage.

"You wanna eat somewhere nice, or you want something small?" he asked as we walked into the house.

"I definitely don't want anything small," I replied and he shook his head at me.

We showered together and then got dressed in warm clothing so that we could go eat dinner at Jack's Bistro. The whole ride there I felt like someone was following us, but no one was ever there when I looked back.

"What happened with Zaria?" I questioned once we were seated.

"Don't worry about all that," he responded dryly.

"Will she be bothering me again?" I quizzed.

"Nah, she ain't gon' bother you, girl. Didn't I tell you I would handle it?" he frowned his sexy face up.

"Yeah, you did," I smirked. I looked around the restaurant at the other people dining, and nothing seemed to be out of the ordinary, so I don't know why I felt uneasy.

The waitress came back after a little while, and she took our orders. I was hungry so I made sure to get an appetizer too.

"I know you say that I don't spend enough time with you, so I'm gonna take you up to my parents' cabin," he smiled.

"Really? That means you won't be running off to work in the middle of the night, or so you say," I replied.

"What you mean or so I say? You know I ain't out running with bitches," he shook his head.

"I know, you're too in love with me," I grinned and so did he.

"Cocky ass," he responded.

"Well, I should be. For the longest you were able to be cocky knowing I had it bad for your ass," I stated seriously.

"I don't mind you being cocky about my love for you. Let these bitches know who I love," he stared into my eyes and my panties became drenched. There were a lot of girls vying for KJ, but I won and I was happy as fuck about it.

"I will let them know every time, especially when I wear this," I tapped my diamond ring I was wearing.

"Where are you gon' put that one when I marry you?" he sipped his drink.

"I don't know, maybe on the other hand. That won't be for a while though," I said trying to see if I was right or not.

"Maybe sooner than you think, shorty." He looked at me and I couldn't contain my smile. "Look at you blushing over there at the thought of me putting a ring on your finger," he chuckled flashing his perfect teeth and deep dimples.

"So!" I smacked my lips at him.

"Have I broken a promise to you yet?" He raised a brow and I shook my head no.

"I know you're gonna marry me KJ, you just better not get me pregnant again before you do," I rolled my neck.

"Maybe if you didn't have such good pussy, I wouldn't always be in that shit," he smirked. "And look at you right now, you're so beautiful, baby," he squinted his eyes as if he was thinking.

"Thank you," I cheesed. "I'm gonna be celibate after I have the baby," I joked.

"And you gon' wake up with my dick in your mouth," he retorted and I almost spit out my water.

"I hate you," I giggled. "So when is this cabin trip?" I asked.

I was excited to be excluded away from the world with KJ. I was so greedy when it came to him and his time. If he could walk around with me on his back while he worked, I would be down for that.

"Next week. We're gonna leave on Tuesday because there may be a blizzard on Thursday, and I wanna already be there," he said.

"So there is a chance we will have to stay longer from being snowed in?" I beamed and he shook his head at me.

"Possibly, but I hope not. I do wanna get back to work," he laughed at me. "You want me to spend all my time with you, hunh?" he questioned with a smile, and then got up to sit next to me.

"Yeah I do, but I understand you have to work," I shrugged.

"And sometimes you even have to do styling jobs, so I have to be away from you," he said.

"You miss me when I'm working?" I looked up into his eyes.

"Yeah I do. I miss you even when I'm working. The best nights are when I come home from a long day, to some food you made and then get to fuck you all night," he pecked me. I just smiled up at him and he kissed me again. "I love you, shorty," he pushed my hair behind my ear.

"I love you more, Kendrick," I whispered as I got lost in his seaweed colored eyes. We just stared at one another until the waitress came and set our plates down for the appetizer.

We scarfed it all down, and did the same to the food because we both had the same idea. We rushed right home, turned on the fireplace, and then got to fucking right by it.

My alarm woke me up at 9am while I was knocked out in Kaleeini's bed. I hadn't slept in my own bed in weeks, and I was not complaining. I damn near lived here.

I sat up and walked over to my duffle bag, so I could fish out my clothes and toiletries for a nice hot shower. When I opened it, I saw an envelope on top of my stuff that read *Shop*. I shook my head at Kaleeini always disregarding my job, and then proceeded to gather my things.

When I stood up I felt light headed, and my throat started to jump. I rushed to the bathroom once my mouth became salty, and then threw up violently into the toilet. I hadn't even eaten yet, so nothing of substance was coming up after awhile. I felt horrible all of sudden like I was dying. I stood to my feet, but then lost my balance and fell onto the clothes hamper.

Once I felt like I could stand again, I stood up and rushed downstairs to get myself a drink of water. I downed the water and then poured myself another. I couldn't even finish the second one before I threw up again into the trashcan. I stared out the window at the cold weather, and knew not only did I not feel like going to work, but also

I was sick as a damn dog. I walked up the stairs to call my job, all the while trying to remember what I had eaten last night.

"Must've been that Chinese we ordered last night," I said as I dialed on my phone.

I never missed work, so my manager knew I must've been sick if I was calling out. I grabbed my phone and dialed Gianna so that I could check on her. I was weird like that; I called my friends every morning to check on them for some reason.

"Hello?" she answered and before I could respond, I was throwing up all over my side of the bed and floor. *What the fuck!* "Aysia!" I heard Gianna yelling over the phone.

I thought I was dying as I dry heaved on the floor. I crawled to the bathroom, and then washed my mouth out with water. I cleaned my hands and arms, and then carefully went to get my phone.

"Gigi, I'm sick as fuck and I need to go to the doctor," I sniffled because I was crying now. I didn't know what the fuck was wrong with me.

"Okay, are you at Kaleeini's?" she quizzed.

"Yes," I replied and wiped my nose.

"Okay, Shannon is over here and we're gonna be there soon," she replied.

"Okay," I whispered and hung up.

I looked around because I didn't know what to do about the mess I'd made. I knew Kaleeini was gonna strangle me once he saw my throw up all over the bed and floor. I gathered the bedding, hoping to remove it before it caused any more damage, but I didn't know what to do about the throw up on the floor. I decided I would just buy some of that powder they used to use in middle school, so that I could sweep it up when I got back, hopefully before Kaleeini could see it.

I quickly showered and got dressed, then munched on a banana as I waited for Shannon and Gianna to arrive.

Gigi: *Outside.*

I rushed outside, and directed them to my physician's office. She didn't have any appointments, but once I explained my symptoms she made time for me. Thank God, because I felt like my body was rotting from the inside out.

———

"Terrence!" The nurse called my last name so I could go to the back. Gianna and Shannon stayed seated as I went to the back. "Step on the scale please," the nurse said. I climbed on and she moved the little things around to get the accurate weight number. "Okay, one hundred and thirty," she wrote down and my eyes almost popped out of my head.

"Are you sure? I was one hundred and twenty pounds when I came a month and a half ago," I chuckled nervously.

"Yes, I'm sure, honey," she half smiled and then handed me my UGG boots to put on. I took them and then followed her to another room. She took some blood from me and had me pee in a cup. "Okay Ms. Terrence, are you sexually active?" she quizzed once I returned with the pee cup.

"Umm, yes," I replied. She wasn't even the doctor, so why was she asking me this.

"Alrighty, and when was your last menstrual? And the duration?" she inquired.

"Umm, I would say on November the third to the fifth," I nodded.

"So you're twelve days late? It's December fifteenth." She cocked her head at me after jotting down my previous answer.

"It's happened before," I responded. "I get stressed a lot," I added and she nodded.

"Alright, well the doctor will be in once the results from your blood and urine come back. Would you like some tea or anything?" she offered.

"No, no thank you," I half smiled and she left.

I sat there for a bit, and then decided to pull out my phone. Group text with Gianna, Willow, and Shannon was popping as always, so I decided to catch up on that before scanning Instagram.

Willow was mad that she wasn't here, so we promised to meet up with her afterwards. She didn't seem depressed like she had been these past few days for some reason.

"Ms. Terrence," my doctor walked in and smiled at me.

"Hi, Dr. Naison," I cleared my throat. She took a seat on her doctor stool, and then clicked around on her computer.

"So we ran your blood and urine to test you for STDs, HIV, pregnancy, and a couple other things that may have caused those symptoms," she began and I gripped the examination table with my sweaty hands. Had I trusted Kaleeini too much? *This nigga better not have given me the clap*, I thought. "Ms. Terrence, were you aware that you're four weeks pregnant?" she furrowed her brows.

"I-I am?" I bucked my eyes and she nodded with a chuckle.

"I'm guessing the answer to my question is no. So yes, you're pregnant. Did you wanna keep the baby? Or do you need time to think?" she asked.

"No, I don't need time to think. I'm gonna keep it. I'm just surprised," I blinked a couple times.

"Yes, I know honey, is the father around? Is he your boyfriend?" she inquired.

"Yes, he's my boyfriend," I smiled at the thought of Kaleeini.

"Well that's great that you have him. Now, I will write you a prescription for prenatal pills," she said and then stood up. "But let me just listen to your heart and breathing," she added.

Kaleeini and I used condoms *most* of the time, but the last few times we were kind of reckless and in the moment. I hoped he was prepared for what I had to tell him.

I WASN'T TAKING that bitch Rosalind seriously at fucking all. Girls had claimed to be pregnant by me plenty of times before I got with Willow, and as usual, the shit always turned out to be a lie. When you had money, presence, and good looks, it came with the territory. I wasn't no reckless ass nigga that went around Baltimore raw dogging random hoes, so nobody would be having my baby but my wife, which I was hoping would be Willow one day.

Speaking of my baby, she still seemed to be bothered by what that hoe had approached her with, and in turn it was bothering me. This is exactly why I didn't want Willow to know I smashed that bitch. I knew she had an inkling since she saw us conversing at the party that night, but her knowing for sure was a big difference. I could kill Rosalind right now.

I drove over to my parents' house, because I wanted to talk with my father and see if he could give me some advice. Shit, he was used to these crazy hoes going ape shit, so I needed some guidance.

"What's up, son?" my dad smiled when I walked into the den.

My fifteen-year-old little sister, Kendria, was lying on his shoulder; she was such a daddy's girl. Ever since she was little, she would cling to my dad like a damn cell phone clip. Even now, if he's running small errands, she always wants to go.

"You're always trying to use up daddy's free time," Kendria joked and stood up. I hugged her and kissed her cheek before she left out.

Once she was gone, I went to the small fridge to grab a bottle of water, and then sat down next to my dad.

"So what's good boy?" my dad looked over at me.

"Man, not too much is good right now," I shook my head and took another sip of my water.

"What's going on?" he quizzed.

"Shit, too much. I took a break from Willow, and while on that break I smashed another girl. Now that girl is saying she's pregnant," I explained. He stared at me confused. "I swear she's lying though. I only hit once and I strapped up. The condom was in tact when I finished too," I told him so that his expression would change. I knew he would be so disappointed in me if I had slipped up with some random.

"Oh, aight. Have you told Willow?" he questioned.

"Willow told me! The girl approached her and told her, and Willow came home crying and shit," I shook my head.

"And what did this girl say when you put her ass in check?" he furrowed his brows.

"That's the thing, I haven't said anything to Rosalind. I've just been ignoring her because I know she's lying Pop," I frowned at the thought.

"Understandable, but you need to put her ass in check, Kendrin. She went way too far approaching your damn girlfriend. You need to let her know what type of nigga you are, and how she will respect you as such," he said and I nodded. "As your woman, Willow should feel protected from all that shit. These girls on the outside have to know that girlfriends and wives are not to be approached under any circumstances," he added.

"Nobody ever approached Mom?" I inquired.

"No, they knew better. And plus, your mama was too fucking

crazy. I mean girls tried to say little shit when she was around, but they never walked up to her on no bullshit saying stuff like that. I nipped any contact hoes tried to have with your mama, in a bud," he answered. He was speaking some real shit. Willow was above these hoes and I wanted her to feel and know that.

"Thanks Pop," I tapped him and he nodded.

"Handle your shit, son," he raised a brow at me.

"I am," I said before standing up. Just then, my mom walked in and slid into my dad's lap. I leaned down to kiss her cheek, and she caressed my face gently. "See y'all later," I said.

"You look good, babe," I heard my dad tell my mother right before the sound of kissing. I shook my head and laughed at their asses. I'm glad I wasn't old enough to witness them as teenagers, if they were this bad now.

I hopped into my Range, and then sped to Rosalind's apartment. I called her on the phone while I was in the car, and she damn near answered before it rung.

"Finally!" she yelled.

"Lower your fucking voice and open the damn door." I hung up in her face and climbed out of the car.

When I walked up, she was standing at the door and I could see a slight bulge. This bitch had been pregnant longer than I thought. A smile crept across my face because I really knew it wasn't mine. I was already sure, but this just solidified it.

"Ros, I know what you did, and I'm gon' tell you this once. If you ever approach my girl again with your fucking lies, I'm gon' snap your neck myself," I gritted and she stared up at me in fear.

"So you don't care about our baby?" she sniffled.

"You know got damn well that ain't my fucking baby!" I hollered and she jumped back. "You already fucking showing, shorty! The timeline don't add up!" I barked. She looked away and then plopped down on the couch.

"I'm sorry, Kendrin," she sobbed.

"I don't want your fucking sorry, Rosalind. I want you to leave me and my girl the fuck alone. You need to tell whoever's the real father that he has a baby coming," I huffed.

"Can you tell him for me?" she whispered and smirked.

"What? Are you crazy? Fuck I look like telling some random nigga he got a baby on the way? You for real have lost your mind shorty," I shook my head.

"It's not a random guy." An evil smile was now plastered onto her face.

"Hunh?" I furrowed my brows.

"The baby is Kenzie King's," she rubbed her belly.

I WAS CHILLING in the den with my feet resting in tub of ice. I'd had a long day at practice, and the hot bath in Epsom salt hadn't done much. My body was really taking a beating from all the workouts and practices. I was used to high school practice, but college was way more intense. I wasn't tripping too hard though, because I knew it would all be worth it once I got drafted.

"Shannon is here, baby," my mother peeked into the den and I smiled.

"Thanks ma," I responded.

A few moments later, Shannon walked in looking beautiful as ever. She was pretty covered up because of the weather, but I could still see how gorgeous she was. Her smooth brown skin was glowing, and I couldn't wait to get my hands on her.

"Come here beautiful," I waved her over and she sat next to me.

"How are you feeling, baby?" she quizzed.

"I'm feeling aight, but I'm better now that you're here," I said before sliding my tongue into her mouth. We kissed hungrily for a couple moments, and then I let her go. "Damn, if I wasn't so sore right now I would take your ass to the pool house," I bit my lip.

"It's snowing outside though!" she chuckled.

"So what! You know I make you sweat every time," I replied and we laughed.

Her phone buzzed in her hand and I saw *Rosalind* flash across. I swallowed a lump in my throat, because I hoped it was a different girl. There were plenty of Rosalinds in Baltimore, right?

Shannon opened the text and I tried my best to read it without her realizing it. I couldn't really get the gist of the conversation, but I was fuming. How did they even meet? This was too much.

"Who is that, babe?" I asked as if I had no idea.

"Oh, this girl from school. She texts me every now and then wanting to hang out," she shrugged. Right then it dawned on me that they must've met that day Rosalind showed up at my practice trying to act a fucking fool.

"Have you?" I quizzed.

"No, not yet. I'm not really interested," she shrugged and flashed a smile. "We're gonna have a study group together though on Wednesday, because she has some notes I wanna copy," she added and my stomach dropped. I stood up quickly and stepped out of the ice.

"Kenzie, what are you doing?" she frowned.

"I forgot I have to take care of something baby, don't leave, aight?" I told her. She just stared up at me with her face in a knot. "Aight?" I repeated.

"Okay, I'm not going anywhere," she responded and shook her head.

I dried my feet off, slipped on some socks and then my Nike slide-ins. I grabbed a jacket so that my mom wouldn't say shit, and then got into my Mercedes. I sped to Rosalind's house with all kinds of thoughts racing through my fucking mind. I didn't know what I was gonna say to her ass, but I needed her to cease contact with Shannon. She didn't even go to Morgan State, which let me know she definitely had an ulterior motive by trying to have study sessions. I wasn't even sure how she knew or found out about Shannon honestly.

I finally got to her condo and saw a car that looked like my cousin Kendrin's, parked out front. I shrugged it off because plenty of people had black Range Rovers, just not in this neighborhood. I jogged to Rosalind's door, and beat on it repeatedly. I heard voices and I was alarmed like a muthafucka. Who the fuck did she have in here? Finally, she opened the door, rubbing her small stomach as if it were much bigger. I rushed in and my words got caught in my throat when I spotted my cousin Kendrin.

"What the fuck is going on?" I frowned and looked between he and Rosalind.

"Nigga, you tell me! How the hell you know her?" Kendrin pointed to Rosalind.

"How the fuck do you know her?" I shot back.

"I met her at a party and I fucked once, your turn," he folded his arms. I snapped my neck to look at Rosalind. Ain't this some shit right here.

"While I was at camp?" I wondered and Kendrin nodded to answer for her.

"Who is she to you, Kenzie?" Kendrin barked, anxious to find out.

"She was my girl, or so I thought!" I yelled shooting daggers at Rosalind.

"Your girl? Nigga, what about Shannon?" Kendrin hollered and Rosalind glared at me.

"Don't act like you ain't know Shannon was my girl Ros, I know you been found out. I came here to tell you to stop fucking with her and tryna be friends and shit," I grimaced.

"What the hell is going on right now?" Kendrin said more so to himself. I wasn't in the mood to explain myself to him.

"Fuck you, Kenzie! You can't just ignore me and our baby!" Rosalind screamed with tears rushing down her light cheeks. I hated to do her like this, especially since she was carrying my baby, but now that she had fucked Kendrin, who knows?

"Look, I'm out, I ain't got nothing to do with this shit," Kendrin rushed to the door and dipped out.

"You fucked another nigga, Ros? And my cousin?" I furrowed my brows at her and sat down on the couch.

"Really, Kenzie? You have another girlfriend! Who you dumped me for and couldn't even be honest about!" she shouted.

"You cheated before you found out about Shannon," I scoffed at the thought.

"So what are you gonna do Kenzie, because I'm not gonna let you keep ignoring me," she started to cry again.

"I know shorty, I know. I'm gon' be there for the baby, but as far as us being an *us,* that's not gon' happen. Shit is not gon' happen ever again," I looked into her face. I was gonna get a DNA test too, but she was stressed enough and telling her that would only elevate it.

"Kenzie, how did this happen? You were mine!" she stabbed herself in the chest with her pointing finger.

"I wish I could tell you, Ros. I just fell in love with someone else," I shrugged.

"And that's it? You just break my heart and be done?" she scowled and panted heavily.

"Let's not forget that while I was away at basketball camp, you fucked another guy, Rosalind," I glared at her and she turned away. "Anyway, leave Shannon alone, aight? I will tell her about the baby on my own time, and I promise it will be sooner than later," I rubbed her exposed thigh. She sniffled and nodded, before wiping her tears. "Come here," I said and pulled her into a hug.

I rubbed her back as she sobbed violently. I felt bad, but then when I thought about my cousin smashing her, my empathy vanished. I consoled Rosalind for about twenty minutes longer, gave her some money, and then went home hoping Shannon was still there.

When I walked into the den of my home, she was lying on the couch watching *Love and Hip Hop.*

"I'm glad you stayed, baby," I said and kneeled down in front of her.

"Of course. You okay?" she rubbed my face and I kissed her gently.

"Yeah, I'm good," I half smiled.

"I waited for you to eat. Your mom made some mojo roast chicken," she stood up off the couch. I loved when my mom made Cuban food. "Let's go eat," Shannon pecked me.

Shannon was always down for me, and I loved that shit about her. Rosalind, nor any other woman could ever compare. I had to find a way to tell her about Rosalind without losing her. Us being apart was just not an option.

I'd been pretty depressed since running into that bitch from Tasha's party. I tried hanging out with my friends in order to ignore Kendrin, but it never worked. Gianna was the only one who knew anything about the situation, and I made her promise not to tell Shannon and Aysia. I was too embarrassed, and didn't want everyone knowing my man had gotten another hoe pregnant. Shit, if Gianna hadn't been there she wouldn't have known either. Gianna and Kendrin swore up and down that the girl was lying, but for some reason my heart was still in pain. It was like this whole time I knew he would ruin our relationship, and he proved me right.

It was Tuesday and I had decided to skip my community college classes. I just wanted to lie in my bed and sulk. I knew it wasn't good for me, but I did it anyway. I just didn't have the energy to do anything else.

My phone rang and I looked down to see it was Kendrin calling again. Tears seeped out of my eyes as I thought about our relationship. I loved him but I couldn't be with him knowing he had a baby with someone else. I let my phone ring constantly until it finally just stopped. I heard someone beating on the front door, and my mom yelled for me to answer it. I rolled my eyes, and then grabbed a tissue so that I could wipe my face. I padded to the front, and when I opened the door, there stood my love Kendrin.

"What?" I looked down.

"Come with me for a little bit shorty," he licked his lips and shivered. I exhaled heavily and looked around before slipping on my UGGs and grabbing my jacket.

I followed him to his car, and got in after he opened the door for me. I didn't say anything as he drove me to his home, because I was too wrapped up in my own thoughts as I watched the snow fall.

He pulled into his garage, and we walked inside. He led me to his dining room, and the place was surrounded with white roses spray painted in gold. He had some candles lit, and a couple gift bags.

"Kendrin, what is all this?" I quizzed as I took in the beautiful atmosphere.

"Open the gifts, Lo," he responded and gestured towards them.

I grabbed the biggest box first and he chuckled. I ripped it open, and it was a pretty orange dress by Givenchy. I opened another box containing some nude Louboutins and I was screaming on the inside. There were two more really small ones, so I grabbed one of them. I pulled out a red velvet box, and inside was a pear shaped diamond ring. I looked up at Kendrin with my mouth ajar, and he walked closer to me. He took his jacket off and then got down on one knee.

"Oh my God!" I squealed.

"Willow Shaniece Jameson, you know I love you no matter what you do. I know I wanna be with you forever, even though you're crazy as hell. And baby, I swear on my life and everything I love that old girl is not carrying my baby. I have solid proof baby, and I need you to believe me. I've always been honest with you for the most part, and I wouldn't lie to you about something like this. Most importantly, I would never be so heedless, that I would impregnate another woman. I love you way too much to dog you out like that, whether you were my girl at the time or not. And I wanna show you that I'm serious as fuck about you, shorty. So will you marry me, beautiful?" He looked up into my eyes, as tears fell out of mine. I was crying like a little ass baby.

"Yes babe, of course," I sniffled and smiled.

He took the ring box from me, removed the ring, and then slid it onto my finger. I stared down at the eleven-carat diamond ring and almost blinded myself.

"That's over two and a half million dollars on your finger," he said and my jaw hit the floor. "Open the last one," he told me after kissing me softly. I took the other one, and then opened it to see a key.

"A key to your heart?" I blushed.

"Nah, that's corny as fuck. This is a key to the crib shorty," he grinned and we laughed. "You gon' come live with your man?" he pursed his lips.

"Of course, I've been waiting for you to ask me," I said while rubbing his face. "Ah!" I squealed. "I'm so happy," I cheesed and so did he.

"Well, go put your dress on baby. I know it's too nippy to go anywhere, so we're gonna have dinner here," he said and helped me up.

I rushed off to the bathroom to wash up and change into my dress, but when I walked into the bathroom, he'd set out a basket of bath bombs and bubble bath from LUSH. My baby knew I loved LUSH. I looked around the huge ass bathroom, and then spotted him in the doorway.

"Did you need any help?" he smiled.

"Yes, please," I put my hand on my hip.

He walked in and turned on the bathwater. I looked at the choice of bath bombs, and then tossed in the one I wanted to use. A smile spread across my face as I watched it spin around and turn the water all kinds of colors.

"Come with me," I said as I stripped out of my clothes.

He admired my body for a little bit, then pulled a lighter from the drawer to light some candles. He stripped down, exposing his perfectly chiseled toffee colored body. My nigga was so fucking fine.

Jealous and crazy was the only way to be fucking with a nigga like Kendrin King. He got in, and we cuddled for a little bit before he started to clean me off.

"Mmmm," he moaned as he sucked on my nipples.

I ran my hands all over his strong shoulders as he devoured them gently. Once he was done, he looked up at me so that we could kiss. I draped my arms around his neck, and we sucked on each other's lips as he gently slid me down onto his rock hard rod.

"Fuck, Willow," he exhaled and wrapped his strong arms around my torso. "You gon' have my baby?" he asked in a low tone.

"Yes daddy!" I cried out.

I moved up and down on him slowly, and then pulled back a little so that I could feel his lips against mine.

"Ahh, uuh, Kendriinn," I whimpered as he slipped his finger into my ass. The feeling of his dick filling me up, and the minor anal play had me on one. "I-I'm gonna, aaahh," I couldn't even get it out before I exploded.

"Shit," he whispered and sucked on my bottom lip. "I love you, wife," he cooed, and the sound of him calling me that made my clit throb.

"Ugghh," he gripped my body as he shot his seeds up in me.

He caught his breath, and then picked me up off of his dick. He kissed my forehead, and then got out of the tub and left the bathroom. I cleaned myself again, and then got out to put on some body oil.

Once I was finished, I came down to the same dining room, and there was food on the table. Kendrin held my chair out, and I sat down. Once he sat across from me, he grabbed my hands into his.

"Baby, I want you to know that I'm sorry about old girl coming at you like that. You know that's not my baby, and that's for sure, for sure," he rubbed my hands to reassure me. "I want you to know that I only have eyes for you and that no one else matters to me, so you don't have to be so worked up all the time," he added. I just stared at him with a half smile. "I love you, Willow, and for as long as I'm with you,

you will never have to deal with a girl approaching you like that again," he finished.

"I love you too, Kendrin," I sniffled.

"I know, shorty, and I love how hard you love me too," he smirked.

"I love how hard you love me too," I giggled.

"I'm gon' love you hard as fuck tonight," he squinted his eyes lustfully.

"We just did it though," I tapped his hand.

"I know, but I didn't get to eat it." He licked his lips and then leaned over to kiss my neck making me giggle.

"Let's eat the actual food first," I smiled.

I was in bliss right now, and that bitch had better stay far away from me and my nigga if she knew what was good for her.

I WAS LEAVING my apartment building headed to class, and I was not in the mood to go, but I wasn't the type to miss a class. As soon as I walked into the hallway of my apartment, I spotted Rosalind. She was rubbing her belly and frowning.

"Rosalind? What are you doing at my house?" I shook my head in confusion.

"I came to confront you," she smirked.

"Confront me about what?" I quizzed and adjusted my book bag strap. This bitch had been weird since the day I met her ass.

"About my man that you've stolen from me," she said and then got up off the banister.

"Okay, I knew your ass was crazy from day one," I scoffed.

"Kenzie didn't seem to think so. At least not until you came along and stole him," she grimaced. What the fuck was she talking about?

"Kenzie has been my man for over a year, and as much time as we spend together, it's impossible for him to have another bitch. Especially one that acts and dresses like you," I waved her off.

"He's been mine for about two years, boo," she cocked her head and held two fingers up. "Let me prove it to you," she added and dug into her purse.

She retrieved an envelope of photos and handed them to me. I looked through pictures of she and Kenzie all in love, and some were dated two years ago, and some were dated as recent as this past summer. My heart rate sped up, and my skin became hot. I had never been this angry and confused in my life. I suddenly felt like I had no idea who Kenzie was.

"Take your fucking pictures. You can have these and Kenzie's lying ass!" I hollered and shoved the pictures into her chest. I tried to go down the stairs but she stood in my way.

"Wait, I'm not done with you," she folded her arms.

"Bitch, get the fuck out of my way," I frowned up and went down the steps. She rushed after me and grabbed my arm. I tried to snatch away, and she slipped from my arm and down the stairs.

"Aaahhhh!" she screamed and clutched her stomach, as blood oozed from under her.

Gianna and I had just arrived to the cabin yesterday, and we were already snowed in. She was happy as hell that we were stuck here together, and I was too, somewhat. I loved spending time with my girl, but I wanted to make sure I made it back to the city to work. I made her believe I was just as excited as she was so I wouldn't hurt her pregnant ass feelings.

"I got the fireplace going," she walked up to me and I palmed her small belly. "Let's make hot chocolate," she beamed and grabbed my hand with her small soft one.

I followed her to the kitchen, and we both made the hot chocolate together. We went into the living room by the fireplace, and I tried to turn on the TV but she stopped me.

"No, let's talk," she smiled and scooted closer to me. I pulled her in between my legs, making sure not to spill the hot chocolate.

"What do you wanna talk about?" I quizzed and kissed her head.

"What are we gonna name the baby?" she questioned.

"We don't even know what it is, Gigi," I chuckled at her before sipping the contents of my cup.

"That's why we can pick two names," she responded.

"Aight, if it's a guy then we can name it Kendrick, obviously. If it's a girl, you can pick what you want," I offered.

"That works for me," she turned around to look at me and I pressed my lips against hers. I set my cup down, and then took hers as well. I got up and then scooped her up so I could carry her to the bedroom. "Already KJ?" she giggled and I nodded.

I laid her down on the bed, and then pulled her tights down her smooth brown sugar legs. She took her shirt and sweater off as I slid her panties down. I spread her legs and kissed her lower lips gently, making her arch her back. I stood up and pushed her to the middle of the bed, and then got on the bed as well. I kissed her full lips as she rubbed my biceps, and then trailed kisses down her face to her neck, belly, and of course the tattoo of my name right by her pussy. I got comfortable and then placed her soft legs on my shoulders, and immediately started sucking on her clit while groping her thighs. She was juicing up nicely, and I was taking it all down.

"You taste so good, Gigi," I moaned in between licks and sucks.

"Mmmmm, uuuuh," she cooed as she released fairly quickly.

I spread her legs some more so that I could see and taste more, and went in for the kill. I could hear her fresh nails scraping the sheets as she called to the high heavens.

"Uuuh, Kendrick, I love you baby," she whimpered as her legs trembled.

Her nectar gushed into my mouth again, and I slurped it up. I licked her clean, and then sat up on my knees, in which she tried to suck my dick but I stopped her.

"I will stop before you cum," she looked up at me. I didn't wanna nut in her mouth while she had my baby inside her body. I rubbed her long hair back and she took my dick into her small hands. She swirled her tongue on the tip, and then slowly worked it into her mouth. I palmed the back of her head and let my dick glide in and out of her warm wet mouth.

"Gianna, shit," I whispered. She looked up at me as she worked her jaws, and that shit was so sexy. I began to hump her face while staring down at her naked and sucking me off. "Get on your knees baby," I told her. She got off her butt and onto her knees, and for some reason that shit intensified the sensation. She slid her mouth off of my dick, and then flicked her tongue over my balls. "Gigi," I grunted. She took my dick back into her mouth and started to go ham. I felt myself about to nut, so I took her off of me so that it could settle down.

She laid back, and I climbed between her legs to enter her. Pregnant pussy was the best shit around. I wiggled into her walls, and had to pause for a couple seconds so that I wouldn't nut. The combination of her pussy and that head she'd just given me had me on one. Once I calmed myself down by thinking about dead possums, I started to stroke her nice and slowly.

"Kendriiick, you're gonna make me cum already," she cried and twisted up her pretty face. I pinned her hands behind her head, and then wound my hips into her while sucking her lips.

"You're so fucking bad, Gianna," I whispered and kissed her neck.

"I love you, Kendrick," she responded before I started to tongue her down. She was so wet, and then she released so she was now soaking.

"Gianna, fuck, shorty," I groaned. I licked the side of her face, and then started to beat it up.

"Aaah, uuuh, aaaahh, Kendrick, aaaahh!" she cried out as I pulverized her pussy. I loved hearing her say my full name.

"Uuuggghhh!" I called out and I felt my toes curl up as my body jerked. Fuck! She made my toes curl in missionary. Crazy. "Shit!" I said before kissing her hungrily. She wrapped her arms around my neck, while my dick rested inside her. "And you wonder how I got you pregnant," I smirked and she laughed, before we started kissing again.

I was sitting in the den waiting for Aysia to bring the snacks for the movies. She was taking a cool minute, so I took that time to reply to a couple texts and shit. I was just happy she was over here, so I wasn't gonna rush her. For these past few days, she was sick and saying that she couldn't come over, so I had to settle for all night phone conversations and FaceTime. I would've been suspicious if I hadn't come home to her barf all over some bedding.

All of a sudden, a bunch of sweetness hit my nose, and I looked up to see her walking in with a big bag of chips, a bowl of chips, drinks, and a bowl of popcorn.

"Damn, shorty," I chuckled.

"What?" she frowned.

"You brought all the snacks," I chuckled and so did she.

"Is it that much?" she frowned and sat down with the popcorn in her lap.

"Nah, you good," I kissed her cheek.

I turned the movie on, and she began tearing into the popcorn. I reached over to grab some and it was sticky as hell.

"What the fuck? Marshmallows and syrup on popcorn Aysia?" I turned my lip up in disgust as I wiped my hands with a paper towel.

"What? It's not good?" she looked at me with a worried expression.

"Hell nah, it's not. And it looks disgusting." I stared down into the bowl in horror. It looked like someone threw up in the bowl. "And jalapenos? Your stomach is gonna fucking flip with this horrible ass combination," I added.

"I'm sorry, Kaleeini, I can make you your own," she offered.

"Nah, I will just eat the chips, babe," I replied and reached for the bowl of chips she'd brought in. I glanced over at her and she was eating the popcorn like it wasn't covered in bullshit.

We'd eaten popcorn plenty of times and she had never made it that way. I would've thought she was pranking me, but she was fucking it up. I looked down into the chips I was about to eat, and there was caramel sauce all over them. Who puts caramel on cheese puffs?

"Aysia, shorty, please tell me this is a joke," I said and showed her the chips.

"I've had it before Kaleeini, it's good," she smiled.

"When the hell have you ever eaten cheese puffs drizzled with caramel?" I quizzed, as the thought made my stomach turn.

"Yesterday night," she shrugged and chuckled nervously.

"What's up with you eating all this nasty shit?" I frowned. I was starting to think she was on drugs or some shit.

"It's not nasty, Kaleeini, stop saying that! It's rude to call people's food nasty!" She wrinkled her forehead but was still killing the popcorn. I looked into the wooden bowl and she was only a few kernels away from being done.

"Aysia, are you okay?" I inquired. She looked at me while shoving popcorn into her mouth, and then paused. She put the bowl on the table in front of us, and then licked her fingertips. Her caramel complexion looked a little flushed.

"Umm, Kaleeini, I was sick earlier this week, a-and I went to the doctor. A-and I'm pregnant," she gave me a fake grin. I just stared at her until it faded away.

"By whom?" I asked and her jaw dropped. "I'm kidding shorty, come here," I smiled and pulled her close.

"Why are you just now telling me?" I wondered.

"I couldn't think of the right time, until now I guess," she shrugged one shoulder. I kissed her supple lips, and she caressed my face with her sticky ass hand.

"Aye, watch your hands," I laughed and moved them out of the way.

We kept kissing until I leaned her all the way on her back. She only had on one of my t-shirts, so I reached under to pull down her panties. I lifted my shirt off of her head, and then kissed her flat stomach. I took her nipple into my mouth, and sucked it hungrily before moving to do the same to the other. I got onto the floor, and pulled her bottom half to the edge of the couch so that I could feast on her. I placed her legs on my shoulders, and began sucking the life out of her.

"Aaahh, uuuuh," she cooed and massaged my dreads. I gripped her waist, and she began to wind her hips into my face the way I liked. I fucked her with my tongue, and then brought it back up to flick and suck her button. "Uuuh, uuuh, aaah!" she called out in a high-pitched voice as she exploded.

I stood up and she pushed down my basketball shorts. Since I was already shirtless, I just watched her work. I stepped out of my boxers and shorts, and my dick was staring her right in the face. She deep throated it immediately, and I almost burst on contact. She bobbed up and down on it, letting her saliva flow freely. I rubbed her head as she worked her magic, and soon enough I was releasing. I sat down on the couch, and she straddled me, sliding her tight pussy down onto my dick.

"Damn, you're gripping Aysia," I moaned referring to her walls.

She paused halfway down, giving herself time to adjust, and then finally made it all the way down on my pole. Her upper half collapsed against me once I was all the way in, and she gripped my neck in her arms. I grabbed her waist, and moved her up and down since she couldn't do it herself yet, and then she finally sat back so she could take over. I watched her perfect perky B cups bounce as she went up and down in my lap.

"You're so sexy, baby," I looked up into her twisted up face. She gave me a quick half smile, before biting her full bottom lip.

I sucked on her nipples, and then bear hugged her so that I could beat it up at the same time. I started humping upward, and because of the position she was in, with her legs spread widely on my lap, she couldn't move. We hugged each other tightly as I slammed in an upward motion.

"Oh, oh my gosh, Kaleeini!" she screamed as she gushed on my dick.

I sucked on her neck, and then she looked at me so we could kiss. I squeezed her ass with one of my hands, and then brought the other down to spread her ass cheeks. I went even harder in the paint, and a couple moments later we released together. I loosened my grip on her body, and she pulled back so we could kiss passionately.

"I fucking love you," I grunted as I took her hair out of the bun it was in. Once her hair fell down, I put my hands in it while kissing her.

I LOVED this whole cabin thing with KJ. Even better was that we were snowed in! KJ couldn't go anywhere and I loved it, because I could be all up under him, over him, and on him.

It was around 9pm at night, and it was snowing super heavy outside. You could see the pretty white snow falling down out the window; it was perfect. KJ and I were lying in bed, and he was rubbing my small stomach as we listened to music. I caressed his smooth hair as I slowly rocked my head to the Jazz that filled the room.

"Are you hungry?" he asked me and kissed my belly.

"Of course," I chuckled.

On the way up here, we'd bought a lot of groceries just in case we got snowed in and couldn't leave. We both got out of bed, and put on something to go into the kitchen with. He wore boxers only, and I had slipped on a little nightgown.

"You want shredded chicken tacos?" I asked and he nodded happily. Tacos were his favorite food, and homemade cinnamon buns were his favorite dessert. I whipped up the food, along with some salsa, and then pulled down the tortilla chips from the cabinet. "Here you go, baby," I said and set the plate in KJ's lap, and then went to get our cups of juice. I sat down next to him with mine, and then we held hands so that we could pray.

"Damn shorty, I'm glad you made me five," he chuckled and bit one.

"There is more stuff in there, so let me know if you want more," I smiled. "The cinnamon buns are cooling right now."

"You tryna get that ring ASAP, hunh?" he raised a brow and sipped his juice.

"Not even, I can't cook for my man?" I frowned playfully.

"Nah, you definitely can. And I wasn't saying it like that. I meant you gon' make me give you one on my own," he kissed my face. We scarfed the food down and then ate some of the cinnamon buns. We then made some hot chocolate, and then cuddled up to watch some TV.

"Gimme a kiss," I said to him after he cut the lamp off, making the room more romantic. He looked down at me, and then kissed me gently before sucking my lips. I cupped his face, and played with his chin hairs as we made love with our mouths.

"I love you, Gianna," he whispered in between kisses and rubbed my stomach.

I climbed into his lap, straddled him, and then brought the cover over us. We bear hugged and then began kissing hungrily again.

"I love you so much, Kendrick," I whispered back as he caressed my backside. Suddenly, the lights came on, so KJ pushed the covers off of us.

"What the fuck!" he called out when he saw London standing there. He moved me off of his lap, and I was dumbfounded by this old bitch.

"KJ, you can't do this!" she sobbed hysterically. Her mascara was running down her face, but her hair was in perfect condition.

"London, are you fucking crazy?" KJ frowned and stood up. I was frozen in place because I had no idea what the fuck to do.

"KJ, I love you, why can't you see that?" she cried and threw her hands out.

"Yo London, you have to go shorty. I don't care if it's a blizzard out there," KJ shook his head and started towards her.

"Well if I can't have you," she said and retrieved a gun from her waist.

"No!" I screamed.

POP!

www.ingramcontent.com/pod-product-compliance
Lightning Source LLC
Chambersburg PA
CBHW061347310726
48974CB00001B/231